The Key of Lost Things

ALSO BY SEAN EASLEY

The Hotel Between

The Sequel to THE HOTEL BETWEEN

The Key of Lost Things

‹ SEAN EASLEY ›

Simon & Schuster Books for Young Readers

NEW YORK   LONDON   TORONTO   SYDNEY   NEW DELHI

SIMON & SCHUSTER BOOKS FOR YOUNG READERS
An imprint of Simon & Schuster Children's Publishing Division
1230 Avenue of the Americas, New York, New York 10020

SIMON & SCHUSTER BOOKS FOR YOUNG READERS
is a trademark of Simon & Schuster, Inc.
For information about special discounts for bulk purchases,
please contact Simon & Schuster Special Sales at 1-866-506-1949 or business@simonandschuster.com.
The Simon & Schuster Speakers Bureau can bring authors to your live event.
For more information or to book an event, contact the Simon & Schuster Speakers Bureau at
1-866-248-3049 or visit our website at www.simonspeakers.com.
Jacket design by Chloë Foglia
Interior design by Hilary Zarycky
The text for this book was set in Goudy Oldstyle.
Manufactured in the United States of America
0819 FFG
First Edition
2 4 6 8 10 9 7 5 3 1
CIP data for this book is available from the Library of Congress.
ISBN 978-1-5344-3787-6
ISBN 978-1-5344-3789-0 (eBook)

For Kendrick, whose generosity and self-assuredness inspire me.
No mountain can stand in your path. The world is yours.

1

Holy Cats!

Doors don't always lead where you think they will. When you live in a hotel full of enchanted doorways, you have to get used to your life being a little . . . weird.

For instance, this morning I walked through a door in New York that took me directly into a bakery in Germany, where I picked up some spaetzle for a woman whose grandmother used to make it. Then I ferried a lovey-dovey couple from Venice, Italy, to Buñol, Spain, so that they could attend a festival where people throw tomatoes at one another. After that I took a door from South Africa to a pink-sanded beach in Indonesia, where I ate grilled bananas with dark chocolate syrup and worked on my most recent assignment: a list of awards to give my hotel staff at the end of the summer—things like Tidiest Bellhop, and Most Likely to Crack a Joke with Guests, or Most Creative Use of Binding.

But the door before me now—the one I do *not* want to go through—leads to cats. Lots and lots of cats. And *I'm* the one who has to fix the situation.

I swallow hard and ease open the door.

"I came back from dinner, and there they were," a guest with pouty lips tells me. Her neck drips with pearls, and her earrings cast rainbows against her brown skin. "Where could they have come from?"

When I took this job, no one said anything about animal control. If they had, I'd have told them about the time when my aunt's cat peed in my suitcase. And yet, here I am somewhere in South America on the twentieth floor of the Hotel, faced with more cats than I've ever seen in one place. They're all over. Sharpening their claws on the king-size bed, drinking from the bronze fixture of the bathroom sink, climbing the complimentary bathrobes like pirates swinging from the rigging.

One of the cats is licking at a playing card that's stuck to its back with the magic glue that comes from a source of power everyone here calls "the binding." All the cats have playing cards like this one attached to their fur, and those cards tell me exactly who sent these felines to terrorize the guests of The Hotel Between.

Nico. He's the one with all the tricks. It was his cards that first lured me into the Hotel seven months ago, and now he's using them once again to send me a message. Only, I can't quite figure out what the message is.

A yellow-striped tabby with a three of hearts scurries past, followed by three others. I reach to grab the last one, but it wriggles free and races down the hall. Ugh. It's hard enough being Concierge-in-Training without having to deal with Nico's endless pranks. This isn't the first—malfunctioning equipment, missing furniture, minor changes to the decorations—but this clue finally drives home who's responsible.

I ask the guest to step back into the hall and shut the door on the shrieking cat den, but not before the seven of spades squeezes past, tail whisking back and forth as the cat chases down the hall after the first escapees. That's one more we're going to have to track down, and quickly, preferably before the Maid Service finds out.

"We'll have your room cleaned up as soon as possible, madam," I say, flattening the vest under my coat. A concierge must be dignified at all times, or so the Old Man keeps telling me. Of course, I'm anything *but* dignified. "Until we get your room in order, may I invite you to dine at our finest restaurant, the Four Corners? Complimentary, of course—order anything you like."

"Did you not hear me?" the woman says with a pointed stare. "I just had dinner. I don't want to have dinner again."

I wish the Hotel would invite some nice people for once. Seems it only ever invites those it wants to change. Then again, I guess that's kind of the point—changing the hearts of the world, one vacationer at a time. . . .

"Maybe you'd like to take advantage of our spa service instead? The stones are bound to volcanic pumice, so they're always toasty."

She groans. "Why am I speaking with a child? I'd like to talk to your supervisor."

I squish my lips together to hold back my tongue. That's the third time today that someone's called me a child. I'm almost thirteen—definitely *not* a child anymore. "I *am* the supervisor, ma'am. I can handle whatever needs you have on my own."

"No wonder this place is falling apart."

I clench my fists behind my back. *Keep it under control, Cam. You can handle this.* "You're welcome to lodge a complaint when you check out. We take guest feedback very seriously."

I pull the pad and pen from my pocket, lick the pen tip to infuse it with my binding, and write out a royal-treatment voucher for the spa. As a source of magic, the binding works itself out in many ways, but they all involve connections—the gluing of two objects together, the invisible bonds that link people, the rules that hold everything safely in place. Signing my name to the page with my own binding in this way seals the message, like a contract. It's an agreement that links me to the magic that runs this place—and that agreement must be followed, or else we risk breaking those bonds. And violating the treaty we've made with the magics of the world is something none of us ever wants to do.

"Our masseuse will take good care of you," I tell her as I hand her the voucher and start down the hall.

Fifty-two cards in a normal deck. That means there are probably fifty-two cats that Nico has loosed on the Hotel. As long as he didn't include jokers—

"Wait," the woman calls. "Where are you going?"

I turn to face her. "I have five more guests experiencing the same issue, and reports of cats all over the Hotel." I give her one last bow. "Good evening, madam. I hope you find your destination."

• • •

The next few guests aren't any happier to find their rooms overrun by squatters of the feline kind. I thought people loved cats? After all, tons of folks spend hours and hours watching videos of them online. Though, I guess it's a little different when cats take over the vacation of your dreams.

A small gray calico marked with the queen of clubs galumphs past me down the sixth-floor hall.

"Grab her!" Sev yells as he stumbles behind the cat, struggling to keep his bag over his shoulder.

The queen rounds the corner, and I dash to follow.

We pass under a wooden arch, and my ears pop as the décor changes, teal-and-white floor tile giving way to plush green carpet with amber swirls. Nearby, a timber-framed window displays a grand view of the Swiss Alps, topped with snow like the frosting on the mini Bundt cakes served in the dining hall. The air inside is thick and dry despite the cold landscape outside, and there's a slight rotten smell coming from one of the nearby vents. One more thing I'll have to check on once I've taken care of *this* problem.

The cat sprints through another arch and down a set of ancient-looking stone stairs.

"Is that one of the cats from 2332?" I shout as Sev rounds the corner behind me.

He pulls up next to me, huffing and wiping a bead of sweat from his dark brow. "Yes," he says in a thick Russian accent. "Guest found me in the hall and asked what to do about that rat-chasing *koshka*. The rest escaped when he opened the door."

"We have to catch them all," I tell him.

"Like Pokémon." Sev laughs. "I am the very best."

We race through the next arch, out of the humid hallway and into the cool stairwell beyond.

The Hotel Between isn't like other hotels. Normal hotels exist only in one place—you drive there, or fly, and stay until it's time to go home. Ours is more like a hodgepodge of places from all over the world stitched together by magic. Each arch Sev and I pass through takes us from one spot on the globe to another. Which, when I think about it, means we're literally chasing this dumb cat across the world.

Kinda like last year, when I first joined the Hotel in search of my dad. I found him—I'll find these cats, too.

"That way!" Sev yells as we draw up to a Y-junction that connects to corridors in New Zealand and Taiwan. We take the left arch into a hall decorated with watercolor landscapes of tiny people and enormous hills, paintings framed by twisting, snakelike dragons, and scrolls etched with fancy Chinese letters.

I rush up to the corner and peek around the ornamented pillar into the hall beyond. The cat's still trotting away, but I smile. "It's a dead end," I whisper, noting the solid, arched wall at the far side.

Sev leans his head against the wall. "We need a plan."

Plans. Something I'm good at. As long as I can control all the pieces, my plans typically come together. Unfortunately, so do Nico's.

I shirk out of my tailcoat and hand it to Sev. "I'll scare it back this way. You catch it when it hits the corner."

Sev steels his jaw. "I will be ready."

"Don't worry," I say, as much to myself as to him. "I've got everything under control." I give him an encouraging clap on the shoulder—the way Nico used to do to me—and race through the arch into the next hall.

But it's empty. The corridor is quiet, dark, undisturbed.

Sev steps out behind me and scratches his cheek. "Odd. Are you sure it came down here?"

"I saw it." I walk down the hall, tracing the bricks that curve overhead to form a kind of low tunnel. Gray doors are set into the walls every few feet. The ancient wood floor creaks with every step. The Hotel is full of old passages like this—forgotten branches that aren't quite as impressive as the other halls. Most are hidden where only staff can access them. These doors are all locked and unbound, so . . .

"You must have been mistaken." Sev tosses my tailcoat over his shoulder. "Maybe it went the other way."

I know that cat came down this hall. I feel the doors, listening for the familiar hum of the binding, but find none. They're just doors. Plain, locked doors in an empty hall.

"Oh no," Sev says, leaning back around the corner that we just passed.

"What?"

He crinkles his nose. *"Beda ne prikhodit odna."*

"Trouble never comes alone," I say, remembering the translation.

I join him to see two suited figures marching down the hall toward us. The first is my friend Rahki, dressed in her usual tailcoat, headscarf, and white gloves of the Maid Service. A frown creases her face—the seriousness of her expression a stark contrast to the playful purple cat-ear headphones hanging around her neck.

But it's the woman behind her that I need to worry about. The Maid Commander pounds the carpet in heavy boots, burn-scarred brow chiseled into an intense scowl, silvery hair pulled back in the world's tightest ponytail. Her sword hangs stiffly at her hip—the only weapon I've ever seen carried inside the Hotel.

"It's *him*, isn't it?" the Maid Commander booms in her gruff French accent. "Your little friend, playing endless *games* at the Hotel's expense."

I bristle at her calling Nico my "little friend," but I don't correct her. I'd rather face a world-killing asteroid than deal with the MC's wrath.

"You don't know it's him," I say.

Rahki crosses her arms. "The playing cards kinda give it away, don't you think?"

I grip the wooden coin that hangs from my necklace. Despite having become one of my closest friends, Rahki still sides with the Maid Commander on all things Nico. It has something to do with the Maid Service's contract, and their commitment to "Trust the Hotel, trust the mission, no matter what." Never mind that Nico is the one who put the Hotel's enemies on the run, or the one who freed Sev and the others—even me—from the Competition's control. The maids didn't see what Nico did to stop Mr. Stripe. They don't know that Nico almost gave up his own freedom to save us all.

The MC narrows her eyes at me. "I will find Nico Flores and make him pay for all these endless inconveniences," she grumbles. I should nominate her for the Longest-Running Display of Anger award.

"It's just pranks."

"It is a declaration of war!" she exclaims. "He assaults the very mission of the Hotel, and anyone who threatens our mission must be stopped."

I'm about to argue, but a look from Rahki warns me to keep quiet. For all her rule following, she knows how to handle the MC better than anyone else.

I straighten my shoulders. I have to remember to be *dignified*. "The Old Man says we should focus on what's *inside* the Hotel, not what's outside. He doesn't believe Nico's our enemy, and neither do I."

The Maid Commander stares me down, resting a hand on the hilt of her sword.

Rahki glances back and forth between us. Sev shifts nervously.

Finally the MC huffs. "Rahki, please ensure that this disaster is handled properly. If Mr. *Cameron* won't safeguard the Hotel against his friend,"—she casts me a side-eye—"then *we* must."

She swivels on her heel and marches out of sight.

Sev releases a bottled breath. "That could have gone better."

"She's not going to quit until she's found a way to punish Nico for everything that's happened." I sigh. "It's like she has some sort of vendetta against him."

"Good. He deserves it," Rahki says, and starts down the hall, back the way we came.

"Where are you going?"

"To take care of this mess, like she said." A mischievous smile forms on her lips as she turns back. "How about a contest? Guys versus girls. I bet we catch more cats than you do."

There's the Rahki that I like to see. "You're on."

But as she races down the hall to round up our strays and Sev chases after her to get ahead, I turn back to face the dead end hall. I *know* that cat was here. The queen of clubs—I didn't imagine it. So where could it have gone?

2

The Aging Gardener

"How many is that?" Sev asks, closing the bag on yet another feline intruder. We've been hunting for hours, and herding cats really isn't in my skill set.

Sev's new magic bag has been indispensable, though. A "have-sack," he called it, so named because he made it from a leather haversack. The bag is tailored with the same binding magic that links the Hotel doors to two different places at once; only in this case it's linking the mouth of the sack with the door to my bedroom. As long as the have-sack stays closed, the cats we've caught remain trapped in my room. Not a perfect solution, but I have to work with what I've got.

Though, I'm pretty sure that the last time we opened the satchel I smelled cat pee, which doesn't bode well.

"We've caught nineteen," I tell him, handing over the list. "Not even close to done."

The Pacific Lobby is furnished almost completely with wood—sandalwood, mahogany, rosewood—pieced together into intricate designs on the walls, ceiling, and floor. Guests mill about, lounging on leather couches near fireplaces, meeting with tour guides, handing their luggage off to porters. A few of them watch us, probably curious about why a bunch of hotel staff are chasing down loose animals.

"At least we know how many we have to find," Sev says, scanning the list.

I run my fingers through my hair. There's still the question of what to do with those we've caught. Our friend Orban is off looking for a shelter that will take them, but where's he going to find a place willing or even *able* to handle this many animals at once? "We need more help."

"No, you don't," a voice says from the arch to the Asiatic Lobby. Rahki's holding a plastic cat carrier—complete with angry cat—as she weaves through the guests to join us. "This makes thirty-one for us girls."

My jaw drops. "Thirty-one?"

"Add in your nineteen, and we've found all but two." Rahki takes the magical sack from me and places the end over the cat carrier door, sending the creature through. "With you two running around the place screaming like wild goats, it's a miracle that you caught any at all. Face it, boys—you lost."

"She always outsmarts us." Sev chuckles and points to the cat-ear headphones around her neck. "Or maybe those have turned her into a real cat."

Rahki scoffs. "Maybe *you* were raised by wolves."

"A distinct possibility," Sev laughs.

Rahki flips through the cards that the girls collected, comparing them to our list. "All that's left is the queen of clubs and the four of diamonds."

The queen is the one that vanished, but . . . the four of diamonds? Something seems familiar about that one.

I turn and shout to the front desk, "Cass, could you come out here?"

Cass doesn't respond.

Instead a head with braided hair adorned with colorful beads pops up in the counter window.

"She's not here," Elizabeth says in her long, wavy tones. "I came to check on her when she stopped answering our calls."

"Okay?" I say. "Then, where is she?"

Elizabeth shrugs.

A growl gurgles in my throat. That's the third time this week that Cass hasn't shown up for duty. I know she doesn't want to work the front desk, but this is getting ridiculous.

"Do you see any reports of the two missing cats in there?" Rahki asks.

"Nope," Elizabeth says, checking the notepads. "Maybe Nico didn't start with a full deck?"

"Nico's *never* working with a full deck," Rahki jokes.

"No," Sev says. "Nico does not do anything halfway. Those last two cards are somewhere."

"By the way," Elizabeth adds, "looks like Cass left a note for you, Mistah Cam." She holds the paper out for me to see. "It reads,

'Tell my dork brother that the Old Man is looking for his stupid head.'"

The others chuckle. Not at my sister calling me a dork, or a stupid head—that's just the way Cass and I are together. But if there's one thing I don't need after a day like today, it's another assignment from the boss.

Rahki takes the have-sack from me. "We'll track down those last two while you report in. What should we do about your room?"

"Nothing until Orban finds that shelter." Oma's so going to kill me.

I head toward the elevators and the Old Man's inevitable disappointment when he hears about the cat crisis.

"Are you coming to dinner afterward?" Sev calls out.

"Not tonight," I holler back. "Family dinner night."

"Oh." He and Rahki both give me knowing looks.

Can this day get any worse?

The rickety, open-air platform of the staff elevator drops into the Shaft, and my stomach drops with it.

Wind from the pit below whooshes through the metal cage, sending a shiver from my cuff links to my coattails. High above, the mouth of the dormant Shaft volcano opens up to a bright blue circle of sky, but precious little of that warm light makes it this deep. I guess the cold is better than having this whole chasm blow up and torch us to a crisp.

Hanging metal cages and gold boxes travel along rails around the cylindrical chamber, stopping every once in a while at the hundreds of elevator doors carved into the rock to pick up or drop off their riders. It's a strange mixture of binding magic and modern technology that carries our guests to the Hotel halls scattered all over the world. I don't fully understand how the elevator system works, but even if I did, I doubt I could ever be comfortable in this creepy volcanic hole.

I pull my arms in, resisting the urge to look down into the darkness. Whenever I do, I'm always reminded of things I never wanted to see: memories of my mom and that night long ago when we lost her.

The cage creaks to a stop, and I draw the metal grill aside to leave the Shaft behind and enter the twilight Courtyard, in the central ring of the Hotel.

The sparkling marble-and-gold tree statue rises from the pool before me, its gurgling boughs shading the ornate doors on the eastern side of the Courtyard. The Shadedial Fountain. Each of the doors arrayed around the fountain lead to different time zones scattered all over the world. The angle of the fountain tree's shadow tells me which of those places are experiencing nighttime right now, like an enormous sundial. It's a useful way to tell time when traveling from day to night as often as we do.

I'm not headed through any of those doors right now, though. I go along a different path, past the fountain, to the double doors on the southern side of the yard.

The new doorway curls up from the fresh-cut grass like tree

roots, as if the double doors had grown from the land itself. More roots wind around the gnarled door and away from it in every direction, reaching out toward the frames on the outer Mezzanine wall to carry the Hotel's magic to every hidden nook and alcove.

I pull my pearl key from an inner pocket of my tailcoat, fingering it reverently. Mom's topscrew—which gives me access to all areas of the Hotel. There is no keyhole in the door before me, but this key doesn't need one. I insert the topscrew directly into the wood, enjoying the tissue-paper crackle of the binding as glittery foam expands to form a magic keyhole around it.

The crisscrossing roots and branches retract, and the heavy doors creak open. I try not to gag as the hot garbage stench of the Greenhouse rushes through and curls down my throat. On the other side of the door, dusky yellow sky filters through the glass dome overhead, casting amber sunbeams across the massive tree before me.

I follow the winding dirt path past tables of herbs and flowers that I can't even begin to identify. Groundskeepers in paper masks tend to the plants—spraying and snipping and fertilizing—hoping to grow new sources of the magic that runs the Hotel.

We all hope they find something soon. The Vesima tree is dying.

Unlike the Shadedial Fountain tree, the Vesima is very real. It stands before me, several stories tall, so expansive that its branches obscure the sky. But despite its grandeur, the Vesima's limbs droop like wilted celery, dripping with sickness ever since we took it back from the Hotel's enemies. The fruits—like rotten, oversize pears—dangle loosely from the branches.

An image flashes through me—memories of a man in a pin-striped suit biting into one of the tree's nasty fruits just inches from my face, black goop dribbling from his mouth, his teeth gummy with tar, the rancid smell of his breath as he tries to make me his indentured servant.

Mr. Stripe's not here, I remind myself. The Hotel's magic prevents him from entering through its doors uninvited.

Standing right where Stripe stood the last time I saw him, I instead find the frail, twiggy figure of Agapios Panotierri tending to the weeds at the foot of the tree. The Old Man—as the junior hoteliers affectionately call him—has exchanged his Grand Concierge coattails and formal gloves for a pair of jean overalls and gardening gloves.

Agapios removes his sunhat and wipes the sweat from his forehead. Everything about him—from his sharp cheekbones to his pale complexion and knobby frame—always looks so grave.

"Mr. Cameron," he says in his crisp accent, "I believe you have news."

I tell him about the angry guests, and about the cats and how we're still missing two of them. I leave out the part about the one that disappeared, though. Maybe I did imagine it after all.

Agapios eases himself up and brushes the dirt from his gloves. "It appears your friend has been very busy. Tell me, why do you think Mr. Nico insists on disrupting the peace of our Hotel?"

I almost laugh. The Hotel is a lot of things, but I'd never consider it *peaceful.*

"It's who he is," I say, clasping my hands behind my back in parade rest, like Agapios taught me. He says it's a *proper* stance, but it makes me feel itchy. "Nico likes mischief."

Of course, that's the understatement of the year. If Nico were still on staff, he'd surely win Most Likely to Burn the Hotel Down to Get a Laugh.

Agapios carries a pail to an old spigot and pumps the lever. A squeal of water pours from the spout. "What did he say he intended to do with Stripe's Museum after he took control of it?"

Back to this. It doesn't matter that Nico came through for us in the end—all anyone cares about is that he betrayed us in the first place. He never came back to clear his name like Orban and Sev did, and that makes it hard for those in the Hotel to believe he ever had our best interests at heart. If he had returned, I wonder whether they would still distrust him.

"Nico said he was going to build his 'empire,'" I tell Agapios, again, like I have a thousand times before. I should get stickers made.

"Ah, right. His own, personal empire . . ."

I wince against the screech of the water pump as Agapios fills the bucket. "Nico believes in our mission, sir," I say. "He just . . ." What? Doesn't belong here? Isn't like the rest of us? It's hard to think with the pump shrieking like that.

"Nico has led you to believe many things, but I wonder how you can be so sure that he is not our enemy." Agapios glances up at the dying tree. "Much has happened since you saw him last. His disposition may have changed."

"He gave us back the Greenhouse, remember? He saved me, and Cass, and all those kids. Nico just . . . he is who he is."

Agapios carries the pail to the foot of the tree and pours the water onto a section of the roots that isn't darkened with the tree's sickness. The roots soak up the water hungrily, and an unseen wind whispers through the wilted leaves above.

I gaze up into those sickly branches. The Vesima is the heart of the Hotel's magic. Without it, the whole place would fall apart. Without her . . .

I'm not sure how to think of my mom these days. She's not dead, exactly. Years ago Dad made an agreement with Mr. Stripe that threatened the Hotel and everyone in it, and Mom entangled her spirit with the Hotel and the tree, to save me and my sister and everyone else. She sacrificed herself to fix Dad's mistakes, and now she's all around us. Guarding the Hotel's secrets. She's in the tree that holds it all together. In a way, she *is* the tree, and the Hotel, and the magic itself.

Which scares me. If the groundskeepers aren't able to cure the tree's sickness, will she die along with it? If the Hotel falls apart, do I lose her forever?

The Old Man waves to one of the groundskeepers across the Greenhouse. Not just any groundskeeper, though. It's Reinhart. My dad. The man who's at least partially responsible for what happened to Mom.

My chest tightens as Dad sets down his pallet of herbs and rushes over to join us.

"Mr. Kuhn," Agapios says, handing him the empty pail. "Return this to the toolshed for me, please."

Dad responds with a bow, and glances over at me.

I look away.

He doesn't seem to know how to act around me sometimes, but I don't know how to act around him either. I mean, I've only known my dad for a few months. After a lifetime of longing to meet him, I expected that this whole "being a family" thing would be easier. I thought I would know what to do. Sometimes I regret asking Agapios to take him in, because now that he's here it feels like we're farther apart than we were when he was missing. Then I regret regretting, because what kind of person finds what they've wanted all their lives and then wishes it would go away?

"You coming to dinner tonight?" I ask him.

"Of course," Dad says.

Of course? He's only remembered to come to a couple of our family nights, and he was late both times. Even though we're living in the same house, I don't really see him all that often. It's like after years away, he still doesn't want to be around us.

"Just don't forget again," I tell him. "Please. Oma really wants you there."

He grimaces and heads off toward the shed.

Agapios watches me for a moment, but at least this time he doesn't offer all his sage wisdom about "giving him time" and how

Dad "went through a lot" during those missing years. Maybe he's realizing too that after a lifetime of not knowing each other, Dad and I might just be . . . incompatible.

The Old Man clears his voice. "I have a new task for you, Mr. Cameron."

I perk up at the prospect of anything that'll take my mind off this heavy feeling in my gut.

"The Hotel has been in need of an event coordinator for a few years now," he says. "I have done my best to fill this gap, but,"—he looks up at the tree—"the Greenhouse and my other duties consume my attention as of late."

"You want me to find a new event coordinator?" Piece of cake. There should be plenty of staffers who know what it takes to plan parties. I just have to pick someone, like with the assignment Agapios gave me to pick the awards. Best Event Coordinator goes to . . .

But he's shaking his head. "No, I want *you* to serve as event coordinator."

I don't like where this is going. "I thought I was Concierge-in-Training. I can't be both, can I?"

"I have been performing event coordinator duties along with my other responsibilities for quite some time. As future concierge, you will need to fill many roles. This will give you opportunity and experience."

"But . . . what do I do?" I'm only now starting to get this concierge thing under control, and now he's changing the rules.

"You'll start by planning our upcoming Embassy gala," he says. "Think of it as a big party to end the summer season. We'll be celebrating the binding day of one of the Embassy's ambassadors—Admiral Dare, of the Fleet Marines. She has done much for the Hotel over the years, and deserves the recognition. You'll need to speak with Chef Silva about food, coordinate security with the Maid Commander, arrange entertainment, organize arriving guests—"

"I don't know how to do all that! I'm not even sure what the Embassy is."

Agapios draws his lips into a thin line. "This is precisely my point. The most important job a leader has is to open the door for others to succeed. You are surrounded by very talented people. You must learn who they are, and how to work with them."

I can't hold in my groan. Everybody wants me to *learn*. Why can't I just master what I already know?

He answers my unspoken question. "When I brought you on staff, I told you that this position would challenge you. Challenges shape us into who we are meant to be." He turns his attention back to the tools on the table at the foot of the tree. "You have two months to prepare. Please take this task seriously if you wish to continue your path toward becoming concierge. You will not get a second chance to make a good impression on the Embassy. I will provide more details at our next session."

And with that, the discussion is over.

3

Dinner Plans

The Embassy Gala—a giant party for a bunch of big, important people I don't know. They'll need places to stay—that's easy at least. They'll have to eat, too. Do I need to make up a menu to give to the kitchen staff? I'll have to plan security, send out invitations, make sure everyone knows the program, entertain the guests while they're here, and somehow prevent Nico from spoiling it all.

Oh yeah. This is going to go very badly.

There's a bright side, though—after seven long months on staff, I might finally start getting answers to all my questions about the Hotel, and the Embassy, and the magics that make it all possible. Maybe then I'll understand why Nico chose not to come back with us.

By the time I get back to my bedroom on the seventeenth floor, this gala thing has made me forget all about the cats, which was definitely a mistake.

I crack my bedroom door and am instantly greeted by a chorus of yowls and hisses. I've never seen so many hateful creatures in such a small, confined space. They've already shredded the bed-clothes and the curtains, and have even started turning the legs of my desk into scratching posts.

The stench of cat waste crawls up into my nose and forces a sneeze.

"What is that racket?" Oma shouts down the hall.

I shut the bedroom door and lock it with my topscrew. "Noth-ing!" I call back as the silvery foam recedes and the noise of the cats is whisked far, far away. The key turns cold. Using the topscrew will hide the mess from Oma for at least a little while. Hopefully Orban can deal with this cat problem soon.

Oma huffs from the other room. "Always nothing with you. Your father was the same. Always nothing. Always up to trouble, I think. As if we don't . . ."

I hold back a smile as she rounds the corner. It's a good sign when Oma jabbers like this. It means that for once she's not wor-ried. Though, I'm pretty sure that fifty balls of destructive fluff using your bedroom as a communal toilet is a good reason to worry.

"I keep saying, 'Don't look for trouble,'" she continues as she marches past without a glance at me, "but no one listens. Where is your father?"

"Last I saw, he was in the Greenhouse."

She bangs on Dad's door at the end of the hall. "Reinhart! Are you in there?" It's strange hearing her talk to our dad like she talks to us. It's as if all three of us are her kids that she's trying to keep in line, especially now that we're all living under one roof.

"Maybe he's still there?" Cass offers, rolling out of her room in her sleek black wheelchair.

Oma hoists her hands to her hips, staring at his door as if it's going to open by the sheer power of her indomitable will. Then she stomps back to the living room in a hurry.

Cass and I follow. Cass is dressed in her usual Hotel-formal getup, coattails hanging out the back of her wheelchair. The suit's been her outfit of choice ever since she started hopping through the Hotel doors, exploring all the places where she was never allowed to go before. It's amazing how clean her suit stays, considering all her traipsing around.

"Oma's gonna fry you like a fish when she finds out what you're hiding in there," she whispers as her magic-propelled wheelchair rolls past me.

"What about when she finds out that you skipped duties, again?" I warn, drawing a finger across my throat.

She bobbles her head—a South Asian gesture she picked up from her new best friend, Sana. "She already knows."

"Pick up the pace," Oma calls. "We're late!"

I hurry to the living room, catching a glimpse of myself in the wall mirror as I pass—scratches all over my face, a bit of dried blood at the collar of my button-down shirt, another stain from who-knows-what sprinkled on my tie.

Cass pulls a small comb out of the hidden space next to her seat cushion and runs it through her ponytail. It's a secret message to me that says, *You better fix your hair before Oma sees.*

I scramble to flatten my cowlick, but it's too late.

"Oh, Cammy," Oma says, finally looking me over when we reach the door. "You look a mess. Go change."

I picture the zoo that is my room right now and shudder at the thought of braving a trip inside. "All my other clothes are with the Laundry Service."

"Meow," Cass says, lifting a mischievous eyebrow. I shoot her a *Don't you dare* glare. Cass's love of torturing me borders on being a sport. I'm dreading the day when she finally organizes an Annoy-Cam Olympics so that she can win all the medals. First place in Making Cam's Life Miserable goes to . . .

Oma sighs. "It'll have to do, then. Come on. I've left your father a note."

I roll my eyes. "Did you tell him not to bother?"

She furrows her brow—the Oma-brow is her signature warning to shut my mouth before I get Oma-chopped—and uses her key on the front door to activate the binding to the Hotel. One of her conditions in allowing us to join the Hotel staff was that we keep the Texas house as our primary residence. She said she went through too much trouble making this place a home to "abandon it willy-nilly," though I'm pretty sure she just didn't want to move all her junk. The end result was that the doormen bound the front door of our house directly to the Hotel itself so we could have our home and the Hotel too.

The familiar crackle of the binding zips us from our house in Texas to a hall in the Netherlands.

"Where's dinner tonight?" Cass asks.

"Someplace warm," Oma replies in her usual, cryptic way. Family dinner nights always take us to some surprise location. Now that we've got the whole world at our feet, Oma says we ought to take advantage of it.

As soon as Oma drops the first clue, Cass starts throwing out wild guesses like "Zimbabwe!" and "Samoa!" Even though the destination is always a secret until we get there, Cass still asks. Every. Single. Time.

We hop onto the elevator, and my thoughts wander back to the gala. Agapios's events are always grand. Last time, it was a parade of magical stone statues tromping through an Amazonian jungle. Before that, we had the Ice-&-Sands exhibit at the Hotel pool, where guests could walk through life-size sandcastles that opened into glistening snowy wonderlands. Then came the spectacle that was the International Fashion Show. I can't possibly compete with stuff like that.

"Someplace wet," Oma says, giving Cass another useless clue. I mean, come on. Two thirds of the earth is covered with water.

I wonder why Agapios would make my first event be one for the *Embassy*? Our last Embassy event was the biggest we've ever hosted—a huge celebration of our victory over the Competition and the return of the Greenhouse back in January. The doormen—hotel staff responsible for binding the magic doors—even set up a special venue by intertwining sections of different cities from each continent into one location.

"Cammy," Oma says, "is something wrong?"

"No," I lie.

"He's just grumpy about his new assignment," Cass adds.

I shoot her a particularly rancid stink-eye. "What would you know about it?"

"I'm a clerk, remember? What was it you said earlier? Oh right, it's my *job*."

"Yeah, because you always do what you're supposed to."

"Stop bickering." Oma places one hand on my arm and the other on Cass's back. "Family night means no fighting."

Cass sticks her tongue out, and I bite my cheek to keep from returning fire.

"What assignment, Cammy?" Oma asks.

I replay my conversation with Agapios as we head out under the colorful banners of the African Lobby.

There are eight massive Hotel lobbies, all connected in succession to form the Lobby Ring, the outermost section of the Hotel. Each is decorated to reflect the part of the world that it's connected to. On the outer wall of the Lobby Ring stands a row of doors that we call knockers, which lead outside the Hotel—not to be confused with turners, which connect the rooms and halls *inside*.

The lobby looks especially polished tonight. It's thanks to all the input I've been giving the Housekeeping staff lately, I'm sure: upgrades like the expanded safety pamphlet display, and repositioning the icon statues that guard the entrances, and the little station I had Maintenance add so that Cass can see over the front desk.

Oma stops under the domed ceiling near the center of the lobby, relishing Cass's frustration at not being able to guess our destination, while I finish explaining my gala predicament. "Cammy," Oma says, "this sounds exactly like what you should be doing. Agapios is preparing you for your future."

"I can barely keep my current responsibilities straight as it is," I say, and cringe, realizing just how whiny it sounds.

"Are you going to decline, then?"

One of the terms of every staff member's contract is that we can decline any task at any time. No one here can *make* us do anything, except maybe force us to leave if we ever endanger the mission of the Hotel.

"No," I say, "I won't decline." I will prove to Agapios that I can handle whatever he throws at me. I don't want to let him down.

"Well then, stop worrying. You'll figure it out." Oma scans the row of knockers, rubbing her chin. "Now . . . where was it? Chad? Nigeria? Oh, that's right. It's in Asia, not Africa. Silly me."

Cass and I groan in unison.

Moments later we're riding a cyclo—a three-wheeled bicycle taxi—through the streets of Cambodia. Our driver drops us off after a few blocks, and we enter a discreet door at the back of a building. Portals like these are hidden all over the world. The global door network is much bigger than the Hotel. Anyone can freely use the doors outside the Hotel's knockers, but most never see them. People who've never bonded with a magic—the mundanes, we call them—don't even realize that those secret doors are right under their noses.

We end up in a small building overlooking green, terraced hills that resemble misshapen thirty-layer cakes. "Rice fields," Oma tells us. "Welcome to Vietnam."

"It's gorgeous!" Cass exclaims. "Is it morning-time here?"

Oma leans in. "Tonight's dinner is actually a breakfast."

A woman brings out several bowls and a big pot from the kitchen.

"Soup?" I ask.

"It's phở," Oma says. "Very common for breakfast here."

I twist my lips in disappointment. I've never had soup for breakfast, nor have I ever wanted to. It's warm outside too. I glance over to see my sister eyeing her phở hungrily. Does she always have to be excited about everything?

"You should have been at the front desk for your assignment," I tell her. "What if we'd really needed you?"

Her expression dims. "I was busy."

"Doing what? The front desk is your job. That's what you should have been busy with."

Cass shrugs. "An opportunity came up."

I narrow my eyes at her, then look to Oma for assistance. "Will you please tell her she's supposed to do her job?"

But Oma is motioning for the lady who brought us the phở. "We'll discuss that later. First I want to introduce our host, Aijin."

The woman brushes her long, straight hair out of her face to greet us with a warm smile.

"Aijin invited us to dine with her after I met her last week,"

THE KEY OF LOST THINGS

Oma tells us. "Agapios told me she could help with my class preparations. She's an ambassador."

"Really?" Cass says, excited.

Aijin smiles. "Really."

An ambassador. I've only met a few. Some of the leaders of
the Hotel double as Embassy ambassadors, though I've never really
understood what that means. There's so much about the Embassy—
and the Hotel—that I still don't know. Maybe that's why Nico left;
he hates not being in control, probably more than I do.

Cass's eyes almost glow with interest. "What's it like? Danger
around every corner? Binding and contracts? Saving the world?"

The ambassador laughs. "It's not quite so dramatic."

"Aijin is not one of the members-in-permanent, like the Old
Man or the Maid Commander," Oma continues.

"What do you do for them?" Cass asks.

The ambassador raises an eyebrow at Oma. "I . . . write. I'm
a journalist, of sorts. I make sure the right stories get told, so the
right people can be helped." She looks around. "Where is your
fourth this morning?"

"It may be just the three of us after all," Oma tells her. Dad
doesn't exactly have the best track record with making it to where
he's supposed to be at any given time.

"So," I say, "an ambassador. What does that mean, exactly?"

Again, Aijin looks to Oma, as if seeking permission. "In order
to be welcomed into the Embassy, one of the world's . . . friend-
lier magics has to first reveal itself to you. Those magics make an

agreement with individuals who then represent it to the world. As long as I don't break the contract between the magic and myself, I can tap into its power."

"Do all ambassadors have a magic they're bound to?" I ask.

"It's a requirement for ambassadorship, isn't it?" Oma says, clarifying.

Aijin nods.

I stare at the pot of broth. "So, Admiral Dare—"

"Ah," she says. "Admiral Dare is no mere ambassador. She is a *member-in-permanent* of the Embassy. Those ambassadors have bonded with some of the wilder magics. Admiral Dare doesn't have a contract in the traditional sense. The bonds between members-in-permanent and their magics run much, much deeper."

"Which magic are you connected to?" Cass asks.

Aijin doesn't answer.

Instead Oma responds for her. "It's rude to ask a person directly what magic they're tied to. I only learned that recently too."

"Magics are protective of themselves and their secrets," Aijin says, arranging the dishes on the table. "They are very careful about who they choose to reveal themselves to, and often prevent those bound to them from sharing their secrets. It is a part of the contract we make to keep the magics safe."

Cass blinks. "Safe from what?"

Again, Aijin doesn't respond. She doesn't have to, though. As she heads back into the kitchen for the ginger and onions, the implication is clear: the magics are trying to keep themselves safe from the likes of Mr. Stripe, and whatever war happened long, long ago. Which makes me wonder, where is Mr. Stripe now that we took his home away from him? What is he doing? And isn't that something I should be worrying about, rather than planning parties?

4

Stealing Time in China

S he went *where?*"

Elizabeth gives me a sour expression from behind the front desk. "You heard me. Your sister went with Rahki."

"On a *mission*," I clarify. "To *China.*"

"It's no big deal," Elizabeth says. "They've got the Maid Service with them. They'll be fine."

"Which door?"

Minutes later I'm sweating in southern China, stomping through the woods outside an expansive villa that serves as the target for today's Maid Service mission. I haven't been on one of these excursions since my first few trial weeks on staff, and for good reason— they're dangerous. I'm not trained for the kind of perilous antics the maids get up to, and neither is Cass.

Rahki should know better. The Maid Service—of which Rahki serves as the Maid-Commander-in-Training—isn't safe at all. It's more a military battalion than a cleaning force, people who've signed service contracts to support and trust the mission of the

Hotel above all else. But Cass hasn't signed a Maid Service con-tract, because her safety comes before the Hotel's, always. At least it does in my mind.

I spy the two of them up ahead, creeping behind a hedgerow, and my stomach clenches.

"What do you think you're doing?"

They both turn—Rahki crouching behind the privets, my sis-ter leaning forward beside her. Cass touches a finger to her lips, warning me to be quiet.

I narrow my eyes at her. "You're supposed to be at the front desk," I whisper.

"The front desk is covered," she says. "Elizabeth actually *likes* working the desk, and Rahki said she wouldn't mind if I tagged along on an easy mission."

My anger switches its focus. "You encouraged her?" I say to Rahki.

Rahki shrugs. "I could use the help."

"I wanted to try out being a maid," Cass says. "I think I'm bet-ter suited to it."

"You're better suited to staying inside," I snap. I know it's not fair—that I'm wrong for treating her like something that's breakable—but this is what I do. I worry about her. If she stays in the Hotel, it will keep her safe, always.

Cass scowls. "I can take care of myself."

"And yet you don't."

"Keep your voice down," Rahki says, and strikes her gloved

hand along the length of her wooden duster. "They'll hear you."

Rahki's baton is made entirely of wood from the Vesima, with one flared, splintered end that gives it that feather-duster shape. She sands off a handful of binding dust and, fingers sparkling, pulls the branches in front of us aside. Leaves and wood stick together, giving a better view of the villa.

"Go back to the Hotel." Cass folds her arms. "We've got this."

"I'm not going anywhere," I say. "Just . . . tell me what we're doing."

"Fine." Rahki passes me Sev's have-sack from her shoulder. "You can carry my bag."

She lays out a rushed overview of the plan as we peek through the hole in the hedgerow. The prize we're here to claim is in the building on the other side of the rock garden. Our enemy is the Competition's docents—servants tasked with protecting Mr. Stripe's "property." If everything goes according to plan, the maids around front will draw the docents out, allowing us to sneak in the rear door and take back what should never have belonged to him, or to anyone, in the first place.

"Any questions?" she asks.

I motion to Cass, who's rolling along the hedgerow with a glass bottle in hand, drizzling a bright blue liquid on the ground beside the privets. "What is she doing?"

Cass's eyes shimmer as she stoppers the half-empty bottle. "You'll see."

I hate surprises.

As we sneak into position, I'm painfully aware of how much I don't belong here. Rahki's Chucks make no sound. Cass's chair is silent too—I guess sound dampening was one of the features Sana had the artificers add to it. My shoes, on the other hand, crunch the grass like I'm marching on plastic grocery bags.

I'm going to have to tell Oma about this when we get home. Maybe then she'll finally realize I'm right about keeping Cass from running off whenever she feels like it.

The charge of the frontline maids echoes across the villa grounds. More shouts—in Mandarin, I think—respond from inside the villa as the docents spill out of the front doors to fight off the intruders.

Rahki hops the railing onto the porch. "Cass," she says coolly, as if we're totally not breaking into an enemy hideout, "want to show him your upgrades?"

"You bet," Cass says, and flips her brake. Though she twists it the opposite way from what she usually does. Her seat rises from the back wheels, lifting her up and pushing the front end over the railing to deposit her chair on the porch next to Rahki. The rear axle draws up and over the rail behind it to catch up with the front end of the chair in an almost elastic way, snapping the wheels home where they belong, like magic. No, not *like* magic—that *was* magic.

Cass giggles when she sees the dumbfounded look on my face.

"What was that?" I ask.

"Mobility upgrades," she says. "The artificers are *really* good at the shaping. I've been learning a lot."

I smirk. "You think you're so cool."

She holds her head high. "I think therefore I am," she says, and blows a raspberry before continuing through the door.

The shaping—that's another of the magics that built a relationship with humans. A magic that I don't know much about. I know that the binding is like an invisible force that draws power from the connections between things, but is that how the shaping works too?

I glance over to Rahki. "A few magical upgrades to her chair don't make this a good idea."

"That's not up to you," Rahki says, and runs her hand along the stem of her duster to shave another shimmer of binding dust over the floor just inside the door. A trap. Anyone who steps in that will be stuck like a fly in honey. "Stay close. I don't want to have to save you. Again."

The villa's interior is ultra-modern. Sleek sliding doors, polished wood and slate surfaces, and TVs in every room, featuring Chinese celebrities playing party games. It's all everyday things that everyday people would have, and watch. You'd never guess that the people staying here are enemies of the Hotel, doing nefarious deeds for Mr. Stripe.

We creep down the paper-paneled hall, listening to the fighting out front. If those maids can't keep the docents occupied until we complete our task, there'll be no one to stop them from coming for us next. And while Rahki's a prime candidate for Most Likely to Beat Any Obstacle into Submission, a single Maid-Commander-in-Training is no match for a bunch of zombie-like docents armed with slivers.

"I know that look," Rahki says as she and Cass slide open door after door, searching for the package. "Stop worrying."

"I'm not worrying."

"Yes, you are. You're not in control, so you're worrying. We'll be out of here sooner than you think. With Stripe evicted from his Museum, his hold over the docents is weaker than ever. We'll be fine."

Stripe. It's been seven months since he lost his Museum, and we're still cleaning up the messes he left behind. Or are these new messes?

We find our prize tucked off the main hallway—eight small cribs, each cradling a sleeping baby.

"Watch the hall," Rahki tells Cass. "Raise the alarm if trouble starts heading our way."

Cass spins to face the corridor, squaring her shoulders with a look of determination.

I move to enter the room—ready to get this over with—but Rahki throws out a protective hand to stop me and points inside.

There's a girl in there. A girl our age—dressed in tweed pants and a leather vest, peering into the corner crib. Her shirtsleeves are rolled up, and there's a flat cap situated over her frizzy braids. It's not your typical Competition getup, but I guess enemies don't always look the same.

The girl turns and flashes a smile. "Oi, what do we have 'ere?"

Rahki raises her duster in a defensive stance. Cass peeks around the corner to see.

The girl at the crib stretches her back. "Relax, doll. The name's Beatrice. Bee, if you like."

"She could be a docent," I murmur.

Bee laughs. "Me, a dosie? Mate, I wouldn't sign one of those contracts for the world. And believe me, it's been offered." She turns her attention to the shelves along the far wall. "That's a difference between us Hoppers and you hoteliers: there's nobody can get me under terms of indenture."

Terms of indenture. That's what gave Stripe the power to control Dad all those years when he was missing, and what Stripe uses to force the docents to obey him.

This girl knows about binding contracts.

Bee makes her way around the edge of the room, picking at the items on the shelves. "Besides, I was the one who tipped you off 'bout these kids. Would a dosie do that?"

She slides a lamp off a table and presses the base into her pocket. The lamp shrinks as she does, and disappears into the pocket without a trace. She does the same with a stack of books, a watch, a stonework tea set—her pockets are like Sev's have-sack. Which means . . .

"You're a thief," I say. Rahki's glare intensifies.

"So are you," Bee replies, stuffing a couple of cups, a handful of pens, and a box of tissues into her pocks, which don't seem to be getting any fuller. "Only we Hoppers got different ways of going about it." She pulls a crisp suit jacket off a nearby chair and tries it on, admires herself in the wall mirror. "You folks should hurry. Sounds like your maids're having a bit of trouble."

I stop to listen. The shouting outside has faded.

Cass leans around the corner to confirm. "I think the docents slivered our maids."

"We've got to get these kids out of here," Rahki says.

"And fast," Bee adds as she swipes a whole box of junk into her pock.

I hurry to check on the babies. They're all so little. I pull one of the girls out of her crib, and she yawns and wraps her tiny hand around my index finger, like she's holding on for dear life. Which, given what I know about Stripe and the Competition, isn't far off.

This is the Hotel's secret mission—to save kids like these from people like Stripe. The Hotel Between lifts high the low, helps the helpless. We do whatever we can to make the world a bit better, standing up for those who can't protect themselves, bringing homes to the homeless. That mission must be protected at all costs.

"Why would anyone want to take kids this young?" I ask, more to myself than anything else.

"Because they grow up," Rahki says, checking the doors for hinges to speed our escape. "Bind them when they're babes, and you can mold them into whatever you want them to be."

Like Stripe tried to do with Nico. But Nico and I beat Stripe at his own game. Together we got the leader of the Competition to nullify his contracts, and now Nico, Cass, and I are protected by a new contract—one that ensures that we are free from Stripe, forever.

I touch the coin at my neck. Nico's coin, which he gave me when he left the Hotel for good. It contains all his memories of his time with the Hotel. Without it, he might not remember everything that happened. If he's forgotten all that—forgotten me—all he'd have left is what Stripe taught him. What Stripe *made* him. But Nico's stronger than that. I know he is.

Bee dumps over a hamper full of dirty diapers, and the weirdly sweet smell of baby powder and poo fills the air. "You ain't gonna find any hinges. They got smart after you evicted Ol' Stripey."

Rahki casts her some side-eye and pulls a pin from a specific pocket in her jacket, her pin-sleeves. "Cam, the sack."

I swing the have-sack off my shoulder. "What are we going to do with it? We can't just toss babies into my bedroom."

She hands me a pin and gently lifts one of the children from its crib. "No time to explain. Just pin the bag already."

An electric current zips through my fingers as I slide the pin into the have-sack's inner sleeve, and a wave of light bursts across the opening before giving way to an incandescent glow. A room fades into view on the other side. It's the Hotel Nursery, lined with cribs and toys and sparkly chandelier mobiles dangling with gold and crystal animals.

Oddly enough, the room appears to be lying on its side, and seems way smaller than it should be. A pair of miniature maids inside run for the bound portal, but they're upside down, and . . . distorted. I

THE KEY OF LOST THINGS

don't think I'll ever get used to the physics-defying nature of binding one place to another.

A woman's face pops up in the mouth of the have-sack. Countess Physiker, who runs the Hotel's nurse station. She looks like she's hanging from the ceiling. I flip the bag around so that the world inside appears right-side-up, but the have-sack and the door on the other side are two different sizes, so the maids beyond still look like tiny toy soldiers.

"What's happening over there?" Countess Physiker asks.

Rahki peers into the sack with me. "Docents are on us," she says. "We have to hurry."

The sound of voices filters through from the hall, followed by a worried, "Uh, guys," from Cass. "A little faster would be great."

I lower the first little girl into the hole, and the woman in the bag extends minuscule hands to receive her. Both the baby and my arms seem to shrink as they pass through the have-sack portal. It's like looking through a glass of water, where two things don't quite match up.

The maids rush the baby to one of the cribs as Rahki passes me another.

"Sounds like they're searching the house," Bee whispers, pulling a narrow, wooden spike from her vest pocket.

A sliver. A weapon.

She leans her ear against the wall. "Not searching smartly, though. They must be trying to let us get away without breaking their terms."

"Good," Rahki says as I hand the next baby through. "Their resistance against Stripe's influence might just give us the time we need."

The bond of Law is the first, and most important, of the three fundamental bonds that limit the power that magics have over people. The bond of Law states that no magic may ever break an agreement made between it and humans, no matter how powerful a magic might be. This rule applies to magical contracts between people, as well. There are other bindings—rules meant to keep people safe from rogue magics—but the bond of Law is the one on which all the others are founded.

Right now that means the docents are only required to obey the exact wording of their contracts with Stripe—no more, no less. Docents are just people, after all. They don't typically *want* to be evil; they're forced by magical contracts. Most had no idea what they were getting into when they became indentured to Mr. Stripe.

Thankfully, people like that can sometimes find loopholes and bend the rules just enough to let good guys like us get away.

Again, it strikes me that this Bee girl knows an awful lot about magical contracts for someone who's not a hotelier.

"Hurry," Cass whispers through the doorway. "They're almost here."

Rahki passes the last baby through and stands to face Bee. "All right. That bag won't fit us, so we'll have to go through the docents," she says. "But first I need to know, are you a friend, or an enemy?"

Bee's crooked smile grows. "Which do you want me to be, doll?"

I shut the bag and stand beside Rahki. "Friend," I say, and motion to her sliver. "Wouldn't want to be on the receiving end of one of *those*."

She laughs. "I wouldn't sting you with this sliver anyway. I can use it to help get rid of those dosies, though, if you like." She raises the long, sharp spike. "Ready to have a little fun?"

5

Hidden in the Lining

Rahki and I stare on in shock. This can't be happening.

"Oi, you 'bout done back there?" Bee says as if nothing's wrong. But something is very wrong. She slivered a man without a scrap of hesitation, and it was awful. He crumpled up into her sharp spike like a wadded piece of paper.

I thought I wanted Bee's help, but now that I'm faced with the reality of what her help looks like, I'm not so sure. The Hotel banned weapons like hers because they're dangerous. One prick, and a person transports to another location, violently. What's worse, a sliver can be bound to almost anywhere, so for all we know, that docent could be floundering in the waves of the Pacific, or freezing on a tundra, or burning up in a scalding hot spring. And the process of being slivered is supposedly no cakewalk either. I've never had it happen to me, but Rahki has, and she's giving Bee the angriest glare I've ever seen.

Meanwhile Cass has a different glimmer in her eye, like she's seen something truly amazing.

"This is a bad idea," Rahki grumbles as Bee races around the corner and out of sight.

"She'll get us out of here," I say.

"But what's it going to cost us?"

We round the corner in time to see Bee sliver another docent, who vanishes with a ripping cry of pain. Despite our hesitations, Rahki and Bee bind and sliver our way to the back door of the villa, where Bee immediately pokes another docent caught in Rahki's trap. Rahki tries to protest, but the docent—and the section of floor he was bound to—are whooshed away to some hidden corner of the globe before she can get the words out.

I clutch the have-sack to me, unsure what to do. I'm not part of the Maid Service, so I'm not equipped or trained with a duster like Rahki is. And I'm certainly not . . . whatever Bee is. I'm just me. I hate feeling powerless like this.

I glance over at my sister. She's entranced, and has a subtle smile on her face as she watches the girls fight. It's the same look she gets when she's watching *National Geographic*, as though the world is full of wonder and she alone gets to revel in it.

A docent tries to grab her, but Cass grips the seat of her chair, and the handlebar shoots up into the docent's jaw with a solid uppercut. The man stumbles backward, dazed. Cass then removes one of her armrests and jabs it toward the docent, sending the armrest telescoping forward into her attacker. The move actually makes me smile. Now that she can manipulate her chair through her binding, even she's getting in on the action.

Soon we're back in the rock garden, racing for the hedges. Once we're through, Cass skids to a stop.

"What are you doing?" I ask.

"What I came here for." She leans over the side of her chair—one hand clutching her flask, the other coated in a layer of blue liquid. When she touches the ground, her gloved fingers glow, as does the trail of goo she poured out along the hedgerow earlier. I can see where it has seeped into the ground, and more—it soaked into the roots of the hedges and was carried out into the branches. The light grows bright, a sparkling wave traveling along the ground and through the plants.

The hedgerow has changed. No longer do the leaves waft in the breeze. They're not even green anymore—they're gray, like . . .

"Stone," I say. "You turned the hedges into stone."

"Shaping," she tells me, and beams.

There's that word again. Since when does Cass know how to do all these things with the shaping magic? I'm only now beginning to understand the connection we have with the binding as it is, and she's doing transformations and magic tricks like they're nothing.

"That won't keep 'em long," Bee says. "Need to put some distance between us."

We dive through the cherry trees outside the villa grounds and race for several long minutes, my chest heaving as I sweat through my suit jacket. Cass keeps glancing back, chin held high with pride. What she did *was* pretty impressive. I didn't realize all the things the shaping could accomplish.

Finally Bee pulls to a stop at the edge of a clearing near the door that leads back to the Hotel. "Well, mates," she says, "this is where I leave you. Thanks heaps for your help."

Rahki grimaces. "Running off to check out your haul of stolen goods?"

"Only the guilty run, doll."

"Is that what they tell you in thief school?" Rahki snips.

"Don't be like that," I say. *A concierge is always dignified and gracious.* "The Hotel thanks you for your help," I tell Bee. "If there's any way we can repay you—"

"Oh, you'll pay up eventually, boy-o," Bee teases. "By the way, you oughta check that bag of yours. You might find something of interest. The Hopper King sends his regards!"

And with that, Bee jabs the tip of the sliver into her own arm. Her mouth opens in a silent scream as her body folds in on itself and slurps into the tip, and the sliver goes with her.

Cass gapes. "Why would anyone do that?"

"Come on," Rahki says. "Let's get out of here."

But I don't follow. Bee's words echo in my mind. "Something of interest?"

I open the have-sack and see the Nursery. Countess Physiker is tending to the babies we saved. I'm glad the mission was a success. Now these kids can grow up free from Stripe's influence and become whatever they want to be.

But this can't be what Bee was referring to.

I pull the pin from its sleeve, and the Nursery vanishes in a flicker of gold, revealing the empty bag beneath. Wait. It's not empty—something's crinkling in the folds. I press my fingers into the seam, and it parts.

"What is it?" Cass asks.

"I think she slipped something into the lining."

Rahki raises an eyebrow as I pull out an envelope with the words "Mr. Cam" scrawled across it in loopy script.

I read the letter aloud:

> Mr. Cam,
>
> I'm not entirely sure what our connection is, or how I even know you, but I feel compelled to give you a heads-up. The Hotel's days are numbered. Whoever you are, you now have your warning. What you do with it is your business.
>
> Pretty much the greatest,
> Nico, King of the Hoppers

I stare at the page, silent. Rahki's saying something, but I can't hear it. All I hear is Nico's voice in my head, over and over again. *Whoever you are.*

He doesn't remember. Bringing me to the Hotel, signing our contract, working together to foil Stripe's plans to take the Greenhouse. . . . He wanted me to keep his coin safe, and this is the consequence. Why did I think he would be able to remember all that happened? Of course he'd forget. He left his memories hanging around my neck, just like Dad did when he vanished all those years ago. At least he can still feel our connection, but what good does that do if he can't recall why?

"Cam!" Rahki says, snapping me back to reality. "We need to take this message to the MC. Now."

"We can't," I tell her.

"Didn't you read what he said? *The Hotel's days are numbered.* He's our enemy now."

Cass scoffs. "Yeah, right."

"I don't believe it either," I say, glad that Cass and I are on the same side for once. "It's not right. The message, this girl Bee . . . Nico's my friend. My blood-brother. He'd never be my enemy."

"He. Doesn't. Remember. You," Rahki says, speaking slowly as if to make sure my addled brain can understand. "We have it in his own handwriting. You two may still be bound, but if he doesn't understand why—if he doesn't remember the *Hotel*—then he's back to being the guy he was before he came to us. And you know who that was."

I swallow. The Competition's docents are one thing, with their contracts that force them into obedience, but Nico was a suit. They follow Stripe because they want something that he has to offer them. They're not required to obey unless they break some other contract, and even then, Stripe often lets them make their own decisions because he gets more power and satisfaction out of a willing servant than out of those who are forced to obey him.

"Nico wasn't just any suit, Cam," Rahki says. "He was training to be Stripe's replacement. He was going to run the Museum *for* him. Stripe promised him an empire, and Nico *chose* that. He spent months lying to us. He was our enemy before, and he's our enemy again. If he's going to attack the Hotel, we have to stop him."

I look to Cass for backup, but she has stopped paying attention and is now playing with a deck of cards.

"It might not be what it sounds like," I say. "Maybe we can make him remember. We can bring him back."

"He gave you a *warning*." Rahki taps the word on his letter to drive her point home, then pauses. "You're going to try to find him, aren't you?"

My chest aches at the thought. "I . . . I have to."

"No, you don't. If you try, you're going to end up in major trouble." She motions to the coin at my neck. "The Hotel can't take risks when it comes to the mission. The old heads of the Hotel know that you and he are connected. If his attacks keep coming and you're out searching for him, they'll think you're working with him. You'll lose your position, or worse."

"He deserves a chance."

She forces me to look at her. "Promise me you won't go looking for him."

"But . . ."

"Promise. Whatever you think about Nico, whether he really is your friend or not, the Hotel won't put up with anyone who endangers its mission. If you still want to trust him, that's your choice, but for the sake of the Hotel, you absolutely *cannot* seek him out."

"She's right," Cass says, shuffling the deck absently. "They will kick you out if they find out. Especially if Nico *does* make a move against us."

I meet Cass's gaze. She's never been one to avoid risks. If she's urging caution, maybe I should listen.

"Fine," I say, "but on one condition."

Rahki blows out a relieved puff. "Name it."

"You can't tell anyone about the letter."

"Cam, that's not—"

"That's my condition," I tell her. "Nico proved himself to us before. If you tell the MC, she'll hunt him down and we'll never find out the truth. I don't want anyone trying to hurt him just because you're not willing to give him a chance. If I can't go searching for him, no one can. He's earned at least that."

Cass gives me an approving smile.

Rahki stares me down for a long moment, weighing her options. There's no way she'll agree to this. She's too much of a rule follower. But then . . .

"All right. Agreed."

"Really?" I say.

She holds up a hand. "But you can't keep me from preparing for the worst. Nico gave us a warning; it would be stupid not to take it seriously. I'll tell the MC that I'm beefing up security for the gala."

"I can help," Cass adds eagerly.

I can't believe Rahki's considering this. "So, we have a deal, then?"

Rahki places her hand over her heart.

I mirror the gesture, and with that, it's agreed. The bond of Law is taken seriously by everyone here. There's power in the agreements people make with one another—the magic of binding—and they should never be taken lightly.

The two of them head through the door into the Hotel. I sling the have-sack over my shoulder to follow, but when I do, something hard hits my hip. I comb my fingers through the sack and realize there's something else hidden in the lining—a long, sharp spike of wood.

A sliver. Bee must have snuck it into the have-sack along with Nico's note.

I stuff the sliver back into the lining and make sure Rahki and Cass didn't see. What am I supposed to do with this? I don't want to take it into the Hotel, but there's no time to figure out my options before Rahki starts asking questions.

So I close the flap on the sack and head inside carrying one of the Hotel's most forbidden objects with me.

6

A Glow in the Depths

N*u ti dayosh!*" Sev exclaims when he sees me at his door on the twenty-first floor. I expected him to be in bed by now, but he's still dressed in his doorman's uniform. "You look as if the world has exploded."

That's not quite the description I'd use, but it's close. "Can I stay here tonight?" I ask. "Oma said it's okay."

"Of course. But what is the trouble?"

I don't know what to tell him. That Nico has forgotten us? That Rahki is convinced that he's our enemy? That I have no idea how to keep this whole gala thing under control, Cass won't do what I ask her to do, and I can't sleep in my bed because it smells like a cat-o-potty? Right now I don't want to think about any of it.

Sev must see that on my face, because he changes his tone. "Come with me. I have an errand to run and could use the company." He smiles. "It is for you, anyway. For your birthday."

We hop onto the elevator and press the button for the lowest level of the Shaft.

"I've never been down that far," I tell him.

"I would imagine not," he says as the elevator starts its descent. "There is not much down in the caves, and the Old Man discourages most from visiting without good reason."

The elevator cage shifts to another track with a loud, ratcheting *clank*. I watch the enclosed guest lifts travel up, down, side to side, and I try not to think about what awful things lurk in those depths below.

Sev leans against the cage and flicks on a flashlight. "An adventure in spelunking, yes?"

I ready my own light. "Why doesn't Agapios want people coming down here? And where is the Shaft located, anyway? Seems it would be really hard to hide a place like this."

"I do not know the secret of the Shaft's location," Sev says. "As for why staff are encouraged to steer clear,"—he holds his light under his chin menacingly—"this is where the Outliers hide."

"The what?"

Sev doesn't answer. If I hadn't spent the past several months living in a place that had the power to prevent people from discussing its secrets, I would ask him again, but his silence speaks volumes. Whatever these "Outliers" are, they are a mystery that the Hotel intends to keep even from me.

A musty breeze cools my face as the elevator shudders to a stop. When I step out onto the platform, I glance up at the circle of blue sky high above us. The clatter and whir of the elevators fill the air as we creak our way down a set of stairs. The sound is almost musical.

"Do you come down here often?" I ask.

Sev pulls his collar a little tighter. "Only once. The shaping is still new to me."

"The shaping." I didn't get a chance to ask Cass how Sana had used it to make her chair have all those new functions, or how it had turned the hedges into stone.

"It is the magic of artificers." Sev pauses. "The shaping taps into a person's will to transform one thing into another, or to modify the way a thing operates. You know, you really should consider joining the artificer trainings. I have learned quite a bit."

As if I don't have enough to do.

He leads me to a cleft hidden in the shadows along the Shaft wall. I sweep my light over the cave entrance, but can't see how deep it goes. I think I can hear a noise emanating from within—a long, deep groaning sound that makes my teeth hurt. Sev ducks on through, beckoning me to follow.

The tunnel curls away from the Shaft, dropping even lower into the earth. The rocks are slick and slimy, and the whole place smells like wet cheese curds. Bulbous stalactites drip water into our flashlight beams. A droplet pats my head as we duck under a low outcropping.

"What are you getting me for my birthday? A card would have been fine," I say, masking my excitement.

He clucks his tongue. "I cannot tell you. You will find out soon enough."

"But you need this . . . whatever is down here to make the gift?"

"Shaping dye. It is useful for many things. I require only a drop to change the binding on a pin, but artificers use much more to bring the icons to life."

I've seen the statues and machines that Sana and the rest of the Motor Pool staff work on. The artificers specialize in making objects do things they couldn't otherwise, but I'm not sure what that really means. "I've never really understood what it is the artificers do down there in the Motor Pool."

"The shaping re-forms one thing into another," Sev explains. "It allows us to alter the nature of an object so that it can be influenced by the person bound to it."

"Nature," I repeat.

The bond of Nature is one of the three fundamental bindings that restrict the way magics can interact with humans, along with the bond of Life and the bond of Law. The bond of Nature prevents magics from changing the world—and people—to be something that goes against their "nature," the invisible qualities that determine how they operate. That bond is what keeps rogue magics from turning people into handbags or forcing them to crawl around on all fours. The bond of Life is simpler—it keeps magics from harming humans. Without the bond of Life, Mr. Stripe would probably be able to use magics to kill everyone who crossed him. And then there's the bond of Law, that ties it all together. The bond of Law is the original treaty between magics and humans. It's what requires magics to obey the other bonds. If a magic were to ever violate any of those rules, there would be serious consequences.

But wait. "The dye can break fundamental bonds?" I ask.

"Bioluminescent," Sev says. "Glowworms. They have bonded with the dye, and it turned them into something quite unique. These tiny creatures can process even more dye, which is why we have enough to run the Motor Pool. Very few Houses are so lucky."

We pass into a wide, open chamber with a blue pool so large that I can't see the end of it. The water glistens like a galaxy of glowworms. The whooshing, moaning sound from before is louder here—in, out, a wheeze, a whistle—as if some enormous beast is breathing in the darkness on the distant shore of the massive pool, where the shadows seem to dance. The sound is both wonderful and utterly terrifying.

Sev kneels at the water's edge and scoops a jarful of the glowing liquid. "Shaping gives us the power to make a thing *want* to be something else. Like your sister's chair. The shaping makes her chair want to be alive to serve her, and works with her to act as if it is."

Changing someone's nature. Sometimes I want to change myself. To be confident like Nico, or determined like Rahki, or friendly like Cass. If I could control my nature, could I become what Agapios wants me to be?

Sev gazes out over the pool. "Does it not amaze you that there is so much we do not yet know? Unknown wonders always lie just beyond what we can see."

"Yeah," I say as another groan echoes through the chamber. "Why don't we let some of it stay unknown so that we can get back? This place gives me the creeps."

"Bend them," he corrects. "We do not dabble in *breaking* bonds. Much too dangerous." He drags a finger along the cave wall. "The shaping dye comes from water that has been changed through a special process."

"It's just water?"

Sev stops at a split in the tunnel and swings his light back and forth. "Have you considered that water is, itself, something special?"

"Water is water." It's the stuff I avoid in favor of drinks with flavor. The only time it's special is when you can swim in it.

"Water is necessary for life," Sev says, picking a tunnel and continuing on. "It dissolves all things over time. Its magic can change the very shape of the world. Water erodes land, moves shorelines, cracks mountains. It is change itself, in all its forms—liquid, ice, steam—and if you find water that is old enough, distilled by the ages, you can use its magic to shape even greater things. Such dye is very rare indeed."

The passage narrows, and we have to shimmy through to continue on.

Before we reach the exit, Sev stops. "Turn off your light."

"What?"

"Your light." He switches off his flashlight.

I obey, and the world around me goes dark.

"Now"—he steps through and moves aside—"look."

The cavern ceiling glitters with a faint blue glow, a sea of radi ant sapphires.

"They're moving," I say. The lights wiggle, sparkling as th crawl along the stalactites.

7

A Hiccup in the Plan

Hiccu . . . *BURP!*

"Cam!" Rahki shouts. "That is unbelievably gross!"

"I'm sorry. I . . ." No, no, no. Not again, not aga—*hiccu-BURP!* "I can't help it."

Everyone laughs. Sana, Elizabeth, Sev, Rahki, Cass—all of the junior hoteliers with "in-Training" in their job titles are gathered for another of Oma's mandatory educational field trips, and they're all looking at me like my head is a pimple about to pop.

I hold my breath, trying to stop the strange hiccup-burp combination that's been plaguing me lately. Hiccuburps, Cass calls them. Oma says they're caused by stress. All I know is that every single hiccup I have is followed by a door-shattering, world-rending belch that I'm pretty sure can be heard all the way back in Texas.

"It is like a frog lives inside you," Sev says, grabbing his side and wiping an eye. "Would you like me to get him out?"

Cameron Kuhn, Most Likely to Belch up a Toad. "I can handle my own"—*hiccu-BURP!*—"frogs, thank you." I wish Oma would show up already and take everyone's attention off me.

Teaching has always been Oma's thing. When we joined the Hotel, she insisted that she keep on teaching. Thus a contract was formed so that the Hotel could show her what it wants us to learn. Agapios said it's been years since the junior staff had someone to formally teach them. I mean, getting to travel the world provides its own kind of education, but Agapios wants us to learn other things too.

Hiccu-BURP!

The back of my neck warms with irritation as another chorus of laughs echoes through the North American Lobby. Even the giant bear statue next to the front office window looks like it's gripping its belly in a hearty guffaw.

Cass is the only one not joining in the hilarity. She's been extra quiet ever since I came after her on the China mission. Now she's just sitting next to me, shuffling her deck of cards like this is the last place in the world she wants to be.

"Try holding your breath," Rahki says.

"Or rub your chest," suggests Elizabeth.

"I can get some ice water," says Carlee, twisting her thick black braids. She's our Sous-Chef-in-Training. She thinks blanching your head in ice water is the solution to everything.

"I said no"—*hiccu-BURP!*—"thank you!" I shout, way more loudly than I intended. Sana gives a little *Ooh, someone's angry* head bobble.

I can't stand them seeing me out of sorts like this. Thankfully, Oma arrives in her usual whirlwind fashion, handwoven Sherpa sack over her shoulder like she's some sort of mountain guide, and waves her hands to draw everyone's attention.

"Gather, gather!" she calls in her best Mother Goose impression.

"What's our trip today?" Sana asks. She and Rahki exchange an excited grin. The two of them are like Cass—they love learning, maybe even more than working at the Hotel. Rahki once told me that where she grew up, girls weren't allowed to go to school, so attending Oma's classes almost feels like breaking the rules, which makes "learning" pretty much the only rule she's willing to break.

"It's a mystery, of sorts," Oma teases.

Hiccu-BURP!

She shoots me an offended look—the one where her mouth crinkles like a mantis's. Come on! She knows I can't control it.

Oma leads us through a hidden door behind the lobby bear and into a back hall filled with rusty tray carts and dusty popcorn machines. Compared to the glittery facade of the Hotel, these back halls always feel dismal and spooky. They're remnants of places that were bound to the House ages ago, before it was officially dubbed The Hotel Between.

We stop at an old wooden door draped in cobwebs on one side of a cramped chamber. The stonework has an English look, with an arched ceiling similar to the one in the hall where the queen of clubs disappeared. We never did find those last two cats.

"All right," Oma says. "Let's see if you can figure out our destination." And she opens the door.

We step into a hot, woodsy area that smells like rain and salt. Insects trill all around us, and the humid air sticks to me. Instantly I'm sweaty and gross. I glance back to see the rickety doorframe we just passed through, barely hanging on a shack whose roof collapsed long ago. A few trees rise from within the walls, like cowlicks.

"Temperate climate," Sana says, checking her pocket watch to determine the time zone. "Somewhere in the Americas."

"But which"—*hiccu-BURP!*—"America?"

"North." Sev waves his hand through the air. "It feels like summer."

"So . . . hot . . . ," Orban whines.

Oma hums in approval. "What else?"

Carlee runs a finger through the dirt and pops it into her mouth. "United States. East Coast."

"You can't possibly know *that* from eating dirt," I say.

"Everything's made of ingredients," she replies. "Chef Silva's been teaching me the taste of all sorts of places." Okay, I'll just mark Carlee down for the It Tastes Like Chicken award.

Our guessing game continues, everyone but Cass offering helpful tidbits of information. It's weird for her to not participate. Sev comments on the deciduous trees and the loamy soil. Cass fidgets with her cards. Orban notes a strange, long and winding mound that looks man-made. Cass shuffles the deck. The saltwater smell and the sound of waves lead Elizabeth to guess that we're in a coastal region.

Finally Cass blurts, "It's Roanoke Island."

"Very good," Oma replies, sounding genuinely surprised. Cass gets the gold star, again. "Today we're discussing the lost colony of Roanoke."

"How did you get that?" I ask, in almost a whisper.

"Elementary. You know my methods, Watson," Cass replies in a fake British tone. Ever since she read a bunch of Sherlock Holmes stories last year, she's been mastering her accent. "Pay attention. . . . You might learn something."

Oma retrieves a stack of clipboards from her sack and passes them out. Before she's done distributing, Orban uses a pin from his pin-sleeves to draw a cartoonish face with big eyes, a round nose, and sharp mustaches in the bottom corner of his board. An echo of that same face draws itself in sparkling gold ink on all of our boards. He follows with a speech bubble exclaiming something in Hungarian, eliciting a chuckle from those who can read it.

Oma scowls and erases our slates with her pin. "Can anyone think of *why* we'd be talking about the lost colony of Roanoke?"

Silence. I glance over at Cass, expecting her to pipe up again, but she's back to shuffling her deck.

Oma dabs the tip of her pin to her tongue, then touches the pin to the board. Our slates burst to life with swirling gold lines, sparkling as they sketch out a collage of cabins and people in bonnets and linen dresses and rugged pants. A ghostly backdrop of ships sailing the ocean appears behind them.

In the center of the collage, the magic hatches a portrait. At first it looks like a baby girl, but then the drawing ages, growing into a woman dressed in a naval officer's uniform.

"Admiral Dare," Rahki says, her voice soft—almost reverent.

I perk up, taking in every detail of the face on my slate. The woman is old now, with naturally curly hair and a slight smile that makes her look as if she's hiding something.

"Virginia Dare," Oma confirms, "whose four hundredth binding day is the reason for our upcoming event."

The image changes. The woman's face stays the same, but her clothes and hat shift into furs and a coonskin cap.

"What happened to Miss Dare is one of the greatest Embassy mysteries. In 1587 she and her family went missing, along with the rest of the Roanoke colony. She was only a child then, but her father worked for the Embassy. No one knew where they went. And then young Miss Dare resurfaced three decades later, all by herself. Thirty years missing, and still only as old as many of you. To this day, she refuses to tell anyone the truth of what happened."

1587 . . . Admiral Dare is like the Old Man and the Maid Commander—someone who has lived for centuries, thanks to their connection with one of the many magics hidden in our world.

The portrait swirls and vanishes, and is replaced by some story about expeditions to the New World and secret missions to establish a door in the Americas. But none of this will help me plan the gala. If anything, it's making me more nervous. Admiral Dare and the Embassy have been around for so long, and I . . . well, I haven't even been alive a fraction of that time. How am I supposed to throw a party for people like that?

"Maybe the colonists used Mr. Dare's door to go back to England," Rahki says.

Oma shakes her head. "Dare's Door had been cut off. It took two years before the Embassy could reach the colony to investigate, and by then the settlement was entirely gone."

"We had to have found it eventually," I say. "I mean, Miss Dare came back. And what happened to the door's pin? Someone must have taken it."

"*She* did," Oma says. "Miss Dare offered it as proof of her family's history with the Embassy. She said they'd done what was necessary to keep the Embassy safe 'from those who would possess it.'"

"You mean safe from Stripe," Orban adds.

There's a collective gasp as everyone understands the implication. Possessing things—people, places, objects—is the domain of Mr. Stripe. If he had his way, he and those like him would own everything and every*one* in the world.

Orban meets my gaze. He's one of the few around the Hotel who knows what Stripe is really like. I wonder what he's thinking right now. What does he remember?

"I still don't understand," Cass says. "If Dare had the pin, why not come back sooner? What happened to the rest of them?"

"That is the mystery." Oma lifts an eyebrow. "Only Admiral Dare knows the truth. The rest of what happened back then is lost to us."

So many mysteries. There's still so much I don't know about the Hotel, and the Embassy, and yet somehow I'm supposed to be learning how to lead in this place? It's overwhelming. How is one person supposed to keep all this stuff under control? It won't be long before Agapios realizes what a bad decision it was to train me.

No. I can't let that happen. My family has a history with the Hotel, just like the admiral's family was connected to the Embassy. Dare proved she belonged. I can too.

8

Made of Glass

I stare into the glass-walled guest elevator, hands on my hips.

"So," I say, making sure I understand the problem, "the guests went in there . . ."

"But they never came out," Orban says. "At least, not out into the Hotel. Their family got a phone call from Dubai, where the guests ended up. We returned them home and took their coins so that they'll forget their unplanned excursion, but we have to keep it from happening again."

Elevators not going to their correct destination—one more problem to deal with. I wonder if Nico's behind this one too.

Orban finishes posting the stanchions and hanging velvet ropes around the elevator to make sure no one else takes an unexpected trip. It's only one of about forty elevators in the Elevator Bank ring, but even having one OUT OF ORDER sign bothers me. We were supposed to be able to take all those down once we got the Greenhouse and the Vesima back. Those OUT OF ORDER signs seem to scream to everyone who passes, *Look, here's one more thing Cam can't handle.*

"I'll take a ride and see what happens," I tell him. "Maybe I can figure out what's wrong."

"I'm coming too!" Cass's voice calls from around the bend.

I close my eyes and take a deep breath. How is it she always manages to be where she's not supposed to be?

"Aren't you on front desk duty right now?" I ask. "I'm certain that's what the schedule says." After all, I'm the one who wrote the schedule.

"I'm on a break."

Dad rounds the corner behind her. "I figured we'd go for a little walk."

"'Roll,' Dad," Cass corrects. "Sheesh." Dad chuckles.

It's weird seeing the two of them getting along. Growing up, Cass was always the one irritated at him for abandoning us. Now it seems easier for her to talk to him than it is for me to, even though I was the one who invited Dad to stay with us. But I just can't forget all those years we had without him.

"I saw the report of the elevator problem hidden under a bunch of papers in the front office, and I was curious," Cass says. "I want to help."

I hid that sheet under those papers specifically to avoid this. Cass has gotten into a habit of trying to show me just how helpful she can be, so that I'll move her off front desk duty.

"I'm only checking it out," I tell them. "It won't be fun."

"Then you won't mind company," Dad says. "Please."

I twist my lips. "All right," I say, and my family piles onto the elevator as though we're headed to the fair.

Like all the other guest elevators, the three floor-to-ceiling walls of this gold-trimmed box are connected to different views from around the world. These show scenes of rainbow-colored geysers, a pastoral countryside dotted with sleeping goats under a night sky, and a craggy cliff side that drops into an ocean glittering with the sunset. Windows like these are scattered throughout the Hotel, but for some reason they always feel more impressive in the elevators. Maybe it's because we're close enough to press our noses to the glass.

"What do you think is wrong with it?" Cass asks as we start moving.

"I'm not sure *anything* is wrong yet," I tell her.

"But Orban said—"

"I won't know for sure until I see for myself."

She folds her arms. "You don't trust Orban?"

"Of course I trust him."

"But you don't believe him."

I clench my jaw.

Dad shifts uncomfortably. He doesn't jump into our arguments often, which is probably for the best. Every time he's tried, it doesn't end well. "How are your plans for the gala?" he asks. "You haven't talked much about it lately."

"They're fine," I say. Truth is, I haven't done much to talk about—I've looked through Agapios's files from previous Hotel events, come up with some meal ideas to give to Chef Silva. But

I can't let anyone know how behind I feel. Hopefully, during my next meeting with Agapios, I'll get a few more leads on what to do.

"If you need any help from me, you know you can ask, right?" Dad says.

"Yeah."

He takes a deep breath. "Cam, I wanted to talk to you."

Here we go. I knew there had to be another reason for them forcing their way into a small, enclosed box with me.

"Yeah," Cass says, straightening her back. "Dad says you need to cut me some slack with this whole front desk thing."

Dad rests a hand on her shoulder. "Cassia, let me talk." He looks back to me. "I understand that you're looking out for her, but that's not your job."

"But Agapios said it *was* my job," I retort. "I'm supposed to be in charge of the assignments, figure out who belongs where."

"Do you really think the front desk is the best place for her?" he asks. "Or are you putting her there because you're trying to manage her?"

That's not fair. For most of our lives, it was just Oma, Cass, and me. Sometimes Cass had a home health care nurse, but we couldn't always depend on having anyone else. That meant I had to do a lot—*learn* a lot—to take care of things when Cass had one of her many surgeries, or know what to do if anything went wrong. He wasn't there. He wasn't taking care of her, or taking care of *me*, and now he's telling me I shouldn't be taking care of Cass anymore?

The elevator rattles, and the platform shakes beneath our feet.

I place a hand against the warm window of the hot springs to balance myself.

Cass flips on her brake. "Guest elevators don't normally do that, do they?"

"Not as far as I know," I reply. Though, I don't ride the guest lifts very much. Staff are supposed to stick to the service elevators.

The floor shakes again, as though changing rails. Shaft elevators move in all directions to reach the doors, so a rail switch isn't uncommon. Only, this time the box grinds to a complete stop.

We can't have gotten to our floor already.

I hit the button again. Nothing happens. "We're stuck."

Cass pushes me aside. "Let me try."

"There's nothing you can do that I can't."

"There's *lots* I can do that you can't," she says, mashing the console. Then, "Yep, stuck."

I pick up the elevator phone to call the front desk. It rings and rings, but no one picks up. I glare at Cass. "Looks like no one's manning the front desk after all."

She grimaces. "Elizabeth's supposed to be there."

"No," I say, "*you* are supposed to be there."

"We can argue about that later," Dad says. "Right now we need to figure out how to get this thing moving again."

"Maybe there's something on the rail?" Cass guesses. "We should have Maintenance inspect it."

But this is a problem I can deal with. Like Oma says, *it's an opportunity.* A chance for me to prove that I can handle any situation the

73

Hotel throws at me. A way to show that I know what I'm doing. "I'll check. Dad, can you boost me up?"

"Maybe we should wait," he replies.

"We don't need to wait. I'm the CiT. I can do this."

He leans his back against the cliff-view wall, studying me. "If anyone should go, it's me. It's too dangerous up there."

I narrow my eyes. "So it's okay for Cass to do things that are dangerous, but not for me to?" It's a terrible argument, I know, but I need to prove myself. "I can handle it."

Dad twists his lips. "All right," he says finally. "Be careful, though."

He cradles his fingers together to make a foothold and lifts me high enough to reach the escape hatch in the ceiling.

"It's stuck too," I say after a few failed attempts to open it.

"Try this," Cass says, and digs in the space next to her chair cushion to pull out a small Swiss Army knife. She's always pulling stuff out of those crevices, but I've never seen this item before.

"You were sitting on a knife?" I ask, incredulous.

"It was in the crack next to the cushion," she says, ignoring my tone. "Keeps falling out of my pocket. Try it."

One of the built-in accessories—I think it's a can opener—gives me enough leverage to pop the hatch open, and Dad lifts me up the rest of the way.

I pull myself out and duck under the curved metal track that supports the elevator to once again face the empty open-air column.

The mechanism that attaches the elevator to the rails along

the pit wall comes almost up to my stomach. It's so dark that I can barely make out the gears and wheels that allow the elevator to move along it.

A burst of wind cuts through me, and I grab one of the curved tracks to keep from falling into that pit like Mom did. This is a terrible idea. What am I trying to prove, really? That I can face danger and be reckless too? I've never had any desire to be reckless.

"What do you see?" Dad calls from inside.

"I'm not sure," I answer. "It's too dark."

"Here, give him this," Cass says. Moments later Dad hands me a flashlight. Only, it's not a normal flashlight. It's one of the arm-rests from her chair. Another of the Motor Pool's upgrades? Nice.

I pass the flashlight over the rail line and find the problem almost immediately.

"Something's growing across the tracks," I tell them. "Or grew. Some kind of vine or root or something." I run my fingers along the woody mass that's twisted around the metal and wrapped up in the wheel. "I think it's dead."

"Can you cut it loose?" Dad asks.

I use Cass's knife to saw at the piece that's twisted around the rail. It seems unlikely that this thin curl of wood could have diverted the elevator and its passengers to a completely different door, but then again the Hotel's magic does strange things some-times.

The dead growth pulls loose, and I examine it in the flash-light beam. A crisp, brown flower hangs from the branch, like a dark-colored lily that dried in the sun. "Should be good now. I'm coming—"

The elevator lurches.

I stumble and grab for the rail, but miss, and instead end up hooking my arm into what remains of the dead growth.

Cass's armrest tumbles into the darkness. But I'm okay. I'm okay. I just need to get inside before—

The elevator drops again, rolling down the curved incline in the track, and this time my footing slips.

"Cam!" Dad's voice.

I slide off the edge.

A yank on my wrist stops my fall. Pain shouts through my shoulder as my body slams against one of the elevator's windows.

My heart races as I dangle over the darkness. The elevator only dropped a few feet, but it left me hanging from the vine.

I face out into the pit, my back pressed against the surface of the gold-framed glass. Nothing but this thin, dead vine wrapped around my wrist keeps me from falling into the hole below. When I look over my shoulder at the elevator wall behind me, I see the opposite side of the nighttime pasture scene inside the elevator—both sides are bound, only this side faces south instead of north.

I hear a commotion inside the elevator. Dad's saying something, but I can't understand him over the boom of my heartbeat. I could have died. I could have fallen like Mom did, and that would have been it. Thank goodness that vine was there to catch me, but what now? I can't move, can't bring myself to look up or down, can't do anything except hold on.

"Cam," Dad's voice says again, above me now, "I've got you," and there's a tug on the vine as he starts to pull me up.

I spin as I rise, and catch a glimpse of myself reflected in the night sky beyond the glass wall. Only . . . it's not me I see. It's Nico. He's wearing a tweed vest, with a blue flower in his lapel. His hair is longer than I remember, poking out from under his flat cap.

I jerk my head around to look out into the empty air behind me, but he's not there. And when I look back at the glass, I notice there's something else odd about the image too. It's as if the reflection is being hand drawn frame by frame. His outline keeps shifting—inky, haphazard lines with scribbled edges.

Mirror-Nico takes one hand off the vine and puts a finger to his lips as Dad hoists me the rest of the way up onto the elevator.

Immediately I'm engulfed in a bear hug. "I was so scared that I'd lost you again," Dad says, squeezing me hard.

But I'm not even thinking about the fall anymore—I'm too busy processing what I just saw. Was it Nico who twisted that growth up in the rail? Was he the one who put me in danger?

And if so, why is he trying to kill me?

9

Lightning Strikes

Now that the overgrowth has been cut away from the tracks, the elevator is able to take us back to the Elevator Bank.

Once we're out, I head straight for the safety of my room. That night I lie in bed, covers up to my chin, nowhere near asleep. Thank goodness Housekeeping was able to replace my bed, because all I want to do is lose myself under the covers. Nico's troublesome grin haunts me. I probably imagined it. Or maybe it's stress, like Oma keeps saying.

Almost a week has passed since my new assignment, and I don't feel any closer to having this gala thing figured out. There are so many things to consider, like arranging entertainment, and making sure no one with an allergy eats anything that'll kill them. Then there's the whole seating chart thing. . . .

I roll over and open the top drawer of my bedside table to pull out Bee's sliver. A part of me wants to use it, to disappear like that cat vanished down that hallway. Is that why Bee left it with me, so I could follow her to Nico? I can't though; I promised Rahki.

THE KEY OF LOST THINGS

Besides, I have no idea where it would take me, and I have too many responsibilities to deal with at the moment.

The knob on my door turns, and I shove the sliver under the covers, only briefly worrying that being too rough with it will result in my bed performing some tricks of its own.

Cass rolls through the door.

"Don't you knock?" I ask, heart pounding. She's the last person I want knowing I've got a forbidden magical weapon hidden in my bedroom.

"I was coming to see if you were okay. Sheesh," she says, pretending to be offended.

"You were?"

"Of course I was. You almost fell today. I was scared."

"Oh." I'm not sure what to say to that. I lie back, careful to avoid the tip of the sliver next to me. "I'm fine. I didn't die."

She bunches up her lips, waiting for something. "Don't you have something you want to say to me too?"

I glance at the clock. I know she wants me to talk about what Dad said in the elevator—to tell her I'm sorry—but all I really want is to get her out of my room so that I can stow the sliver safely back in its hiding place. "Umm, no, not really. You can go on about your business."

Cass folds her arms. "You mean go back to chaining myself to the front desk? Apparently that's all I'm good for."

"That's not what I—"

"I don't even know why I try with you," she snaps, and leaves,

79

slamming the door behind her. I should go after her. Apologize for being a jerk. She was coming to check that I was okay after my harrowing afternoon, and I repaid her by pushing her away.

But I don't move. If I apologize, she'll know she's right—and she'll know that I know she's right—and she'll keep doing stuff like she did today. What if something worse had happened, and no one had been there to answer the front desk phone? The more I think about it, the angrier it makes me. Everyone else does what I say, so why is she exempt? If anything, what happened on the elevator further proved my point. Surely Dad will see that now.

If Cass doesn't like me, maybe she'll stop trying to convince me to change her assignment. I'm supposed to manage people, right? This is the only way I know how to manage her. She'll stay mad at me, but if that means doing what she's supposed to, maybe it's for the best.

Another week over. Another awkward family dinner night.

This time Oma takes us to a tiny village built on a tributary beside a wide lake surrounded by palm trees. Two dozen or so tin shacks rise out of the water on stilts. A heavy thundercloud hangs over the distant mountains. The lake swooshes beneath us, making the boats bob against the pier.

"It's Catatumbo!" Cass shouts, way too loudly for this quiet place. How on earth is she so good at this?

"*Bienvenidos a Venezuela!*" Oma casts her arms wide like a game show host. "I know you like your storms."

After spraying us down with a layer of bug repellent strong enough to melt plastic, Oma leads us across a series of bridges to a pier under an awning strung with lights, attached to a tin shack. The whole community here is built not *next* to the water, but *on* it—a series of piers and docks all connected into a mishmash of metal and wood. Long lines of blue, triangular flags droop back and forth across the water from building to building across a river leading away from the nearby lake. The flags flutter in the strong wind.

Cass bumps me with her wheelchair when I bend down to tie my Chucks. "Oops," she says as I stumble to the edge of the decking. "Don't fall. Wouldn't want you to become piranha bait."

I glance over at the calm lake. "There are piranha in there?"

"Maybe." She rubs her hands together like a supervillain. Yep, still fighting. Ever since Cass stormed out of my room, it's been even worse. We don't usually fight often, but when we do, it's the stuff of legend.

Storm clouds gather as the last bits of daylight fade. I sit at the table opposite Cass while Oma lights a green anti-mosquito coil. The scent of the repellent mixes with the smell of the metal walls and lake water and aroma of fried fish wafting from the nearby window. The smell reminds me of the time I went on a weekend fishing trip with a friend and his dad a few years ago. In the distance a bolt of purple lightning promises plenty more nerve-tingling thunder for dinner.

"The Catatumbo lightning storms never really end," Cass says, raising a finger to accent her impressive assortment of trivia. "It storms here every night."

I rub the static-y hairs on my arms. "I don't like storms." Lightning is one of the holdovers from the Worst Ways to Die list from last year. Kills you in an instant, and there's nothing you can do to stop it.

Cass sticks out her tongue. "Stop whining."

"I'm not whining."

"Hush, both of you." Oma leans forward to pour our drinks. "Tonight is for Cassia. She's been stuck in that little office for too long, so I picked this place for her."

Oh. Now I see what's happening. "You're punishing me?"

"I'm not punishing you, dear," Oma says. "Just giving your sister a special treat."

"It's not all about *you*, you know," Cass adds.

"It's not like you do the work you're supposed to anyway," I say. "People depend on you being at your station, and you're never there."

"This is *not* about me answering phones. This is about you wanting to keep me on a leash."

I growl at that. "You know what, you're right. As long as you're inside, the Hotel's magic protects you. The whole point of bringing you here was to keep you healthy."

"That's *your* whole point," Cass says.

"What's that supposed to mean?"

"Enough," Oma says. "We're not here to blame anyone. We're here to enjoy dinner."

Our argument dies on our tongues. The only sound is the hiss of the grills inside the shack behind me and the rumbling sky on the horizon.

One of the locals passes through a beaded curtain carrying plastic bowls of fish stew, a plate of shredded dark meat, flat corn cakes, and little piles of brown rice-looking stuff that I don't recognize.

"What's that?" I ask, poking at the rice things in a not-so-subtle attempt to break the silence.

"Try it," Oma says. "You might like it."

"But what *is* it?"

"It's fried ants!" Cass says. "I've been wanting to try those." She dives right in. I take a bite too. The ants taste citrusy, and strangely a little like gas station pork rinds. Not bad.

The door we arrived through across the bridge opens again, and Dad steps through wearing the same grungy jeans and soil-stained shirt he must've been wearing in the Greenhouse today. His arms are speckled with dirt, and sweat glistens across his forehead.

Another flash of lightning, followed by the rumble of thunder.

"Nice of you to join us," Oma says.

"Sorry, sorry." He takes the seat next to me. "Didn't realize what time it was." He even smells like the Greenhouse, which is especially offensive, considering the Vesima's rotting-fruit problem.

I start to say something about his appearance—to remind him that we live in a Hotel, with Housekeeping and Laundry Service and an endless supply of complimentary soaps—but I stop myself. This evening doesn't need to be any more miserable than it already is.

"So, what are we talking about?" Dad asks, stabbing the shredded meat with his fork.

"Just about how Cam still insists on putting me in the most boring job ever," Cass snipes.

A bubble of annoyance rises in my throat, but I swallow it back down with another bite of ants. *Keep it under control. Don't let her get to you.*

Dad looks back and forth between Cass's pursed lips and my scowl. "I think I missed something."

Yeah, about twelve years of something.

"Your brother cares for you," Oma says, reaching for Cass's hand. "He may not show it in the right way all the time, but he cares."

Cass harrumphs. "If it were up to him, I'd be wrapped in bubble wrap and put in storage for the rest of my life."

"That is not true," I snap. Lightning cracks over the edge of the lake. "Sometimes I think you *want* to end up back in the hospital."

"It'd be better than sitting behind that stupid desk while you hang off the side of elevators."

"She has a point, Cam." Dad leans back, glancing between us. "You can't watch her every minute of the day. She has the right to go places too. Make her own mistakes."

The thunder roars in my ears. "Because that worked out so well for you, didn't it."

Oma slaps her hand on the table. "That is enough! Cameron, you do not talk to your father that way."

"He doesn't get to tell me how to take care of my sister," I say, practically shouting. I don't want to yell, but I'm so angry. He missed out on taking care of us, and now he's telling me *I* shouldn't be taking care of things?

"You don't take care of me—" Cass starts.

But I'm not done. "He doesn't know what it was like when he was gone and it was just us. I let him come to the Hotel so that we could try to be a family, but he doesn't even care enough to make it to dinner on time."

He shrinks back at that.

"Stop," Oma says in a tone that definitively says I've crossed the line. But right now I don't care. Dad crossed all the lines already. Ever since he came back, Cass acts like the lines don't even exist. And when I think about it, if it weren't for him, I probably wouldn't even be in a position to hang off the side of elevators in the first place. In fact, everything bad that's ever happened to us is because of what he did that night all those years ago.

"I should've never invited you," I mumble, unable to look anywhere other than my plate of ants.

The table goes silent. The kind-faced lady carrying a tray of desserts slowly backs away into the shack. The only sound is the rumble of the storm and the creak of the waves against the deck.

I ease myself back onto the bench. That was too far. It's not like me to say those things. For that matter, he saved my life on that elevator. And I was always supportive of Cass before we came to the Hotel, even if I did want to take care of everything. But I just feel so . . . tired. I don't know how to be what everyone wants me to be. I thought us being together at the Hotel would fix our relationship—make us one big happy family—but even magics can't fix everything. I'm failing—at being a good son, a good brother. I'm not even a good Concierge-in-Training.

Dad leaves the table. Oma shoots me a glare and follows, leaving me alone with Cass as the first droplets of rain patter across the tin roof of the awning.

"Now you've done it," Cass says after a minute. "He's going to end up leaving, you know."

"What do you care?" I cross my arms and watch the water as the rain begins to fall in sheets. "You never wanted him here in the first place."

I don't know where the rest of my family goes after our disastrous dinner, but I head down to the Greenhouse. To Mom.

The Greenhouse dome is almost empty, despite the bright sky. For some reason, it's always daylight here, as though this place isn't subject to the normal turning of the earth—another of the Hotel's endless mysteries. I like coming here, despite the smell. I'm even starting to get used to the odor.

I flop down onto the roots at the base of the Vesima tree, and the sickly leaves rustle overhead.

"Yeah, I know," I say. "I'm sorry."

Of course, the tree doesn't reply. I like to imagine that Mom sees what goes on in this weird life of mine and tells me the things I need to hear. *You shouldn't have done that, Cam. You need to apologize. You're wrong.*

Why *did* I say all those things? Lately I feel angry all the time.

"I'll try," I say when my mom's imaginary voice tells me to cut Dad some slack. I know he's doing the best he can, and I need to accept that. I'm just not sure how. I don't know how to be less angry at him, or at Cass for wanting me to trust that she can take care of herself. I don't even trust *me* most of the time.

I just want to find a way to get all the chaos of my new life back under control.

"Am I a jerk?" I ask into the air.

I settle into a cleft in the tree's enormous roots and pull out my notepad, anxious for anything to distract me. My list of to-do's for the gala is growing, after my most recent meetings with Agapios. We need security, a theme. He said I'll have to organize the guest list, but I don't even know who's *supposed* to be on the list, or what the Embassy's connection is to the Hotel. The more I think about it, the more overwhelmed I feel. Agapios says he'll be there to help, but if I'm supposed to be concierge one day, shouldn't I be able to do this stuff on my own?

I pick at the bark on the Vesima's trunk. Everyone talks about Mom like she was the best thing that ever happened to this place. She would have been able to keep it all together. Why couldn't I have ended up more like her?

When I pull my hand back, my fingers come away black and sticky. Why are we worried about parties when we can't even fix our tree? If the Vesima dies, there is no gala.

I go to wipe my hand on the grass, but . . . the goop is gone. My hand is clean.

That's strange. It was all over my fingers. I'm imagining things again, like that cat running down the sixth-floor hall, and Nico's reflection in the Shaft.

As I stare up into the branches, a chill runs up my back. I pull Mom's topscrew out of my pocket. The key's cold again—it gets that way whenever I come down here, almost as if it's reacting to its proximity to the tree. I wonder if it can sense its previous owner trapped inside.

"We'll figure everything out," I say. "The gala, and you, Mom. I know we will."

10

The Ledger of Ways

The next morning I take the service elevator to the sublevel—which is an actual war submarine from the 1940s—and head down its dimly lit, metal corridor to the heavy airlock door that leads to Agapios's office.

I've been this way many times to meet with the Old Man, but this is the first time I've noticed the recessed bronze plaque on the wall nearby.

EFS *Atalanta*
"Guard the Roads in the Night"
—Adm. Virginia Dare

Wow. Admiral Dare even has a plaque in her honor. All the more reason to make sure everything's as perfect as it can be for her party.

I spin the wheel lock and step through into the Concierge Retreat.

"Cameron, please, come in."

Agapios sits at his cluttered desk under the dusty clay dome, scribbling something with a long wooden pen. A ceiling fan squeaks overhead. The key cupboard behind his desk is open, revealing the hundreds of keys that the Old Man has collected to keep them out of the hands of the Competition. Very few are topscrews like Mom's, but most have a little magic in them.

"Did you bring your mother's key with you?" he asks.

I dig the pearl topscrew out of my pocket and finger the delicate design on the bow. We rarely discuss Mom, or her key, these days. Topscrews like this are super rare—but I still have no idea why.

The Old Man stands. "I have something for you."

He leads me to one of the four doors arrayed around the Concierge Retreat like directions on a compass. I've only ever been through one of these doors—the southern one, which leads back to the sub-level and the Hotel. Now we pass through the eastern door into a large, bright room. I shield my eyes against the sunlight streaming through the windows, and blink away the spots in my vision. The dry air sucks the moisture out of my hands.

As my eyes adjust, I'm struck by how old this room looks. Everything in it is made of rusty red stone—walls, tables, even the rows and rows of bookshelves. It's as if they've all been carved out of that same curry-colored sandstone I see through the open windows, stretching out into the distance.

The Old Man motions to a bench next to a low stone table. "Please, sit."

I ease myself onto the bench, scanning the ancient-looking books lining the shelves. They're not like the printed books in our town library. These look like they were hand-scribed by someone sitting in a room just like this.

"What is this place?" I ask as Agapios sits on the bench across from me.

"My file room, in a city long forgotten." He waves a hand toward the slab table, where a leather-bound book lies closed. "Have a look."

The cover shimmers as I run my fingers along the artfully carved tree and read the stylized lettering. *The Ledger of Ways.* I flip it open, and see that the pages are crisp and brittle with age. Many are darkened at the edges and are flaking away; some have been torn out completely. Not that it would make any difference— every last page is blank.

"This is one of the Hotel's most important artifacts," the Old Man whispers. "A fountain of knowledge, born from the Hotel itself. You could say it's the Hotel's voice."

I drag my fingers down what should be the title page; images and words burn their way across the surface of the page in golden lines, like on Oma's slates. The glittering ink draws my sister gazing out across a valley. On the next page, Oma rearranges family pictures on the hall table at home.

"What's it doing?"

"The Ledger is reading you," he says.

"*It* is reading *me?*"

He hums in confirmation. "Though I fear it is . . . out of practice. When the Vesima was hidden, the book was unable to read anyone. It needs to be used again in order to reclaim the power and skill it once had."

More images. Me seeing my dad for the first time, and the moment when I realized that he wasn't what I'd hoped. A picture of me writing up the contract that took the Museum away from Mr. Stripe, and Stripe's baleful expression when he realized he'd been tricked.

I pull my hand away, and the ink fades.

"Why would I want to see those awful things all over again?" I ask.

"The Ledger fixates on the reader's strongest memories and emotions. It catalogues them to help the reader remember who they are and better understand those around them. It seems you keep your darkest moments close."

That's what Oma's always saying—that I focus too much on the bad things.

Agapios leans in. "Anyone who wishes to master one of the great Houses must learn to communicate with the House's heart." He taps the page. "Please, touch it again. Only this time, ask it a question. Ask it about the Embassy."

I do as he says, and new sketches form out of the ink. Pictures of men and women I've never met, their names in flowing script on banners beneath them. Dembe Tun. Francesca Corona. Anastasia Romann. Wang Zhenyi. Virginia Dare.

92

"These are ambassadors," I say as the figures of Agapios Panotierri and Jehanna la Pucelle curl into the ink at the bottom of the page. "You and the MC?"

"The Embassy is made up of people from all over the world who have built a relationship with the Hotel's binding magic. It is in the magic's nature to bring people together, and so those who have built a relationship with the binding magic have also formed a unified group to work alongside it. Our organization, the Embassy, is committed to protecting this world from those who would exploit it."

"Like Stripe."

Agapios frowns slightly at the name, but the expression fades almost instantly. "The Ledger contains records of every person who has ever been bound to the Hotel. The Embassy's agents, and representatives of governments who know secrets that they can't share, the builders, fighters—many ambassadors get their start here, but not all. This book should help you better understand some of the people you will be serving."

I remove my hand, and the figures disperse. "Why me? You're giving me all this responsibility, and . . . it seems like you should be the only one to even touch something like this."

"Ah, I can't sneak anything by you." He tents his fingers in front of his pale lips. "Unfortunately, I am no longer able to use the Ledger. I'd hoped my connection to it would return to me once we reclaimed the Greenhouse, but alas, it has not."

"So . . . *you* can't make it work, but *I* can?"

SEAN EASLEY

"It would seem so." The Old Man wets his lips. "I have been with this House for many ages. Perhaps there is too much knowledge locked up in this old brain of mine. Or maybe the Hotel has tired of having me as its master. Regardless, it appears my time as Grand Concierge is drawing to a close. The House seeks a new master."

It's not that Agapios *wants* to choose a replacement—it's that he *has* to. Interesting. "And the other old heads of the Hotel?" I ask. "Surely someone else deserves the position more than I do."

"Something is on the horizon, Mr. Cameron. This House senses it, and wishes to be ready when it comes. But the magics of Houses are wild—they do not let us determine how they're used. Often, *they* use *us*."

"That sounds dangerous."

He smiles. "The Hotel is bound by the magical bond of Law, as are all magics. So long as the power that enforces the bond of Law remains intact, the Hotel is required to honor its agreements with us. That keeps us safe."

Remains intact. He's not talking about just violating some rules—he's talking about keeping the power that created the rules safe. The binding created the treaty between magics and humans, and laid the fundamental bonds as a foundation. Is it possible to destroy the fundamental bonds altogether? To break the magic that the Hotel is founded on, and remove the restrictions that keep the other magics of the world in line?

"And anyway," Agapios continues, "ours is a kind House—it

longs to provide the best for the people in its care. It would never do anything to harm us."

The way he says that makes my teeth clench. *The Hotel would never do anything to harm us.* We've seen that there are magics out there that would, and people who would take advantage of that. People like Stripe.

"*The Ledger of Ways* knows our guests' deepest desires and darkest fears. This is how you will learn to serve the people entrusted to our care." He pauses. "Knowledge and truth are among the sharpest blades in the world. When used together they are a double-edged sword, able to cut deeper than any other."

He taps the Ledger's cover, and I read those same words inscribed across the leather.

"I will provide you with a list of attendees," the Old Man says. "Learn what you can about them, and make haste with your preparations. Many of my Embassy peers do not understand the Hotel as we do—they see its dangers more than its strengths. They will close our doors for good if they sense weakness in these uncertain times."

"Wait, the Embassy can shut down the Hotel?"

Agapios hums. "We are but one small piece in a larger machine. Your actions last year set events in motion that had been still for a very long time. Many of the ambassadors fear this new position we find ourselves in, now that Stripe no longer has a House to call his own. He has not been this desperate for a very long time, and the Hotel is still a merciful House. To the desperate, the merciful seem easy prey."

I haven't heard Agapios talk about Stripe in months. "Do you know where Stripe is?"

He leans back. "No, but he will make himself known eventually, and we must be ready. I recognize the weight of what I'm asking you to do. Remember, when little is expected of us, we become small. Challenges make us grow, and shape us into something grander than we could be otherwise."

With that, he stands to leave.

"Tomorrow morning a Mr. Nagalla will be coming to examine the Hotel's security," he says. "Arrange a nice tour, won't you?"

"Where are you going?" I ask.

"To the Greenhouse." He smiles. "Soon I think we should see a change in our poor tree. The Ledger is in your care now—please, give it and yourself a chance to learn the truth before you decide whether you are ready to be what the Hotel needs of you. You may be surprised by what it reveals."

As the Old Man turns the door handle, my biggest fear bubbles up into one huge burp of a question. "What if I'm not ready?"

He stops, but doesn't look back.

I lick my lips. "What if the Hotel is wrong about me? What if I've changed my mind? What if I . . . decline?"

"Then my search for a successor will continue," he says. "Though, I don't know if this picky old House will be able to choose one in time."

11

Holes, Holes Everywhere

I stand next to the front desk under the guardian dog-lion statues in the Asiatic Lobby, my feet wide, hands behind my back
in parade rest, waiting for this so-called Mr. Nagalla to arrive.
I should have tried to use *The Ledger of Ways* to learn what I could
about this Embassy representative before he got here, but with my
normal concierge duties and all my gala preparations, there wasn't
enough time.

My talk with Agapios keeps replaying in my head. I never once
considered why a several-hundred-year-old hotel manager would
be searching for a successor after all this time. Sure, we call him
the Old Man, but that doesn't mean we really think he's going anywhere. Agapios was running this place long before any of us were
born—we assumed he'd be around long after we left.

Did he do something wrong? Did the Hotel decide that if
Agapios couldn't protect it and the Greenhouse, he didn't deserve
to run it? If that's the case, I can't be the one who lets the Hotel
down again. Rahki was right—I have to make sure the Hotel trusts
me, especially if it no longer trusts Agapios.

"Are you sure you don't want me to give the tour?" Rahki asks, pulling her headphones down to rest around her neck. "There are some things you might not know."

"Like your 'security enhancements'?" She has refused to tell me any of the work she and Cass have been doing to protect the Hotel against Nico. "No, the Old Man asked me to do this, so I'll take care of it on my own." Which isn't entirely true. Agapios asked me to arrange a tour, and yeah, Rahki could lead that, but surely what he meant was for me to. I am CiT, after all.

Rahki sighs "Okay" and motions for Sana to go with her. "Come on, *habibi*. Cam says he doesn't need us."

Sana gives me a wave as they make for the Pacific Lobby.

"Who is this Nagalla person in the first place?" Sev asks as he returns from double-checking the knockers. "Why is he coming here now?"

"Agapios said the Embassy has the power to shut the Hotel down if we pose a risk," I tell him. "So we have to make a good impression."

A knock comes at the Shanghai Door. Sev moves to answer it, but I grab his arm.

"This is on me," I say. "I'll catch you later."

He shrugs and heads off to talk to Elizabeth. Now it's time to show the Hotel exactly how responsible I can be.

When I answer, I'm met by a short, round man with exaggerated features and a pair of really big aviator sunglasses. "Mr. Nagalla?"

The man pushes past me and slams the door behind him with a loud *bang!*

"So," he snaps, whirling to face me, "merely anyone can knock at a door, and you just open it right up? Could you see who stood behind the door before you opened it? No, I think you could not. What if I were the Competition? You would just let the Competition fox-trot in as if they owned the place, hmm?"

He spins and strides away from me—faster than I'd expect from someone of his stature—and heads straight for the front desk.

I trail behind, trying to explain. "Sir, we have cameras that monitor everyone who passes through the knockers, and the Competition couldn't enter without an invitation, so—"

"Is an open door not an invitation? It *seems* like an open door is exactly that. An open door says, 'Come right on in. Take all my secrets.' That's what it seems to me."

"We have the icons too." I motion to the giant stone statues that the staff can control, should an intruder decide to make trouble. "If anyone were to get in, the icons can keep us safe."

"Safe." Nagalla snorts. "There is no safe. Everyone resting their hopes on bonds and rules and magical treaties that can be broken and bent. It's laughable. Downright laughable." He leans over the desk and shouts at Elizabeth, who's talking to Sev. "Girl? Girl!"

Elizabeth's glare could burn a hole through Nagalla's face. No one calls her "girl" and gets away with it. "Yes, Mr. Very Important Person? What can I do for you?"

Nagalla doesn't appear to notice her sarcasm, but I shake my head, silently begging her not to make this guy any angrier than he already is.

Spittle flies from his mouth with every other word. "I need to see a list of all the people who have entered the Hotel today, along with the names of each and every staff member who answered their knock."

"Maybe if you ask nicely," Elizabeth mumbles.

Mr. Nagalla ignores her, pacing the lobby and examining the lions, the swooping sashes of fabric, every little detail as if looking for something. "I understand you had an infestation recently. Cats, was it? Little monsters snuck in, caused havoc everywhere?"

A fake meow comes from behind the front desk window. It's Cass, taunting me like only a sister can.

My insides shrivel. "Yes, sir. We did have a . . . minor incident."

"A fiasco, from what I hear." His voice is sharp, each syllable a mini firecracker.

"Oh yeah," Cass says, joining us in the lobby. "You should have seen it. Cat hair everywhere, hairballs, cat scratch fever."

I shoot her a dirty look. She must be getting back at me for Catatumbo. It's the one time she's where I asked her to be, and I wish she were anywhere else.

Nagalla curls his lip. "And who was responsible for the cleanup of said fiasco?"

"I was, sir," I tell him.

He finally stops moving to look me over. "I will never understand Agapios's insistence on putting *children* in a position of power," he says, clutching a dramatic fist. "Seems to me this House should be run by someone strong. Someone who knows what they're doing. A general. Someone like the Maid Commander, not"—he looks me over again—"you."

Dignified and gracious, dignified and gracious. "Sir, the Hotel has plenty of security measures that I'm sure you'll appreciate," I tell him, stuffing down all the things I really want to say. Maybe Rahki should have handled the tour after all. "And which I'm happy to tell you about. Are you ready for the tour?"

"Indeed." He turns and heads straight for the Elevator Bank. Cass follows, talking his ear off about dusty mantels and squeaky hinges. Please tell me she's not tagging along.

"*Aajh,*" Elizabeth mumbles, "what a jerk."

"She sure can be," I say, and follow Nagalla the Terrible and Cass the Vengeful to start this parade of awfulness.

Mr. Nagalla might as well be leading his own tour, given how well he knows the Hotel already. The portly man marches ahead of me, commenting on the sorry state of everything from the Elevator Bank to the guest rooms. Cass points out every out-of-place thing she can, adding more fuel to his fire.

"You absolutely should change the layout more often," Nagalla muses. "It seems to me a House that can change shape should do so, and regularly. Anyone who's been here in the past thirty years could easily find their way to its vulnerabilities. All it would take is the right coin. Wide open to attack, it is."

"So true," Cass says, smirking impishly. "Cam, you should be taking notes."

I don't indulge Cass and Mr. Nagalla any more than I need to, and decide to let them do the talking instead. I can't exactly confront Cass in front of him. For what feels like hours Nagalla grumbles about how easy it would be to steal icons from the Motor Pool, and how giving a topscrew to a child is "Agapios's biggest mistake since the Château." Staff dormitories shouldn't be all the way up on the top levels, in case of emergency. He even complains that assigning a cruise ship to be the main dining hall is a terrible idea, because "what if guests get seasick?" (I tend to agree on that last point.) All the while Cass confirms his complaints one after another. What a great opportunity for her to enact her revenge.

Finally we end up at the War Room.

"This is where I leave you, Mr. Nagalla," Cass says, offering a hand.

He shakes it eagerly. "A pleasure, Ms. Cassia. Maybe with staff like you around, this place won't end up too bad." And he heads through the metal door.

"That was plain awful," I say once he's through.

"Lighten up." Cass pats my biceps as she passes. "Consider justice delivered, for the time being. Now excuse me while I return to my cage. Have fun!"

I take a deep breath and follow Mr. Nagalla inside.

The sun-shaped light behind the War Room's stained glass globe-dome is high over North America now, and the maids are hard at work. Most of what the maids do is entirely separate from the Hotel's normal operations—as if they were a completely different House. I've never understood why they're so different from the rest of the hotel staff.

Mr. Nagalla marches across the Map Floor, aimed directly at the Maid Commander. "Jehanna!"

The MC is dressed in full regalia—buttoned-up jacket dripping with medals and commendations, gray hair pulled back to accent her frown. Her sword hangs at her side, the silver pommel shining.

She turns to face Nagalla. "Venkat." Her tone is almost . . . welcoming? "I hope you're finding your destination satisfactory today."

"You know exactly how I find my destination," Nagalla replies. "This place is a disaster. Holes! Holes everywhere! It's a wonder the Competition isn't running this place already."

"Please." The MC turns to monitor the screens ahead. "Agapios and I have been keeping this House safe and in action since long before you were even a thought. I assure you that we know quite well what the Hotel wants."

He throws his hands into the air. "It doesn't matter what the Hotel wants! We have to keep the mission safe, and from what I can see, it's never been in more danger. With the Curator loosed from his Museum, we have no idea what he's up to. He could be anywhere!" Nagalla eyes me warily, and adds in what I can only assume is his failed attempt at a whisper, "It was different when we had Melissa."

Did this man know my mom? I really should have consulted the Ledger before all this.

"Honestly," he continues, "how Agapios could make this boy Concierge-in-Training . . . It's irresponsible and careless, and it *will* be the end of us."

"Venkat, you know that in many areas I'm inclined to agree with you," she says, "but in this House we are and have always been beholden to our contracts. The House decides on matters like these. You should know that better than anyone else."

He snorts. "Maybe it's time we forgot the will of the Hotel. It is just a place, after all."

"It's not just a place," I mumble, though I'm not sure either of them notice. Hearing someone talk badly about the Hotel feels wrong, as if he's bad-mouthing my mom.

The MC sighs. "Just because the Hotel didn't choose you doesn't mean it's wrong."

Nagalla huffs loudly. "I know the truth about the Château, Jehanna. The Hotel isn't where you belong. With Stripe removed, it's time you reclaimed your home. The Maid should be strong again."

Stripe removed? Reclaim your home? What does he mean? And what's this Château place he keeps mentioning?

She waves her hand dismissively. "The 'Maid' should remain right where she is," she says. "Mr. Cameron, please show Venkat to his room." She eyes him carefully. "We will discuss this later."

He scrunches his face. "Indeed we will."

. . .

Getting Mr. Nagalla settled into his room feels like inviting a skunk to family dinner night. After I leave, all I want to do is be alone to wash off the smell. So I stop off at home to grab a few things and head for my spot.

When I still lived in a normal town full of normal things, it was easy to find a good alone spot. Bathrooms did the trick pretty well, an empty classroom at lunchtime, a dressing room at the mall, the occasional locker, but that changed when I was granted the whole world to choose from. Suddenly, hiding in random corners felt like I was doing it wrong.

Then I found Socotra.

Socotra Island off the coast of Yemen is both beautiful and almost completely, blissfully uninhabited. It's my own desert island, complete with dust and scrubland brush and no one saddling expectations onto me. There are cacti, too—alien-looking tendrils topped with little red flowers. The trees are my favorite part. Most of them look more like mushrooms, which always makes me smile. They understand me. It's as if we're both expected to be like all the other trees in the world, but nature made us look like a fungus instead.

I clear away rocks at the base of a particularly fungus-looking tree and sit in the shade, retrieving the Ledger from my bag. I pause to feel the carved and cured leather of the cover, the brittle endpapers. A dry wind blows across the hills, causing the ancient pages to flutter.

"Now what?" I ask it. "How do I—"

A swirl of gold and black ink creeps across the page, sketching the outline of a handprint.

Well, that answers that question.

I press my hand to the image, and the ink sparkles to life around my fingers. It's working. The Hotel is communicating with me. Not Agapios or anybody else. Me. Glittering currents zigzag to the opposing page and begin sketching out familiar scenes from my life once again—family, friends, hospitals, Stripe. The process takes longer than I remember from the first time. I hope we don't have to repeat this every time I use it, or else—

The ink fades. Uh-oh. Did my thoughts offend it?

"I'm sorry. I don't know how this works."

A smiling face surfaces on the page, sending a spark up my spine. Mom's face. I've only ever seen it in pictures. But Agapios said that the Ledger fixates on the reader's desires—the book could just be using her image to communicate with me.

"There are so many things I want to tell you," I say.

Frame by frame the drawing of my mother places a hand to her chest, and then like all the others, her image begins to fade.

"No! Wait! Don't leave."

The inky lines darken, and she slides to the bottom corner with a gentle bow. She extends a long hand upward, and the ink spools out from her fingertips, drawing dozens of portraits. A crosshatched banner across the top reads *The Embassy Charter: Members-in-Permanent* in flowing cursive.

I scan the ambassadors in the Ledger's pages, each wrapped in a small banner that bears their name. One by one their inky color deepens as I focus on them. Agapios Panotierri with his sharp features and kind eyes, the Maid Commander with her severe brow. But there are many more whom I don't know. Like Fusu, who serves as head banker for the Bank of Qin, and someone named Odi the Discoverer. The "Master of Locomotion" Babajide seems interesting. And there's Jim the Outlier.

Mom points to a woman in a long coat and boots. There's a distant look in the woman's eyes, as if she's trying to remember something just out of reach. *Adm. Virginia Dare*, the banner reads.

I run my finger over the figure, and the lines around her blur and constrict, crumpling the drawing into a scribble. The transformation is sharp—angry, almost—and all I'm left with is a jagged, inky blot where the image of Admiral Dare once graced the page.

Mom's image frowns, as if she's disappointed. Maybe this is the practice that Agapios was talking about. Or maybe it's something else. Oma did say that no one knows what happened to the colony and young Miss Dare all those years ago.

"Sorry," I say. "Can you show me Mr. Nagalla instead?"

Over the next hour I thumb through the pages, gleaning what I can about the ambassadors, and the Embassy's fleet of ships, and the admiral. I find lots of information about most of the members-in-permanent—scenes and stories and complicated histories—but every time I try to learn more about the woman whose binding day we're celebrating, the images struggle to form. The harder I try, the worse it gets.

After several frustrating minutes, I decide to focus on something else.

"Show me Nico," I say.

No sooner are the words out of my mouth than an angry black slash rips through the page. A few stray ink lines even mar Mom's image in the corner, where she's giving me a pitying look.

"I only wanted to see what he's doing," I say, but the acknowledgment is all it takes. The slash grows into a scribble, and with it comes the acrid smell of smoke.

I snap the Ledger shut, blinking away the ache behind my eyes. Even Mom doesn't want me looking for him. Or maybe it's the Hotel. Regardless, Rahki and Cass were right. I can't jeopardize my relationship with the Hotel.

No more searching. That sliver will have to stay right where it is, and I with it.

12

The Road Behind the Curtain

I cannot work like this!"

Chef Silva throws another copper pan into one of the enormous sinks of the main Hotel kitchen and turns on the hot water. Steam billows around him as he tosses dish after dish into the scalding tubs.

"Nothing works!" he exclaims, hurling a stock pot past me. "There is food caked all over every pot, pan, and plate."

"Can't you just rewash them?"

The executive chef roars his displeasure. "We have tried! The food is stuck! Bound and rotting, no less! And that awful smell . . . I sent Carlee to hunt it down, but she says it's coming through the vents. No one wants to eat around such an odious stench."

The "stench" he's referring to is the overwhelming odor of something like manure that permeates the entire kitchen area. It started out as a minor stink but grew to I'm-going-to-puke levels as soon as the kitchen crew began fifth-dinner preparations.

The chef tearfully eyes a row of his magnificent three-tiered tres leches cakes. "My kitchen smells like poop. It's even in my mouth—like eating poop cookies—and my poor cakes . . ."

"We'll get Chef Chowdhury to cook in a different kitchen tonight," I say, trying to be encouraging.

But mentioning the sous chef only seems to make him more emotional. "Nakul cannot make my dinner. He spices everything with coriander. That's almost as bad."

"It'll be all right," I assure him. "I'll find the source of the smell as quickly as I can. I'll take care of it."

"You better, or I'm going back to Perú."

I start to leave, but then I remember that I never did get an answer to the message I sent him two days ago. "Chef Silva, I was wondering . . . did you get a chance to check the menu I sent over for the gala?"

His eyes narrow. "That monstrosity will not come out of my kitchen."

"But I—"

"No!" He chucks another skillet into an already overflowing sink. "Now please do something about this disaster." He goes back to his dishes, muttering about magic doors and uppity hotel kids being the source of all his worldly woes.

I turn to Orban, who's standing beside me holding a cloth over his face. His eyes are wide and wet with tears.

"Why are *you* crying?" I ask, surprised.

"The smell . . . it burns," Orban says, pinching his nose. "I'll get the housekeepers to help us. Or maybe Cass will know what to do."

I do a double take. "Cass?" He can't be serious. "Why her?"

He looks everywhere but at me.

"Orban," I say, knowing full well that there's something he's not telling me, "why Cass?"

He shrugs. "She always seems to know what to do."

"And I don't?"

Again with the shrugging. "Cass and Rahki have been fixing a lot of things while they are beefing up the security. And if they don't know what to do, they find someone who will. Besides, you're always so busy. . . ."

I clench a fist, but it's not him I'm irritated with. Somehow my sister has managed to turn even Orban into one of her groupies.

The air-conditioning clicks on, and we're engulfed in another sickening burst of stench. "No," I say. "I will handle this. Boost me up."

He glances at the vent. "You really shouldn't, Cam. It's okay. Let us take care of it. You have other preparations to make."

Yeah, but it's my job to make Chef Silva happy, to keep Mr. Nagalla from finding anything *else* wrong with the Hotel, and to prevent Nico from ruining everything. The Hotel's counting on me.

"I've got this. Just help me up."

Orban boosts me up onto his shoulders, giving me enough height to hoist myself into the vent.

The air inside forces me to gag almost immediately. Even *my* eyes are watering, and I have the world's worst sense of smell.

"All right, Hotel," I say. "Time for you to lead me to whatever's causing this mess." I don't feel anything, of course, but I'm hoping I can now get some help from the House without using the Ledger for once. Reading the ancient book has gotten easier over the past few days, but there's still a lot it won't show me.

And still, the Hotel remains silent. Fortunately, the smell's enough to start me in a direction. I crawl forward, scraping knees and elbows and bumping my head a couple of times. I've never liked cramped spaces. There were lots of entries on my Worst Ways to Die list that involved claustrophobic corridors back before I joined the Hotel.

I can't believe Orban would trust Cass to solve this problem before me. It's not that she doesn't have good ideas—even great ones—but this is *my* job. She doesn't even do her own, and he's seeking her help. I don't understand that.

I'll show them. I'll prove that I can keep everything under control just fine on my own.

Oof, it's getting hot in here.

Up ahead, a noise. A quiet, padding sound, like something . . . moving. My arms prickle. It's gotta be rats. I hate rats. I hate rats so much.

I force my eyes shut and take a slow, clawing breath of the rancid air. I can do this. Rats are small. But what if there's more than one? I've got nothing to fight them off. Man, I've gotta get Rahki to teach me how to wield a duster. No matter what Agapios says about knowledge being a weapon, lugging an enormous book around is not the most effective way to defend yourself.

THE KEY OF LOST THINGS

I wipe sweat from my brow. The air-conditioning should be on, so why is it so warm?

The scratching sound grows, and I spot movement at the T-junction up ahead. A shadow turns and looks at me with shiny, green, glowing eyes. That's no rat. It's a cat. And in the dim light coming from the vents below, I can barely make out a card stuck to its back.

A queen.

The cat darts out of sight.

"Oh, no you don't, Queenie," I say, and burst forward on my hands and knees, squeezing around the corner.

The cat with the queen of clubs speeds down to the next junction, and I hurry after her. Is she a part of this prank too? Will she lead me to the source of the smell?

A burning sensation starts to spread from my pocket, and a feeling of dread that's more than just adrenaline, and . . . Wait. Is the crawl space getting smaller?

I jerk to the side as a section of metal dents in toward me.

I freeze, startled by the sudden movement. That's weird. It's as if someone hit it with a hammer from the outside.

"Hello?" I wait for a response. There's no way to tell what part of the Hotel lies below me. Maybe it's Orban—he sometimes does odd things that only he thinks are funny. "Orban, is that you?"

No answer.

But the heat in my pocket is still growing. I reach inside and draw out Mom's key—which stings against my skin. That's new.

I've felt it get cold before, but never hot like this.

Another dent punches up under my knees with a loud screech of bending metal, knocking me forward. My nose smashes into the duct wall ahead, and I almost drop the topscrew.

I roll over onto my back to see the misshapen duct behind me. There's no way I can fit through there anymore. Not good. Very not good.

Another loud metallic shriek as the walls pull in toward my shoulders on either side. I scramble away from the collapsing ducts, stuffing Mom's key into my pocket and diving farther down the already-too-tight tunnel. The sound of bending aluminum echoes down the crawl space, above my head this time. *Screech!* I duck and barely manage to avoid getting hit.

This isn't someone banging on the ducts. The ducts are closing in around me.

I race onward. The cat's shadow stays just out of reach, a silhouette against the light up ahead. But at least there is a light at the end of this.

My knees and palms ache as I clamber for the exit. A sharp edge catches my sleeve, rips my tailcoat. Another scrapes my cheek. But I press on, scrambling as fast as I can toward the slatted vent.

I slam my elbow down into the cover as soon as I reach it, dodging another spike of metal as it shrieks toward my head. Is it *aiming* for me now? I hit the vent cover again, and it falls out beneath me.

I fall with it, and crash to the hardwood floor below.

A shot of pain radiates through my hip, but my yelp is drowned out by the shrill noise of the ducts bending and contracting above me, retreating into the ceiling as they collapse.

The hall goes quiet. The stench dissipates, closed off in the mangled tubes that I can no longer see.

I stand, checking the rip in my jacket. The Laundry Service is going to eat my lunch for ruining yet another suit. Thank the binding that I made it out of the crawl space before it crushed me. But where am I now?

Heart still racing, I take in the old hall around me. Lots of doors, but that's not unusual—could be almost any of the non-dedicated corridors. Though . . .

I spin to find a familiar gray-brick wall at the end of the arched corridor. It's the hall where I lost Queenie more than two weeks ago. It can't be a coincidence that the ducts collapsed over the same exact hall that the cat disappeared in.

If Nagalla finds out that the Hotel's air ducts tried to squeeze me to death, it'll be bad news. He already thinks the Hotel isn't secure. I'll worry about that later, though. Right now, I need to take another look at this hall.

I feel along the walls with one hand, absently rubbing the ache in my side with the other. None of these doors bear the nameplates that most turners and knockers have, because these doors aren't bound. They all lead to useless, dusty rooms. And the hall dead-ends into a solid brick wall. No connection, no binding.

Or is there? When I really listen, I can almost hear something on the other side of the wall at the far end. It's not the hum of the binding; it's more . . . a whistle. Like wind.

My gaze falls to a few tiny green shoots sprouting from the corner where the arch meets the floor at the end of the hall. The flowering growths bend as if caught in a light breeze. That's weird. There's no way a plant could have forced its way in here from the outside.

I squat down and reach for the buds, and the wind behind the wall picks up, rustling the tiny leaves. When my fingers brush the soft, cool petals, the cluster of blossoms retreats.

"Wait," I say. "Come back."

The leaves shudder, as if actually listening. I reach for the blossoms again, and this time they grow toward me, curl around my index finger, and blossom into a brilliant lime-green flower in my hand.

I caress the petals, and the vines tickle my palm. These aren't like the dried, dark things I found outside the elevator—they're warm and damp, like the plants the groundskeepers tend to in the Greenhouse, only without any of the sickness. The flower makes me smile, like I found something truly special and it's all mine.

The vines tense. Tendrils of green draw tight around my hand, swirling up my wrist and squeezing.

No. NO! I lean back and brace my foot against the wall, trying to pull out of the vines' grip, but they keep growing, pressing deep into my skin. Now they're moving up my forearm, around my biceps. I pull harder, struggling to break free, but the vines won't let go.

"Help!" I shout. The vines have reached my shoulder now and are splitting the rip in my sleeve even wider. They wrap around my waist, dig into my pocket.

Then, they stop. The hall is quiet for a long breath.

"Is that—"

A dozen more vines burst from the seam between the wall and the arch, engulf my leg braced against the stone, and pull me toward the heart of the flower. I fight against them, but they're too strong.

Wind gusts through a gap that has finally appeared—a small opening between the vines that glimmers with green iridescence. I struggle to turn away, desperately calling out for anyone, but no help comes. I suck in another breath, ready to scream, but the vines wrap around my mouth, stifling my cry.

I'm gonna die. I'm going to die.

Then, all at once, the vines contract, dragging me into the small, shimmering hole.

My vision explodes in a flash of brilliant emerald light; silhouettes of green tentacles and leafy sprouts hover in the darkness behind my eyelids. Wind roars in my ears and swirls around me.

And then, nothing.

I open my eyes to see an endless, pale green sky speckled with stars. Sand mixed with dirt cools my back as a gentle wind kicks up little swirls of dust around me. I sit up to figure out where I am, but I'm pretty sure that not even Carlee's taste-testing tongue would be able to identify this place.

A single path twists and turns away from me, but a path is all it is—a trail no more than ten feet wide, suspended in a vast, star-strewn sky the color of pistachio ice cream.

Wherever this is, it's not any part of the Hotel I've seen before.

I pull my dangling leg away from the edge of the path as quickly as I can without shifting my weight too much, afraid that one wrong move will send me falling for days into that gaping green empti-ness. When I look over the drop-off, the empty emerald expanse continues beneath me too. It goes on forever, in every direction.

Up ahead the road curves, allowing a glimpse of what lies beneath. The path rests on a massive tangle of green. I'm sitting on a road, atop an enormous twist of vines suspended in the sky. Great.

Prr-r-r-eow.

A weight bumps into me, and to keep from tumbling off the road I squeeze the vines that form the edge.

"Queenie?"

The cat nuzzles me with the top of her head, her purr engine humming. This must be where she went when she vanished.

I take a breath to calm my nerves. Queenie disappeared and came back to the Hotel, so that means I can get back too. I just need to figure out how before some monster with a taste for people decides that I've brought it an afternoon snack.

I go through the steps of Oma's game, trying to discern anything I can about this place, but I'm not even sure this *is* a place. The air's cool, but there's no sun to determine what time zone we're in.

Unless one of those distant, tiny stars *is* our sun, and I'm halfway across the galaxy in a place where time doesn't exist because the sun would change positions so very slowly and—

Deep breaths.

Queenie weaves through halfway-buried bags and shoes and all sorts of weird junk. The path is littered with this stuff—papers and notebooks and old pens peeking out of the soil, a single sock, even a few wallets and one expensive-looking purse tangled up in yellow-green flowers. They look like they've been here forever, just waiting for someone to find them. I wonder who left them here.

I inspect the stone wall behind me. It's the same as the one on the other side. With the doors we have back in the Hotel, each side looks different, depending on where you are. This is more like I'm just on the other side of the wall.

Down near the ground I spy that terrible cluster of lime-green blossoms. They're bigger on this side, growing out from the vines that form the road. Something glistens amidst the tangle of shoots and leaves. I lean close to investigate.

It's a key—an off-white skeleton key that shimmers with a rainbow of colors in the light from the pistachio haze. I feel in my pocket, but Mom's topscrew isn't there, where it belongs. Which means . . . that's *my* key.

I lift my hand tentatively, working up the courage to retrieve it.

The wall before me ripples like waves as soon as I wrap my fingers around the topscrew's pearlescent stem. No, not like waves . . . like fabric. I pull my hand out—key gripped tightly in my fist—and jump back. The wall comes with me. It lifts, as if I'm drawing back a curtain, and I can see the Hotel's sixth floor beyond. I let the curtain fall, and it shimmers as it re-forms into solid wall, leaving the topscrew in my hand.

Relief floods through me, knowing there's a way I can leave. But there's something else. I think that was like shaping magic. Like the icons, and Cass's chair. The wall responded to my touch, and opened the way to the other side.

I face the path ahead, noting the rises and falls, twists and turns in the road, like the body of an enormous snake wrapped in leafy wood-vines. In the distance I can almost make out where the path splits in two, one of the branches leading to another arch like the one behind me. There are more of them beyond.

Those arches all lead somewhere.

"What is this place?" I ask Queenie as she rubs against my leg.

That night I ask the Ledger that same question, and it gives me nothing but black scribbles.

13

You Won't Like What You Find

"Check it now!" I call.

Orban runs to the opposite side of the Shadedial Fountain to turn the pump on again. I wait to see whether we've managed to finally unclog whatever's blocking the giant marble boughs from spraying water.

The tree-shaped courtyard fixture went dry two nights ago. Before that, the doors in the African Lobby all bound themselves to one another—people would go in one and come out to the same place. It's all the latest in what everyone's calling Nico's Prank War, which seems to be escalating ever since I found that strange place behind the wall on the sixth floor.

What's worse, I still have no idea what Nico wants, and Mr. Nagalla keeps showing up to watch each disaster unfold, scribbling notes and lingering like the smell in Chef Silva's kitchen. At least the Vesima seems to be getting better, little by little. Every night less of the black stuff coats its branches.

I've been visiting the vine place too; I think of it as the Night-vine. I haven't told anyone about it. I probably should, but I want to know more first. After all, I'm the one that the Hotel wants to be in charge.

Orban flips on the fountain pump, and there's a guttural *thump* as something clonks its way through the pipes.

"That doesn't sound good," he says, raising a bushy eyebrow.

The stone branches sputter, spritzing a quick mist of water. Then the spray holes darken as sludge oozes from the openings. Globs of brown goop dribble from the marble branches into the fountain pool.

I rush over to turn the pump back off.

"I don't think it's supposed to do that," Orban says. "We really should let Maintenance handle this."

"No need," I tell him. "I can tackle a little fountain mess." The more people we involve in solving these issues, the more everyone will talk about how badly I'm failing to keep the Hotel under control. The Hotel has to like me. I'll make it like me.

I tug on the lever to stop the sludge from flowing, but it doesn't budge.

Orban chuckles. "My friend, you do *not*, in any way, 'have' this."

Sev's voice approaches from the other side. "What is happening here?"

"Just a touch," I say, pulling harder. "I'll have it fixed in a sec. It's all"—*tug*—"under"—*tug*—"control."

I give the lever one last yank, and the fountain's branches sputter to life, muck exploding everywhere. One particularly impressive glob smacks me in the nose.

"Ack!" I shout, wiping it off before it has a chance to dribble into my mouth. "It's in my eyes!"

The intermittent stream of sludge from the fountain tree is almost enough to drown out Sev and Orban's laughter. Almost.

"I am sorry," Sev chuckles as I clear the mess from my face, "but woo, you like to keep the Laundry Service busy." He points at my suit, soaked in a spatter of whatever tarry mess Nico has poisoned the fountain with. Ruined, again. Perfect.

When I get back to my room to change, there's another suit waiting for me—a replacement for the *last* one I sullied while rescuing a group of guests who'd been mysteriously transported to the middle of the Kerala wetlands in India. It's a miracle that no one's been eaten by a tiger, or a crocodile, or any of the other dangers roaming those swamps. And the elevators are still giving us trouble too.

As I'm buttoning my replacement jacket, for a split second I think I see Nico looking back at me from the mirror. Same pin-striped suit he used to have, Nico's slick hair, blue flower in his lapel. But when I blink, he's gone again. I want to believe it's just my imagination, but part of me knows better. There's no such thing as coincidence where Nico's involved.

My attention falls to my nightstand drawer. I could use the sliver. See where it takes me. I could find him and make all this mess stop.

I open the drawer to have another look at it, but . . . Wait. What? *No!* Where is it? I rifle through the pens and notebooks, but there's no sign of the sliver that Bee gave me. It couldn't have just walked away. Then again, I still don't fully understand how slivers work. Maybe after a while they return to wherever they're bound. Coins want to return to the person they're bound to; maybe slivers do too.

A knock comes at my bedroom door. "Hey," Dad says, standing in the doorway.

I slam the drawer shut and turn to face him. "What's up?"

"Just checking to see how you're doing." He glances at the tarred suit on my bed. "Is something . . . new going on?"

"I'm fine. It's all good."

Another thought hits me. What if Oma found the sliver, and Dad's here to talk to me about it? If they've discovered that I've been hiding forbidden magics in the Hotel, this won't be pretty. Dad's already super sensitive about the Hotel's safety after his big screw-up all those years ago. Would he report me? What if they find out about the Nightvine?

There's a moment's pause—me not looking at him, him not leaving—and I can feel every ounce of our uneasy relationship.

At last, he speaks. "I want to show you something."

Guests love traveling the German doors to visit the Alpine mountains, or quaint fairy-tale towns, the castle at Neuschwanstein, even Berlin, where a massive wall was torn down ages ago. But Dad and I don't go to any of those places. Instead he hails a cab to take us to a dingy little train yard in Frankfurt.

He's totally about to break the news that Oma found the sliver.

He's brought me here to tell me that the Hotel doesn't want me, and we're going to have to go back to Texas, and . . .

"What are we doing here?" I ask, to stop my brain from running away with me.

"Remembering," he says.

Red, blue, and orange freight cars sit in rows, stacked two and three cars high in places. We weave through the cargo containers toward a cluster of buildings on the far side of the yard. They're apartments, I think. Only, . . . really, really small apartments. A few doors are propped open, revealing tiny rooms with bunk beds on two walls, littered with plastic bags, threadbare clothes, boxes of food. They remind me of the junk scattered across the Nightvine. There's a bunch of people hanging around too—men, women, even some kids. Many of the men's beards have grown long and bushy.

"Everyone forgets them," Dad says, indicating the people nearby. "They always have."

Everyone forgets. When Dad was returned to us, he'd been homeless for a long time too. These apartments . . . they must be for people in a similar situation. I can't imagine how it would feel to be homeless.

He stops next to a picnic table against the back wall and stares out over the park behind the apartments with a distant, muddy expression. I follow his gaze, tracing the lake and woods.

"I lived here," he says after a long moment. "At least, I think I did. I can't really remember, but the Old Man found this."

He hands me a picture. It's him, sitting at this same picnic table with a bunch of other people. His eyes look tired and he's dirty, like when he's worked a full day in the Greenhouse, but he's actually smiling.

He's not telling me that I don't belong in the Hotel. . . . He's showing me why *he* doesn't belong.

"This picture was taken while you were missing," I say.

It's unfair to say Dad abandoned us. He left to protect us. What happened during all those missing years when he was serving Stripe is still a mystery, even to him.

He continues, speaking softly. "I hoped that by coming down here I'd see someone, or something, familiar. But . . ."

"Stripe said you were in Chicago. That's thousands of miles away."

"I'm sure Stripe used me in many places," he says.

I swallow the lump in my throat. *Used me.* Like Stripe uses the docents. "Can you remember anything?"

Dad runs his hand down the painted white bricks of the shelter. "Not really. I'm not sure I want to. Stripe always leaves something behind."

That thought sends a shudder through me. I was bound to Stripe too, if only for a few minutes. What if Stripe left something behind in me? That might explain why I've been so angry, or why I didn't tell Agapios about the sliver and the Nightvine. Nico was bound to Stripe for most of his life; to think what that might do to him . . .

Dad studies me, then smiles and says, "You remind me so much of her."

We continue walking around the shelter. Dad picks through the twigs and sticks on the ground as we go, examining each as though he's looking for something.

"What was she like?" I ask as we draw near the lake.

He picks up his pace after finding a particularly ugly stick that looks long dead and partially rotten. "She was giving," he says. "*Forgiving*. Your mother had a way of showing others who they could be, and not judging them for what they were."

He pulls one of the Maid Service dusting gloves out of his pocket and slips it on.

I furrow my brow. "Where'd you get that?"

"I picked it up somewhere."

That's a lie. Striking gloves are issued only to the Maid Service. "You're not supposed to have that."

Dad slips a pin from his pin-sleeve and runs a gloved finger along its length, shaving off a layer of dust. I didn't realize it was possible to shave binding dust from pins, too. It looks as if he's done this before; his pin-tip has been sanded to a sharp point.

"Your mom and I used to do this thing," he says, standing the large, dead branch upright in the ground with dust-sparkling fingers. "We'd come out to a park, just the two of us, take the deadest, ugliest stick we could find, and give it a little something . . . extra." He releases the branch to stand on its own, like an ugly miniature tree. "Do you have her key?"

I hesitate, and in that moment I hate my hesitation. He's just my dad, telling me a story about my mom, but sadly it's more than that. After everything he's done, I'm afraid to give him Mom's key. What if what he says is right, and some of Stripe got left behind in him, and giving him the key is a bad idea?

"I'm not asking to take it," he says, looking away. "Touch the key to the stick."

I bite my lip, sorry for everything.

I lift Mom's topscrew to the dead, rotten branch, and a glittering keyhole forms in the wood. A click and a turn, and all the warmth drains out of the key, leaving it icy cold in my hand. The stick shimmers with pearlescent light, and its branches grow to form leaves that bloom and rustle in the wind like on a real, miniature tree.

"It's the shaping," I say, marveling at the transformation.

"It's not." Dad reaches for the tree as it drives new, miniature roots deep into the earth. As he touches it, the image wavers, revealing the ugly stick beneath. "Shaping changes the nature of a thing—makes it want to be something different. This is another kind of magic."

"An illusion."

"Always more than one side to magic. Revealing, and concealing. The magics choose their own nature, you know. That can leave contradictions, quirks, in the way they work." He draws his hand back, and the false tree returns. "People are like that too. They don't naturally all fit into the same codes, so I guess it makes sense. Your mom and I followed different rules as well. At first she didn't like the idea of using her topscrew to craft illusions like this, but once I got her to see the beauty it could add to the ugliness of reality, we started doing this all the time. This is how she hid the Greenhouse from everyone, and how she eventually revealed it to you. But now that she's stuck in that rotten thing . . ."

I turn the key over, watching the sunlight shine off its surface. Revealing and concealing.

Then it hits me. The warmth I felt from Mom's key right before I found the Nightvine—it revealed the hidden connection in the hallway. There's no telling how long that passage had been there, hiding.

"Can the key reveal the memories you forgot?" I ask.

He frowns. "No. Your mother's key has the power to reveal or conceal only what is already there. My memories . . . they're gone. Lost altogether, I think. It takes a different kind of magic to find lost things."

He fingers the illusion, causing it to shimmer and fade. He does that a lot. Lose himself in thought. I never can tell what he's thinking about. Then he breaks the silence.

"You need to apologize to your sister."

I turn to face the ducks floating on the lake. "I did apologize," I say. "Kinda."

"The apologies you've given her are false, like this tree. She deserves a real apology, one that doesn't involve you trying to make yourself or your actions look like something you're not. Let her see the rotten sticks underneath, not the illusion that you want everyone to see. Your mom wouldn't have put up with that kind of fakeness. It stinks, just like the Vesima."

"But the Vesima's getting better."

Dad frowns. He's right, and I know it. I do need to fix things with Cass—really fix them and not skirt around the issue. I just don't know how.

"I . . . I'm not good at this stuff either," he says eventually. "All I can give you is sticks, Son. I don't have a magic key to make everything look pretty, and I certainly don't know what to tell you that'll help make things right. But you have to do better. Don't be like I was. Don't let that rot spread."

"I won't," I say, though I'm not sure how to do better. To *be* better.

I have to try, though.

14

On a Whim and a Dare

Queenie paws forward, her tail wiggling contentedly as we continue our exploration of the Nightvine.

I got a lot done on the gala preparations this morning—invitations confirmed in the Mail Room, Housekeeping has my list of decorations, and I even made corrections to Chef Silva's dessert menu. I finally feel like I'm beginning to understand all the moving parts, even if I don't have a solution for them yet. *The Ledger of Ways* still intimidates me with its magic and its scribbles, too, but I'll get to figuring it out soon enough.

The wind picks up, pushing me down the vine path as Queenie winds through the junk littering the road ahead. We've spent the past week testing the arches, seeing where they lead. Like the Hotel, the Nightvine's connections stretch all over the globe, but while the Hotel's doors lead to grand vistas and popular tourist traps, the Nightvine's lime-colored blossoms always take me to some quiet hideaway or less-trafficked location, like the shelter in Frankfurt. There are so many lost places and missing people. It's enough to make me worry that I'll end up lost one day too. And I wonder, is there more the Hotel could be doing to reach them all?

The cat trots ahead to a branch in the path, then up a rise in the road. She's always waiting for me when I come here through the strange curtain-like veil that separates this place from the Hotel at the arch. She's like my own personal guide to the Nightvine. There are other cats too, lounging amidst the piles of junk that people have lost over the years. The cats slip through the veils scattered throughout the Nightvine easily, as if this place belongs to them.

Queenie disappears into a cluster of bright buds at the corner of a nearby arch, as if ducking under a curtain. Something about this arch seems familiar. It's different from the one that brought me from the Hotel—the wood is rougher, more weathered.

I kneel next to the yellow-tipped buds and find the place where the vines press under the stones. Wind whistles through the tiny hole, smelling like pine trees and mold.

I poke my finger under the veil and pull, and the stone curtain ripples, lifting to reveal the world beyond it. Sunny, blue sky welcomes me, partially obscured by tall evergreens. The air is warm and humid and thick, not at all like on the vine road.

The strange part is, I recognize this place. Oma brought us here. It's Roanoke, where Dare's Door was lost all those years ago—and none but Miss Dare were ever seen or heard from again.

Is the Nightvine road where they went? Could that be the secret that Admiral Dare has kept hidden for four hundred years?

I really should tell Agapios what I've found. Then again, maybe this is something the Hotel doesn't want him to know. After all, it didn't lead him to the Nightvine—only me.

"Do you know where Agapios is?" I ask as soon as I round the corner into Sana's bay. The Motor Pool whirrs and buzzes with the sounds of the artificers working on their machines and statues.

Sana looks up from a stone statue of a strange, long-snouted mammal. She's wearing her tool-sari—that unique coverall-sari combo with built-in tool belt that she made herself. "Good to see you too, Cam. Did you finally decide to drop in for training?"

"Sorry. No training today," I tell her. "I'm late to meet with Admiral Dare, and Agapios is nowhere to be found."

I'm sure a shaping seminar would teach me a lot, but I haven't had enough time to attend any. Now that I know better what Mom's key can do, I doubt I'll even need to bother with the shaping, at least for a while. Two weeks have passed since I realized how useful Mom's topscrew can be in keeping this place running. The key can fix lots of things—cracks in drywall and cat scratches on doors, malfunctioning elevator lights and creaking hinges and dirty water from faucets. Well, maybe "fix" isn't quite the word. More like "hide." And it only works for one problem at a time, so I'll need to find a quicker way if I ever hope to keep up with Nico's meddling. But the key should get us through the gala, at least.

I can't take my eyes off the weird statue that Sana's working on. "What kind of icon is that?"

"Anteater," she says. "Or . . . a termite-eater, considering that's what she'll be used for. Termineater? The doormen have been complaining about infestations on some doors, and this beauty should help."

"Oh." Sev didn't tell me anything about that—I hope this doesn't mean he's started taking his problems to Cass too. "So, *have* you seen Agapios? I've checked everywhere."

Sana shakes her head. "Maybe you should meet with the admiral on your own. I hear she's super nice."

The thought makes my stomach hurt. "I doubt Agapios would want me going without him."

She raises an eyebrow. "Did he say that?"

"Well . . . not exactly. It was Admiral Dare who called the meeting."

"He probably expects you to handle it, then. I doubt he's even in the Hotel."

Agapios not here? That would make sense, considering the fact that the map-boards didn't know where he was either. "Where would he go? I didn't think he ever left the Hotel."

Sana swivels the statue on its pedestal so that she can paint more of the shaping dye onto its snout. The liquid glistens as it soaks into the stone. "He's been checking a lot of icons out of the Motor Pool lately. Very last-minute."

That's strange. "Where's he taking them?"

"Pshh, I don't know." She gives a noncommittal head bobble. "It's not my place to ask. Though, it *has* been more often. And most of them haven't come back—a couple of warrior golems, a gorilla, the onyx rhino. I told Cass to make sure you knew about it."

Cass. I've barely seen her these past few days. Seems like every time I turn around, the map-boards say she's sitting in her room, which of course means she's left her coin behind and gone galli-vanting through the knockers without permission again. Of course, maybe Dad's right, and I shouldn't worry about her. I'd apologize and tell her that, if I ever saw her around except at bedtime and awkward family dinners.

"If you're supposed to be meeting the admiral soon, you'd bet-ter get going." Sana smirks. "It isn't a good idea to keep someone like her waiting."

The appointment with Admiral Dare was scheduled to start fifteen minutes ago, and to get to the meeting place, I have to go all the way to McMurdo Station in Antarctica, one of the most remote places on earth. For nearly nine months out of the year no planes can fly there, and very few ships can break through all that ice, which makes it a great base of operations for the Fleet Marines—or so Agapios says. Even if someone wanted to reach it, they couldn't without a bound door. Perfect for anyone who wants to stay off the world's radar.

But its location also means it's cold. Very cold. And there's a gap between the Hotel and the station—a short, grueling jog through sub-zero temperatures and dry ice-desert winds that'll chap your lips in a frozen second. For a Texas boy like me, that sounds like a death sentence.

I make a quick stop to grab a parka and scarf from the coat

closets, and pull on a pair of heavy gloves and goggles to ready myself for the Antarctic cold.

"Go get 'em, Mistah Cam!" Elizabeth calls from the front desk.

I give her a puffy-gloved thumbs-up and hurry through the door.

My body stiffens as soon as I cross into the frigid night. Frozen winds bite through my many layers of clothing. Nearby, a waddle of penguins huddle together for warmth, too concerned with their own survival to notice me.

I hurry across the icy ground, fighting back shivers. All I have to do is make it to the door. The Fleet Marines are expecting me, though I am late. I hope they didn't give up on me and lock me out.

When I reach the station door, my cheeks are burning cold, and I'm pretty sure ice crystals have started growing inside my lungs. Thankfully, the door opens and I collapse into the shelter of an eighty-degree paradise. I draw in deep, comforting breaths as I curl up in front of the nearby heater. I never want to move away from this heater. I'll just stay here on this warm floor for the rest of eternity, with the heater as my bestest friend, and we'll grow old together and I will never leave it. Never, never, nev—

"You are late," says a familiar voice.

The Maid Commander looms over me, parka draped over one arm.

"I'm . . . sorry . . . ," I say, still catching my breath. "I was . . . looking for . . ."

"The Old Man has other matters to attend to." She offers a hand to help me up. "Now, if you are quite done sullying the Hotel's dignity, let us hurry. Admiral Dare has much to accomplish before this silly 'celebration.'"

The MC leads me through the station—full of people dressed in sharp, turquoise military uniforms—and to a door at the top of a spiraling metal staircase.

As we climb, I can't stop looking at her sword. It has always struck me as strange that the MC would wield a sword while the maids all carry wooden dusters. A weapon like hers feels out of place in the Hotel. Then again, *she* feels out of place.

There's something else today too. Something different about her appearance.

"Is that a flower?" I ask, noticing the midnight-blue bud pinned to her lapel.

She glances down, looking for all the world as though she's just now realized that she spilled hot sauce all over her shirt. "Yes. I thought I'd try something new today."

When we cross the next threshold, the stuffy station air gives way to a pleasantly cool ocean breeze. The ground sways beneath us. It's the deck of a ship. Position of the sun and the time on my watch suggest northern Pacific Ocean, early morning? Without landmarks it's hard to tell.

If this is where we were supposed to go from the beginning, why not go straight here? Of course, the answer is obvious: McMurdo is another buffer to keep the Embassy Fleet Service safe from intruders.

A young man in uniform salutes the Maid Commander. "Welcome aboard the EFS *Roanoke*. The admiral is waiting for you on the bridge."

"Lead the way," the MC says, and adjusts her flower.

"This ship is gigantic," I marvel as we follow the uniformed Fleet Marine.

The Maid Commander's face softens. "The Embassy Fleet is the crown of the oceans, and the *Roanoke*, her prize jewel. We have to have *some* way to fight back."

I've known about the Hotel's mission to save kids since the beginning, but her statement feels like something else entirely. I gaze out over the ocean as we climb the stairs, and spy even more ships—everything from catamarans to battle cruisers—gathered into a flotilla on the shimmering sea.

"Fight back against what?" I ask.

"Our enemies." She shoots me a side-eye. "Or have you bought into the Old Man's naive chatter about changing the world, one vacationer at a time?"

The way she says it almost stops me in my tracks. Yes, I think I have. "It was Mom's vision too. To change the world by influencing the people in it."

The MC scoffs. "Your mother was also starry-eyed. Never saw the truth of our enemies, and it was her downfall."

I frown at her for talking about Mom's death like that, as though it was Mom's fault. I know the MC is a good person, but . . . I wish she didn't have to be so nose-in-the-air all the time.

When we arrive on the bridge, the crew stand at attention and salute the MC just like before. I wonder why they do that. She's a hotelier, not a Fleet Marine.

"Jehanna," a woman says from behind a desk covered in maps. "I'd begun to wonder if you'd forgotten."

The woman looks to be around Dad's age, though her shoulder-length hair is gray with a pale, almost yellow-green cast to it. The windows behind her are bound, showing views of other skies and oceans from ships around the world.

As I stand face-to-face with Admiral Dare, I can't help but picture her as a little girl on that island, her parents ushering her into the Nightvine, the veil dropping behind her. Has she really seen it too? Does she dream about that emerald-green sky?

The Maid Commander bows. "Apologies, Admiral. We had a minor miscommunication." She scowls my way, and it suddenly strikes me that I should probably bow as well.

"Ah, this must be Melissa's son," Admiral Dare says, straightening her coat. "Cameron, is it?"

"Yes, ma'am. Uh . . . I mean . . . Admiral."

The admiral laughs—an oddly musical sound. "'Ma'am' is fine," she says. "So, I'm curious. How does it feel being such a young key-bearer?"

The MC gives me another severe look, then blinks as if to tell me it's okay to discuss my key with the admiral.

"It's . . . different," I say. "I feel strange carrying it sometimes, like I'm not supposed to have it." *Just like I'm not supposed to know where you went all those years ago.* Though, I can't be sure that's where she went, can I? For all I know, the Nightvine was linked to Roanoke after she disappeared.

Admiral Dare smiles. "This one seems like a good egg, Jehanna. Nice to see the Hotel hasn't ruined him yet."

The MC picks a speck of dust from her sleeve. "Yet."

The admiral returns to her maps, shuffling papers as if searching for something. "I understand that you're the one planning my party. I expect a grand affair. Something with balloons, maybe. Plenty of balloons. After all"—her eyes widen when she looks up—"four hundred doesn't come very often."

"Neither does four hundred and one," I blurt. The MC shoots me a foul, angry look.

But the admiral laughs her tinkling laugh again. "True. I suspect my four hundred and second binding day will put them all to shame, then." She traces a line across one of her maps for the officer next to her. "He'll be there. I don't know how long, but for the moment that's what it tells me."

The officer rolls the map and rushes away to the upper deck.

I catch a glimmer of something green and sparkly hanging from a chain at the admiral's neck, just below the collar. A key. An ornate *skeleton* key, made entirely out of emerald gemstone.

As soon as the admiral realizes that it has peeked out from under her collar, she pushes it down under her uniform. She sizes me up with her eyes. "I had a curious notion the other day and wondered if you could clear it up for me, young man."

"A notion?" I ask.

"Yes. An intriguing thought. You see, ever since you kicked our infamous Curator out of his Museum, we've been scrambling to find him. It's not easy. He's quieter than he's ever been, and that has everyone on edge. There are some who would rather he had stayed where he was."

"Do you suggest that Cam should have left him in that House?" the MC says.

I give her a double take. That's the first time I've ever heard her say something nice about what happened back at the Museum.

"You know I don't think that," Admiral Dare says. "He never belonged there. And after all, it gives me the opportunity to use my skills." She leans in and whispers, "I find things. And lose them. Though, lately it seems I spend a great deal more time losing than finding. Which brings me to my notion." She rolls one of her maps, staring me down. "I have an itching feeling that he—or one of his agents—has been inside the Hotel recently."

My skin bristles. Stripe, *inside* the Hotel?

"That's not possible," I say. "No one in the Hotel would invite him. And besides, we'd know."

"It's strange," she continues. "As I said, I'm very good at finding whatever treasure or scoundrel I set my sights on, and my gut keeps telling me that if I want to find the Curator, I need to start with your House. Are you certain one of his associates isn't hiding among you?"

I start to deny it, but I can't be positive. Last year there were a few of Stripe's "associates" working at the Hotel. I was unwittingly one of them. Then there's the question of Nico. Everyone else seems to think he's working with Stripe again. What if they're right?

"We will stay on the lookout," I tell her, "but I really don't think any of Stripe's people have been there. If they are, I'll find them."

"I should hope so."

"Admiral," one of the marines says as he steps up next to her, "we need you to find . . ."

And just like that, the admiral goes back to her maps, pointing and issuing orders to her marines as if she's lost track and forgotten we exist.

"Come along," the MC says, ushering me toward the door and squeezing her temples as if this conversation has brought on a headache. "We won't get any more out of her. This was a waste of time."

"I thought she wanted to talk about the party."

"Don't be ridiculous, boy," she says. "There are more important things than—"

"Mr. Cameron," the admiral calls out.

The MC and I stop and turn to face her.

Admiral Dare removes her glasses and gives me a long stare. "I'm sure you'll find what you've lost, soon enough," she says finally. "And balloons, please. Yes, balloons would be lovely."

15

The Bluestone Henge

Admiral Dare wasn't at all what I thought she'd be. I'm not sure what I expected, but I certainly don't like this idea that an agent of Stripe might be in the Hotel. She couldn't know whether someone like that was here. It had to be a guess, right? Then there was the way she hid that key, and the scribbles in the Ledger, and the arch to Roanoke. . . .

"I am glad you agreed to come to a shaping seminar," Sev says as we head down to the Motor Pool. "Artificer training is useful for everyone who works in the Hotel."

"Yeah," I say, "I hope so." Oma's near-daily field trips are already cutting into my gala preparations, but if I can figure out why the Nightvine is the way it is, maybe I'll be able to learn more about the admiral too, and discover who connected the vine to the Hotel, and how they did it.

"It'll be fun," Sana assures me. "Djhut is wonderful. You'll like him."

"You think everyone's wonderful."

"Well, it's true. Mostly."

The head artificer is waiting at one of the arches at the far end of the Motor Pool garage, where we keep the Hotel's vehicles and icon-bound statues. Djhut is dressed in his usual modern tunic and pants, a thick, gold necklace dangling from his neck.

There's a small crowd of around fifteen juvenile staffers gathered with him, including Cass. I still haven't had the chance to properly apologize, but it seems we've fallen into the "polite awkwardness" zone over the past week. It's a nice change from the "can't stand each other" zone we were living in previously.

"Your sister's been coming to all our shaping seminars lately," Sana says. "She's becoming quite proficient."

This could be a good thing. I mean, if she's happy down in the Motor Pool, who am I to argue? At least the artificers don't flirt with danger like the maids do.

Artificer Djhut raises his voice to grab our attention. "Looks as if we've got quite the turnout today, eh, Sana?" He gives her a wink.

Sana's eyes brighten. "Does that mean . . . ?"

Djhut rubs his hands together. "You betcha," he says, and redirects us to an arch different from the one it appeared we were going to take.

We step into a moonlit field littered with rocks. Not just any rocks, though—these enormous, rugged pillars rise from the grassy earth in concentric circles like ancient stone sentinels. Some even lie on their sides, bridging the upright stones to form massive arches, around thirty feet tall. They're so ancient and weathered that it's a wonder they're still standing.

I check my pocket watch—one designed by the artificers to track the local time wherever we are in the world. A little after nine o'clock at night here, which puts us on the western edge of Europe. Rocky fields, slightly cool temperature. England?

"Welcome to Stonehenge," Djhut says, holding his arms wide, "one of the oldest man-made structures on the planet. Older than I am, if you believe it." He waggles his brow, eliciting a laugh. Djhut is one of the oldest staffers in the Hotel. He might even be the oldest, though he certainly doesn't look it.

"Since we have a larger group than usual today, I thought we might discuss something a little more interesting." His eyes grow wide as he spreads his fingers and says in an eerie voice, "Let's talk about the wild magics."

I stand a little straighter. Sev mentioned the wild magics when we went into the glowworm caves.

"Before we begin," Djhut continues, "can anyone tell me what the fundamental bonds are?"

Cass pipes up right away. "The bond of Law, the bond of Nature, and the bond of Life. They're each a special kind of magic that restricts how all the others work."

"Correct," Djhut says, and Cass beams. "Magics are hard to define. The mundanes believe that everything supernatural comes from some mysterious universal cloud that sorcerers and witches use to make flames sprout from their fingertips and rabbits fall out of hats, but the truth is much simpler. Magics are individuals, like people. That's why we call them "magics" plural, rather than just the singular "magic." No two are the same. They are each born, just as we are born, and live like we live. They grow and change, and sometimes . . . they die. Each has a unique personality, desires, wants, even fears. It's those distinctions—what we call their 'nature'—that determine how they interact with humankind."

Just like the Hotel. *It* decides who it likes and who it doesn't. *It* chooses when and how to communicate with us. From what I've been told, the Hotel itself even helped to determine what form the House would take. But if what Djhut's saying is true, that means there was a time when the magic of the Hotel didn't exist at all, and that the magic is still changing.

Artificer Djhut places a hand on the pockmarked surface of one of the giant stone pillars. "We are only able to tap into these magics because they allow us to. Magics reveal themselves to us, and we bind to them in return. If there is any so-called universal force, like the mundanes believe, it would be in the binding."

As he speaks, a sparkling wave of gold ripples across the space inside the arch, then fades as soon as he pulls his hand back.

"The magic we call the binding was the first of its kind to make itself known to us. Of course, it is in the binding's nature to make connections. It taught us how to use its power to interact with other magics, but only those that felt an affinity toward human-kind in the first place—those that saw hope in us and wanted to help us reach our potential."

"What about the ones that didn't like us?" Cass asks.

Djhut purses his lips. "Unfortunately, many of the wildest

magics refused to be tamed. Some rejected us outright because we bound the others when the treaty was founded between magics and humans. Those magics who rebelled against the rules that the binding's treaty imposed on them still war against us to this day." He looks to me. "I believe you've met one such magic."

I swallow down the shoe-size lump in my throat. "Mr. Stripe is . . . a magic?"

"A very specific kind of magic that we call a False." He pauses, and furrows his brow. The class leans forward, waiting for him to continue, but he moves on. "Anyway, back to the reason why we're here—the *shaping*."

Djhut continues with his lesson, explaining how the blue-stones of Stonehenge were transported from far away to form the first links between people and the binding.

I always thought Stripe was just an evil person who uses magic—not a magic itself. It makes sense, though. I remember the connection Stripe and I shared that day when he bound me to him. He and I were linked for only a few minutes, but in that short time I saw into his past—a dark, confusing place. I wasn't merely seeing into the history of a person. I saw a magic that despises people, *all* people, and wants to make them serve it.

Dad said that Stripe always leaves something behind.

"What happens when magics are bound to us?" I ask.

Everyone turns to face me. It strikes me that I have no idea what Djhut was just talking about, or why everyone has moved closer to the bluestones, carrying jars of the same shaping dye that Sev and I retrieved from the underground lake.

I wish I could reel the question back in, but it's been cast now, and I want to know. "What do they do to us, I mean?"

"The effects of binding differ from magic to magic," Djhut says, taking a curious step toward me. "Each has developed its own nature. Those friendly to us allow the binder to use the magic's specialties. Often we have as much say in the way that connection works as the magic does, like when we operate the icons."

"Then how do we control them?" I ask. "The magics, I mean." Cass scoffs.

"Ah," Djhut says. "Control? No. Influence? Maybe. This is where shaping comes in—two forces, each with their own mind, their own will, working together in tandem. Each influences the other. The magic shapes the wielder; the wielder shapes the magic. And, if a magic can penetrate deep into the heart of the wielder, it can shape every part."

Orban folds his arms. "What if that person doesn't want to be shaped?" When I think about it, he's probably just as concerned as I'd be, if not more. Orban was a docent when we took the Museum, so he knows exactly what it's like to be controlled.

Djhut narrows his eyes. "Shaping is always happening, whether we realize it or not. An object or person who resists shaping is still changed, though the outcome may not be what was intended."

I swallow. "Is it permanent?"

"Few things are truly permanent. As long as the fundamental

bonds that were created by the treaty remain, however, the power of these magics is limited. The bond of Nature prevents magics like Mr. Stripe from imposing their will on us. The bond of Life protects our lives. And no magic can break the agreements made under the bond of Law. This is the single most important relationship between humans and magics. It is the foundation. As long as the bond of Law remains, no magic in the world can force us to do anything against our nature, nor take our life, nor break any other agreements we've made with it."

"Unless someone makes a new agreement," Cass says.

Djhut presses his lips into a line. "Yes. A new contract has the power to alter the old ones. Even the fundamental ones, in some circumstances."

None of this really answers my question, though. And I can't clarify what I meant. What if Stripe really did leave something terrible behind, in me? To ask would let them all know, and they'd distrust me, too.

Artificer Djhut shows us how to use the dye to reshape and redirect the faded, loose bindings on the bluestones to connect the arches with places important to each person. Turns out, Cass is pretty good at this. She has the first success, managing to bind her arch to Disney World, one of the rare, special places we visited when we were younger.

But of course she's had practice. I, on the other hand . . .

"You seem to be having trouble, Mr. Cam."

Djhut steps up to face the bluestone with me. I've been trying for several minutes, but I can't get the image of Mr. Stripe out of my head, and the last thing I want to do is bind the stone to somewhere near him.

"I'm sorry," I say, shivering from the icky chill in my gut. "I'm distracted, I guess."

"Distracted shaping is often the easiest kind. The most natural, because it lets the magic and your emotions do the work." He presses a hand against the bluestone. "You already have a relationship with the binding. Tap into that. Feel the tie between this stone and all the places it's been. The dust and rock that it was carved from, scattered across the world. You need only to tell those scattered pieces where you want them to go, and let them do the work for you."

I try to do as he says, and I can feel . . . something. A low buzz. Pictures of places form in my mind, but they're all jumbled. Like a knot, twisting in on itself and pulled taut. Like the Nightvine. Part of me wonders if I'm just imagining it, but I can even see the hazy green sky, and hear the powder crunch of the dirt beneath my Chucks, and feel the soft, cool blossoms against my fingers.

Still, nothing happens.

"Interesting." Djhut inspects the stone, fingering the gold chain at his neck. There's a strangely-shaped charm hanging from it: a bent rod of blue stone flecked with black and gold, with a series of short spikes at one end.

Not spikes. . . . They're teeth. The teeth of a key, made from some kind of blue rock. Artificer Djhut is a keybearer.

He sees me noticing, and pulls it away from his chest to give me a better view. The cloudy blue key looks at home in his hand.

"Sometimes magics break off a piece of themselves to give their power to a human," he says. "We call these broken bits of power 'artifacts.' Keys are one of the more common forms, though all artifacts are rare. The artifact binding is a near-permanent change for the magic—they only do it if they are fully committed to making their power accessible to another."

"Why keys?" I ask.

"I suspect because keys are such a strong symbol for us humans. We view things we can't have as 'locked away.' In giving a piece of themselves to us, magics are 'unlocking' their power. The magic of an artifact can be used by anyone, so long as the key and the user have a connection." He turns the key over in his hand. "I call this one the Sky Key."

"Admiral Dare has one too," I say, remembering the emerald key around her neck. "She said something about finding others and objects."

"Ah, hers is the Key of Lost Things. No one knows where it came from—only that she had it with her when she returned from wherever she disappeared to all those years ago. A lost little girl full of secrets." He cocks an eyebrow. "She was a bit of an imp back then."

"You remember when she came back?" I don't know why that surprises me—Artificer Djhut is older than most hills.

"'Remember' is . . . not quite the word. I can grasp pieces of it, but human minds aren't meant to hold as many years as mine has. Everything becomes foggy past thirty years ago. We old heads have to write a thing down or else we lose it. Many of us have lost whole lifetimes. Reading my old journals often feels like reading someone else's diary." He glances to the coin around my neck. "That's one reason why it's good to have a person around who can remind us of who we were."

I wish Nico had a journal of what happened in the Hotel before he left, so that we wouldn't have to wonder whether he's forgotten. I could give his coin back to remind him of who he was, so that he'd stop making everybody's life so difficult, but in order to do that I'd have to find him first.

All I can do is wait for him to come to me.

16

No More Games

Our group sits at the edge of the Arkade—a brightly colored lounge somewhere in India that's connected to the hotel; it's full of felt tables and live performances. It's a popular hangout spot—there are even video games in the back room. Orban's been getting a bunch of us to come down here more often, ever since the Old Man put him in charge of "making sure the rest of the stuffy trainees have a little fun." (Orban's words, not Agapios's.)

"Pay attention," Orban says, dealing cards onto the table. "If you want to learn how to play the game, you've got to listen."

The little tower of cards I'm building collapses, despite the binding dust I used to hold it together. I'd hoped that this time Mom's key would make my little card tower look like an actual castle, but once again, nothing is proving to be a quick fix.

Djhut's explanation about keys and artifacts made me realize that I still don't fully understand Mom's key. Admiral Dare has the Key of Lost Things, and Djhut said his was the Sky Key, but what is mine called? The Key of Concealment? The Illusion Key?

I've been practicing what Dad showed me in Germany, but I'm discovering that there are some limitations. Hiding the sludge in the Shadedial Fountain was a touch, and the cracks in the upstairs hallways and the HOPPERS 4 LYFE graffiti in the Elevator Bank both vanished with ease, but making one thing look like something entirely different never seems to work out. It's as if the world wants to stay as close to its original appearance as possible.

"I don't get it," I say, gathering up the cards. "I can't get them to do what I want. There's got to be a trick to this."

"It's the Nature bond," Elizabeth says, sitting across from me, petting the felt. "You're trying to make the cards look like a castle. But they are not a castle, or even stones. All things want to be what they already are."

"It is like inertia," Sev adds. "The further you try to stray from an object's nature, the more difficult it is."

So it worked before because I was making the fountain look like a cleaner fountain, or making a stick look like the tree it came from. "But isn't changing one thing into another the whole point of shaping?"

Elizabeth laughs. "What you're doing isn't shaping. I don't even know what it is."

"Now is time for *playing* cards, not building hotels out of them," Orban says, dealing another hand.

I stuff Mom's key back into my pocket. It's probably best if I don't let everyone know all I've been doing with it. They might not understand why I've been using its power to keep things running smoothly before the gala. But in a few days the gala will be over. Everything's almost done. Chef Silva approved the menu (though I'm pretty sure it's not the one I gave him), the music selections have been made, bright green decorations and signs have been hung throughout the Hotel. Once the event is over, I can deal with all the problems I've been putting off, without the added stress of the Embassy guests and Mr. Nagalla.

"Now, see this?" Orban points to an ace of hearts. "Aces are the only cards that affect the entire table, unless you have a king of the same suit. King is the only card that can shape an ace."

"Let's just play already!" Elizabeth exclaims.

Sev agrees. "Cam can figure it out as we go."

The lights dim and the music starts up. Dancers slip out onto the nearby stage, glittering with dangly sequins and jewels. Orban continues explaining the game as the Bollywood crew spin and dance in the spotlights. Their costumes are mobster themed tonight—an Eastern twist on striped suits and fedoras and glittery nightclub gowns.

I spy Rahki, Sana, and Cass at a table of their own closer to the stage. Rahki's doing her usual crosswords, bobbing her head to the music in her headphones, while Sana doodles on Cass's hand with a strange pen thing. I've seen those doodles before on Sana's arms. Most of the time she draws things like math equations, but today she's going full swirls and flowers.

"What is that stuff?" I ask.

"Mehndi," Orban says, dealing the cards.

"It's like temporary tattoos," Elizabeth adds. "Some people put it on for weddings and special events. Sana's been talking for weeks about wearing some nice mehndi to your birthday party."

Cass's and my birthday is tomorrow. Sharing our birthday was always something I enjoyed when we were little, but this year has not been as fun as previous ones. I still can't bring myself to apologize to her, partly because I'm a little jealous. I know I need to get over how she's become everyone's go-to fixer, but whenever I think about apologizing, I get annoyed all over again. She's got that way of talking to people that makes them warm up to her, and the bizarre part is that people like her even when she doesn't know what she's doing. She freely admits it, as though there's nothing wrong with her not being able to solve their problems. And I shouldn't be mad—I don't even *want* to be mad—but that doesn't change the fact that I am.

I watch as Sana squeezes the dye onto Cass's fingers. "Is it okay for Cass to wear that?"

Elizabeth shrugs. "Sana offered, so I'm sure it's fine."

As the music crescendos, we all pause to watch the spectacle of lights and flowing fabric. The whole stage shimmers as a glittery, lemon-scented fog billows around the performers. It's really impressive—maybe I can get an extra show added to the gala schedule.

"We do not get to celebrate birthdays often," Sev says, rearranging the cards in his hand. "Two birthdays at once is a rare prize."

Why? We've celebrated plenty of birthdays, including Sev's own.

No, wait. We celebrated his *binding day*, the anniversary of the day when Sev joined the Hotel. There was cake and everything, but it wasn't his birthday. Come to think of it, all of the celebrations we've had have been binding days.

The dancing onstage intensifies in a riot of color and crashing drums. They've brought out props now, including a wall-size frame with an old Gothic scene on the other side. Another frame up high shows the full moon, shining like a spotlight onto the stage.

"Sev," I ask, "when is your actual birthday?"

"I do not know."

I look to Orban, then to Elizabeth. All three of them shake their heads. "*None* of you know your birthdays?"

"It's not that unusual," Orban says. "Around here you're the odd duck."

"Remember," Elizabeth adds, "most of us who work here are orphans. We didn't have anyone to tell us the date of our births, so we celebrate binding days instead."

They're so easygoing about it. I can't imagine not knowing when I was born. "How do you know how old you are?"

Orban shrugs. "We don't. We can only guess."

"It is not a bad thing." Sev chuckles. "We remember our binding days, which makes those extra special. It is not as if you remember the day you were born."

I never thought about that before.

All at once, the lights go out. The music stops. Total blackout, save for the eerie light of the moon-frame shining through the stage fog.

The jangling of bells from the stage dies down almost instantly. Guests mutter questions in the dark like "What happened?" and "Is someone turning the lights back on?" The hair prickles on the back of my neck. Is this another one of Nico's pranks?

"Has this happened before?" I ask.

"Never," Elizabeth replies.

Orban flicks on a flashlight. One of the dancers' sparkly dresses catches the beam and casts reflections around the Arkade like a disco ball. "I'll check the fuse box," he says.

Before he can go, however, the house lights come back on. Or at least, they *start* to. They only brighten a bit—a dim, grayish light—but it's enough for everyone to start making their way to the exits.

"Something's wrong," Rahki says as she, Sana, and Cass join us.

"I agree," I tell her.

The speakers stutter to life, playing a drawn-out version of the previous tune. The sound drags, a warbling slur that sounds more like a moan than dance music.

"Uh," Orban says, "is anyone else's arm hair standing on end?"

Cass motions to the crowd. "Someone should talk to them. Tell them what's going on. I can do it if you want."

And let her fix one more thing? No, thank you. If she keeps on, the Hotel is going to decide that it should have chosen her instead of me.

I hop up onto the stage and stand in the beam of moonlight. "Nothing to worry about, everyone. We're just experiencing some . . . technical difficulties."

"Technical difficulties?" Cass scoffs.

"Please make your way to the exits," I continue, ignoring her. "If you like, you can drop by the café for a cuppa, on the House. Again, this is nothing to worry about."

"Is it something to worry about?" Orban asks when I hop back down.

I don't know, but I don't want to cause a panic. "I'm sure it's fine."

"We'll get the guests out of here," Rahki says, and motions for Sana and Sev to follow her.

"It's Nico, isn't it?" Elizabeth asks.

"Probably."

"We should wait and see what happens," Cass says. "Maybe he'll tell us what he's up to?"

"No." I clench my teeth. Even with all the work I've been doing to cover up these pranks, it's getting to be too hard to keep them quiet. It's one thing to play jokes with fountains and smells and cats—it's another to endanger our guests. "I've had about enough of him. Everyone, stay here. I'm going to check things out backstage."

When I peek behind the heavy stage curtain, I'm struck by how dark it is back there. I need a light. The suspended frame showing that big beautiful moon catches my attention. That'll work.

I lower the frame to the stage and unclip it from its harness. The wood is surprisingly light, and the air coming through it is crisp, despite the lingering warmth from the stage lights. Using the moon-frame as an oversize flashlight, I continue around the curtain.

Backstage, sandbags and weights hang at various heights from metal cables that reflect the moonlight. The sound of the fleeing guests on the other side of the curtain mixes with the stagnant tones playing through the speakers, to form an eerie tightness in my chest.

A gust of wind blows past, smelling like soil and plants. I stick my hand into the frame to test the air on the other side, but the breeze isn't coming from there, so where—

A loud flutter smacks me in the face, and I jump. Membrane wings slap at my head and pull at my hair before disappearing into the rafters. My shoulders tingle with adrenaline. I close my eyes, struggling to calm myself down. It was just a bat, flying through from wherever the frame leads.

When I open my eyes, I see a figure in the shadows at the opposite side of the stage. A boy, shorter than me, and wearing a pin-striped suit.

"Nico?" I think it's him, and yet something's not quite right. It's as if the edges of his shape are being drawn and redrawn over and over again by hand. Like the image I saw in the elevator glass.

The figure mirrors my movement, grabbing the coin at his chest and clenching his teeth just like me. It *is* him. We're still connected.

The shadow bolts, disappearing into the darkness.

"Wait!"

I dart after him, but I'm stopped short when my face smashes into something solid. The sound of breaking glass showers all around me as I stumble backward, shielding my face against the rain of shards.

When it stops, I carefully reach for the moon-frame for light to see the damage.

A mirror. It was a mirror, and I ran headlong into it. The black-painted floor is covered with broken reflections of the moon in my hands.

He was here, though. I'm sure of it. Does he realize what he's doing to me? Does he care? I kick the bricks of the wall next to me in frustration, stubbing my toe in the process.

The lights flicker on, and a sharp voice assaults me from behind.

"There you are!" Cass rolls toward me, eyes narrowed in suspicion. "I heard a crash and called for you, but you didn't answer. I got worried, and—you're bleeding!" She moves as close as she can without crunching the broken glass, to hand me a handkerchief.

I reach up to feel the trickle coming from the spot where my forehead smashed into the mirror. "Sorry. I didn't hear you. Hold on. You were *worried* about me?"

"Well, yeah." She turns to head back to the Arkade. "Now let's take care of the guests."

I grab the handles of her chair to stop her. I know she hates that, but we need to talk. The death-glare she gives me tells me that stopping her chair probably wasn't the best way to start up a meaningful conversation, but I'm not going to let her get away this time.

"I'm sorry," I tell her.

Her scowl remains. "Fine. Now will you let go?"

"No, I mean, I'm sorry about everything," I say. "I know I've been a jerk, and I'm not great at being a good brother sometimes. It's just . . ." I remember what Dad said in Germany. "I'm only a stick, you know?"

She squints, as if trying to puzzle out what I mean. "A stick?"

"I mean . . . I'm only a common stick. I'm not a tree." Ugh, this is going really, really badly. I fix my gaze on the mirror shards scattered around us. "I mean I don't know why I do stuff sometimes. It's in my nature, maybe. Only, I'm trying to change my nature. I'm just a bunch of cards, and I don't know the rules. . . ."

When I look up, she's smiling, almost laughing.

"You're such a dork," she says. "It's okay. I only want you to give me some space, all right? I know what I'm doing, and I'm not going to break. But thank you for apologizing." She turns and heads for the curtain.

I blink. It can't be that easy, can it?

"That's it?" I ask, jogging to keep up with her. "You forgive me?"

"Sure. That's what sisters do, right?"

"Well, yeah, but . . ."

"Do you *want* me to hold a grudge?"

I hold up my hands in surrender. "No. Nooooo. I guess I just figured it would take more convincing." Like, a lot more convincing.
Like, groveling-at-the-feet-of-Queen-Cass convincing. "Besides, I
know you think—"

"You don't know what you think you know, Cam," she says
sternly. "I've got more important things to worry about than my
overprotective brother being annoying. So yeah, that's it. You're
forgiven." She flashes a smile. "Now. There's a couple of things I
need to take care of before our party tomorrow, and you need to get
that cut on your head looked at. We good?"

"Yeah," I say, smiling for the first time in a while. "We're good."

That night, rather than sneak around using Mom's key to hide
all the things that went wrong today one by one—concealing the
cracks in the Russian staircase, covering up another malfunctioning door, or dispersing the smell in the corridors on the eighteenth
floor—I head straight to the empty Greenhouse.

Djhut's words won't leave me alone. He said that when a
magic penetrates deep into the heart of a thing, the magic can
affect every part of that thing. And then there's what Elizabeth
said about things wanting to stay close to their nature. They want
to be what they already are.

Or what they *were*.

We have the heart of the Hotel right here. Mom's key can't
fix all the problems in the Hotel, but what if it doesn't have to?
The Hotel wants to look like it's supposed to, right? The Vesima

has been looking better lately. I've been using the key to make the situation look like I know what I'm doing—like everything's running smoothly and properly. Magic shapes the wielder; the wielder shapes the magic. Maybe by hiding all these problems, I'm healing her. Mom.

And if that's the case, what if I use the key directly on the Hotel's heart?

I press my hand against the bark at the foot of the tree—it's sticky with sap—and I try to feel the network of connections like Djhut instructed. I visualize all of the Hotel doors at once—the knockers to the outside, the turners inside, even the door that's bound to Oma's house way up on the seventeenth floor, far away from the rest of the knockers.

No more games. I raise Mom's topscrew to the massive trunk, and a keyhole glitters to life. Just a few more days, and I can get to the business of fixing each of these problems one by one once everyone goes home.

I insert the key and turn.

Everything's going to be just fine.

17

Unexpected Guests

The morning of our big birthday party, I sit cross-legged on my bed, *The Ledger of Ways* between my knees. It's all I can do, really. The rest of the trainees made Cass and me promise that we'd take our birthday to chill and "under no circumstances, work."

For once, I'm okay with that. Everyone's been talking about how it looks as though the Vesima is finally healed, which is great news for the Hotel. When Nagalla comes, I'll be able to stand up to his scrutiny with pride. Kinda. I'm still not sure whether using the key actually fixed things or just hid them like Dad's illusion of the tree, but it doesn't matter. We just have to make it through the gala and everything will be fine.

Of course, there's still the final matter of getting to know all the ambassadors before the gala, and that requires the Ledger.

Reading the Ledger has gotten easier, and has given me loads of info that I need to prepare for this event, but sometimes I still don't feel like I know what I'm doing. It's not like the book came with an instruction guide—it's just a bunch of pages full of hidden information. The better I get at finding what I'm looking for, the more I realize that I don't know *what* to look for. Mom hasn't shown up again since that first time, but that's okay. I know she's in there. Agapios has been so busy lately that I never see him, which means he can't tell me what I'm looking for either. And for some reason the Ledger still doesn't want to tell me much more about Admiral Dare. It's not just that the info is missing. Every time I try to look her up, the ink goes wild with scribbles, as if the book itself is in pain.

Then there's Nico.

"I'm not 'looking' for him, exactly," I tell it. "I only want to know if he's going to try anything at the gala. Can you at least show me that?"

I press my fingers to the page, and the ink swirls, golden light turning to black as the magic draws across the page. I can't make heads or tails out of what it sketches. There's a shape that looks like it might be Nico, but that gets scribbled out too, like someone got angry and decided to strike his image out of existence.

It's weird how similar this is to when I search for Admiral Dare. For most people in the Ledger, I receive too much information—their whole life story, it seems—but with these two the details are so limited. Big chunks of their pasts are missing, the pages dark or scratched out. Especially with the admiral—whole decades just blotted out. Is there a connection between the admiral and Nico?

A knock comes at my bedroom door. I glance reflexively to my nightstand to make sure the drawer is closed, but then I remember that the sliver's still gone. I never did find it after it vanished.

I open the door. "Sev?"

"Happy birthday!" he says, and instantly starts tugging on my ears. "One, two, three . . ."

"What are you doing?" I ask, trying to back away from the assault on my ear lobes.

". . . eleven, twelve, thirteen!" He lets go, and I stumble back. "It is tradition. I pull your ears for the number of years—ha-ha, I rhyme—and then I say, 'Grow up. Don't be noodles!' . . . or something like that."

Wow, he's enthusiastic this morning. "What does that even mean, 'Don't be noodles'?"

"I do not know. I have never actually heard anyone say it in person before."

"Then how do . . . Oh, never mind." I peek around him to see if he's hiding anything. "Didn't you say you had a present for me?"

Sev smiles widely. "Later. Trust me. Today will be a good day. We have much planned for you."

The hotel phone on my bedside table rings, one of the lights indicating that the call is coming from the front desk. Probably Elizabeth, wanting to wish me a happy birthday too. I could get used to this.

I pick up the receiver. "Hello?"

"Cam, get down to the front desk. Now." There's an edge to Elizabeth's voice that makes my skin prickle. "They're here."

• • •

Sev and I hurry down to the Lobby Level, where people are piled up in a line all the way to the knockers.

I push my way into the front office, where all eight windows show the same thing—long queues in each of the lobbies, people waiting to be checked in. We never have this many people arrive at once. "What's going on?"

Elizabeth sits behind the Pacific Lobby counter, helping a spindly woman wearing a sparkly sari and bottlecap glasses. Elizabeth holds up a finger to the woman and whips around to face me. "Cameron. Good. Your gala guests have arrived."

"It's two days early!"

"I know," she says, "and we are operatin' at half staff because everyone else is gettin' ready for your birthday party. No one's even given us the room assignments yet, and many of the rooms still need to be cleaned anyway."

I was hoping to finalize the room assignments tomorrow morning. "This isn't possible," I say, scratching my head. "I told the ambassadors when to arrive. It was on their invitations."

"You gave them the wrong date." She thrusts a folded invitation into my hands.

I take a hard swallow, reading it over and over, but there's no denying what it says. "This says the gala is today." I typed out the message myself—double- and triple-checked everything. "Do they all say this?"

"Every last one."

There's no way I'd write my own birthday on every single invitation.

I scan the crowd of people from around the world, all squished together in the lobby. These folks don't look like "dignitaries." I mean, some do—dressed in fancy clothes and all—but the rest look completely normal, like ambassador Aijin, whom we met at dinner. I spent so much time reading about the members-in-permanent, like the Maid Commander and the admiral, that I've barely started learning about the others.

"We've got to find somewhere to put them," I say, thinking fast. Agapios said the ambassadors were a notoriously finicky bunch; part of the reason he gave me the Ledger was so I could accurately accommodate them. Now we don't have that luxury.

Or do we?

"I'll be right back." I head for the door, but stop to add, "Call Rahki down here. We'll need her help."

"What's that?" Elizabeth asks when I return, her voice even louder than usual, to compete with a few grumbling ambassadors.

I lug *The Ledger of Ways* onto the counter. "It's what we're going to use to fix this mess."

Rahki's already here, and Sev pulled Orban away from party preparations to help too. But someone's missing.

"This is an all-hands-on-deck situation. Where's Cass?" I ask, knowing full well that she didn't have anything else planned for today.

"I couldn't reach her," Elizabeth says.

Again? "It doesn't matter. We've got enough to deal with." I take a seat at the counter facing the Eastern European Lobby. "Rahki, you're on translation duty. Elizabeth, Sev, and Orban, get all the ambassadors to move their lines over here. We'll sign them in one by one."

The ambassadors grow more sullen as they're asked to form an even longer line that wraps through the entire Lobby Ring. Rahki translates as each guest steps up to the window, and I use the Ledger to glean what I can about them before assigning each a room, a dining time, and everything else included in the Hotel super-luxury package. The line seems to be dwindling, but there are still so many people.

"Mr. Thanapoom Siripopungul," Rahki tells me, translating for the next person in line. "He says his wife brought their dog."

The man points to a woman seated in a domed chair, nuzzling a small, copper-colored shar-pei puppy.

I hold the man's name in my mind and press my fingers to the Ledger; the ink blooms with information. *Thanapoom Siripopungul: Thai ambassador working as an Embassy spy within the local police force to root out Competition loyalists in East Asia.*

I glance back up at pudgy Mr. Siripopungul, who gives me a wide, dopey smile. This guy is a spy? He looks like our Texas neighbor's dad.

A woman near the back of the line hollers something I can't understand.

"Can we move this along?" Rahki proposes. "They're growing impatient."

Apparently Thanapoom loves graphic novels and Vegemite, and always dreamed of singing opera professionally. I assign him room 973, overlooking the Sydney Opera House. "One of our staff members will take you up to your room. Hope you find your destination. Next."

Out of the corner of my eye, I notice a small shadow slinking across the furniture around the edge of the room. Another cat now? Please, *please* tell me Nico didn't send another feline plague for me to deal with on top of this fiasco.

Mrs. Siripopungul's dog perks up. Oh no. It lets out a squeaky yap before scrambling out of the woman's lap and leaping after the cat.

The chase continues through all eight lobbies around the Lobby Ring—cat and dog weaving through the ambassadors' legs and under the furniture.

"Has anyone found Agapios yet?" I ask, fairly certain I already know the answer.

"Just keep it moving," Rahki says. "We've got a long way to go."

We slowly whittle the line down. Imre Tüske to room 2489 in Egypt. Etiene Greco to 1333, New Amsterdam. Yuki Uehara, Neumann Darby, San Domain. Some guy who goes by "Sagocero the Sorcerer" asks for a room with lots of plants, and Cristina

Corallo would like to stay somewhere that has "mixed martial arts on the telly, if you please."

It's interesting reading the Ledger's descriptions. These people aren't at all like Agapios, or the MC, or Admiral Dare. They live all over the world, working in secret to help people and fight against Stripe's brand of greed. They protect governments from docent infiltrators, search for children in danger, even seek out new magics that might be friendly toward us humans. There are dangers mentioned in the ledger that don't make sense and names that slip from my memory almost as soon as I read them.

The mission is so much bigger than I thought, and each of these ambassadors plays a small role.

After a while, Elizabeth and Sev return from getting some of the guests situated.

"This is takin' way too long," Elizabeth says. "The ambassadors are gettin' hungry."

"We've got another problem too," Sana says, entering from the African Lobby. "The *Accommodation* reeks."

"Again?" I ask.

She weaves her fingers through her braid in concern. "The smell is worse than before. There's no way we can feed them in the banquet hall."

I'm going to strangle Nico if I ever find him.

"No problem," Rahki says, perking up. "We'll just throw the ambassadors a party. That's what they're here for, isn't it?"

"*Blizok lokotok, da ne ukusish*," Sev says ruefully. "We are barely holding our own. It would be easier to bite our own elbows than plan another party on top of all this."

"That's it! We've already planned one," I say, realizing what she's suggesting. "Or, you have. The birthday party y'all set up for Cass and me in the garden. It's perfect. The Kinder Garden is brand new, the topiaries are freshly clipped. . . . It'll be as if we expected them to arrive when they did. We will give them all a grand Hotel Between welcome." This might actually work.

Rahki smiles, bolstering my resolve. "Let's make it happen!"

18

A Grand Hotel Welcome

A couple of hours and a none-too-happy Chef Silva later, the ambassadors are gathered in the Kinder Garden, snacking on a buffet spread of treats like sweet alfajores and savory ceviche, appreciating the perfectly shaped topiaries all decorated with streamers and balloons. Everyone's laughing and drinking in honor of Admiral Dare's binding day celebration, which is now just over twenty-four hours away. There's still the *actual* gala to look forward to, but those preparations are set. The hard part is over.

"You've done well, considering," the MC says, walking up behind me. It's not like her to offer a compliment.

"They're here early," I say.

"But they are here." She gives me that rare, knotted smile of hers. "I wasn't sure you'd accomplish that. It seems they might even be having a good time."

"I still don't know how we'll entertain them before the gala tomorrow. What if they get upset and leave?"

The MC snorts. "Agapios may promise 'the vacation of their

dreams,' but I think that's a load of hogwash. What those ambassadors really need is a good kick in the pants to get their heads on straight. They will get what they need."

I flash her a confused glance.

"Don't give me that look, boy." She waves a hand at the crowd admiring the animal-shaped bushes scattered around the garden. "They all *say* they want to do right by our mission, but here they are drinking cocktails and talking about sports instead. Stripe is out there, and he's got something planned. Whatever his scheme, it will result in more loss for us all." She pulls a deep breath. "I suppose it's our fault for wrapping the mission in trinkets and travel and happy feelings."

I'm shocked. The MC never shares her personal feelings about the mission, or the Hotel, aside from declaring her unwavering trust and faith in what we're doing. This doesn't sound like trust, though. It sounds like she's bothered by the way the Hotel operates.

"Mr. Nagalla said something about 'the Château,'" I say, recognizing an opportunity to ask her a question that's been bothering me. "He said he knew the truth about it. What did he mean?"

She closes her eyes, takes a breath. "The Château was my House, just as the Hotel belongs to the Old Man."

"You had one of the great Houses?"

The MC nods. "It was stolen from me. My greatest defeat." She scans the crowd as if searching for threats. "I lacked diligence, and our enemies took advantage of that. After it happened, Agapios gave me a home here, and allowed me to continue to pursue the mission in my own way."

The Maid Service. The way she runs them must be a remnant of how she ran the Château before it was taken, and this must be too why the Fleet Marines saluted her like they did. She was more than just an ambassador, and whatever rank she once held within the Embassy before must have remained when she lost the Château and joined the Hotel. Did all of the members-in-permanent once have Houses like this one?

"I will honor my contract with the Hotel so long as it stands," she says. "After all it has done for me, that's all I can do. Ever the Hotel's servant. That is what I require of the maids, and what I will hold to, myself. I only hope that one day this House will claim the power it was meant to have." She straightens her jacket. "I guess you have this handled, so I will take my leave. Happy birthday, Mr. Cameron."

With that, she exits through the nearest pergola—an arch formed by tree roots that have grown up out of the ground—leaving me to wonder if maybe one day she and I might actually get along.

Almost as soon as she's gone, Admiral Dare enters through the same floral archway, dressed in a gossamer dress with gold accents. At once, she's surrounded by ambassadors congratulating her on reaching her four hundredth binding day.

When she sees me, she motions to the balloons and mouths, "Thank you."

All those blank pages and scribbles in the Ledger—all I can see about her is stuff everyone else already knows. What is she hiding?

Is it the Nightvine, or something more? When we first met, she asked about an agent of Stripe's hiding in the Hotel, but what if she was trying to throw me off? What if—

"Aren't you going to go say hello?" Sana asks, standing under a giraffe-shaped bush with Sev, who's picking at the table of hors d'oeuvres. Sana motions toward the admiral. "Or are you just going to lurk?"

"All these people are here to celebrate her," I say, motioning to the admiral. "She should hang out with them, not me."

"You're the host," Sana adds. "This is what you're supposed to do, when you're not too busy doing everyone else's jobs."

"You think you're not important enough to speak with her?" Sev prods, munching on chocolate-stuffed dates as a cat squeezes between his legs and disappears under the table. Sev groans and rolls his eyes, but the presence of cats in the Hotel is starting to become a given ever since Nico's cat prank.

"It's not that I'm not important enough," I reply. But what is it, then? I'd much rather do my job from the sidelines, especially when I mess everything up all the time. But isn't it my job to keep everyone else from botching things up too? "Everyone's telling me I did a good job, but it's not true. Y'all arranged this party, not me. The only thing I did was send out faulty invitations."

"We prepared this together," Sev says. "As for the invitations, you said that wasn't you, so maybe it was Nico. Your blood-brother tends to add chaos to almost everything recently. Besides, it is your birthday! Nothing can be your fault."

I relax, but just a little. "Thanks, Sev."

"It is what I am here for. Once we get this evening sorted, I will give you your gift. Deal?"

"Deal."

Sana motions to the crowd. "You should address your guests. Give them that grand Hotel welcome you promised, yeah?"

"Maybe." That's what a good concierge would do, and it's what the Hotel probably expects. But addressing the Embassy is still Agapios's role, for now. Which raises the question: Where is he? Maybe this is like the appointment with Admiral Dare, where he expects me to take care of things on my own.

I straighten my suit jacket and steel my nerves. "Wish me luck."

Sev claps me on the back. *"Ni puha, ni pera."*

"What does *that* one mean?"

He pauses. "I think it roughly translates to . . . 'No fluff, no feathers'?"

Sev, King of Obscure Idioms. "Ni pooka to you too."

The hot sun warms my jacket, and if I wasn't already sweating, I am now. I step up onto the raised stone platform at the center of the garden—my Chucks squeaking on the polished marble—and grab the small wooden microphone. I lick my palm and wrap my fingers around the grip as the crowd takes their seats in the arranged white metal chairs. Everyone stills as my voice is transmitted through the wooden barrels spaced around the garden.

"Ambassadors, guests, and friends," I say as the shuffling of the sitting guests dies down. "I'm very . . . uh . . . happy, to welcome you to The Hotel Between." All those eyes, looking at me, judging me. But I've got this under control. The Hotel chose me. I can prove that I'm worthy, that I belong.

Admiral Dare smiles at me, and somehow that makes me more *un*comfortable. Mr. Stripe smiled like that . . . encouraging me to trust that he had my best interests at heart, when really he only cared about his own.

"Thank you all for coming. We've got some great events planned for the next couple of days in honor of Admiral Dare's four hundredth binding day."

As I scan the crowd, my gaze is drawn to one person in particular. At least, I think it's a person. My eyes can't quite focus.

My lungs freeze when the image shifts into clarity. It's him. Nico, standing right in the middle of all these people, a midnight-blue flower pinned to the lapel of his pin-striped suit. He looks straight at me. I cock my head in confusion, and he does the same—just like in the mirror at the Arkade.

Then I blink, and he's gone. I search the faces in the crowd, but I can't find him. No one else seemed to notice the boy standing in their midst, who popped out of nowhere and vanished just as quickly.

Sev clears his throat to drag my attention back to the ambassadors, who are all watching me with confused stares. A woman in a colorful wrap coughs.

"It's been a . . . challenging day for us, but it's been a challenging year, too." *Breathe, Cam. Breathe.* "The Competition is on the defensive for the first time in ages, so that's good. But having the Competition on the run doesn't make our mission any less urgent. If anything, we—"

"Oi!" a girl shouts from one of the root-grown arches at the back of the garden. "Everyone stay still, and no one gets hurt!"

Bee. Nico's Hopper groupie saunters forward, tweed vest over her white button-down, a flat cap over her braids. She's not alone either. A dozen other kids stand in the arches at north, south, east, and west, their arms folded.

Some of the ambassadors jump to their feet, sending white plastic chairs toppling onto the grass. Everyone can tell that this is *not* what we had planned.

One of the ambassadors takes a step into the aisle between the rows to face the intruders. It's the ambassador with the puppy—Mr. Siripopungul. The pudgy man settles into a stance, ready for a fight.

Bee casually pulls a long, pointed sliver from her belt. "You'll want to stay right where you are, mister, or you might end up on an unexpected safari."

The other Hoppers follow her lead, each readying their own slivers. We took all the ambassadors' weapons when they came to the Hotel—one of Cass's suggestions, if I remember correctly. If Mr. Siripopungul fights, it'll be fists versus slivers, and my money's not on his fists.

He must realize that too, because he stands down.

Rahki and Sev appear beside me on the dais. "That girl," Rahki snarls, unholstering her duster.

"What happened to those new security measures?" I ask.

"Most weren't supposed to be implemented until tomorrow. We didn't expect they would attack *before* the gala."

Now all the chaos of the past few hours makes sense. Nico wanted to catch us off guard. The time has come for his grand scheme to unfurl.

"What should we do?" Sev asks.

"Nothing yet," I say. "One wrong move, and they'll start scattering ambassadors all over the world with those slivers." Where's the Maid Commander when you need her?

The admiral meets my gaze. There's a question in that look. Is she offering to help? I shake my head. Too risky, and I'm not sure I trust her yet. We'll just have to see how this plays out.

Near the back, a Kenyan ambassador bolts for an arch on the edge of the garden.

Bee dashes to intercept him and jabs the man with the tip of her sliver just as he reaches the pergola. The ambassador crumples into the tip like a wadded sheet of paper and vanishes with a muffled cry.

A gasp whispers through the crowd.

"This particular sliver is bound to a glacier I visited a while back," Bee says, addressing the group as if she's talking to children. "The glacier is about seventy miles from the nearest paved road. Anyone else want to do a little exploring? Maybe two or more will weather the cold better together than that poor bloke will alone."

"We need help," I whisper to Rahki. "Do you have a way to call the maids?"

Rahki shakes her head, and motions to the pergola arches that connect the garden to the Hotel. "They can't get in anyway. The Hoppers took over the bindings on all the arches. We're cut off."

She's right. The arch behind Bee should show the Pyramid Foyer on the other side, but instead it's a sunny, blue sky. They . . . reshaped the doors, just like Artificer Djhut taught us.

"Ayyyy!" Bee says, noticing Rahki and me on the stage. "Ain't seen you in a while. How are you going?"

She marches toward the dais, and shoos Rahki and Sev away as she steps up in front of me. When Rahki hesitates, Bee raises her sliver and gives it a playful wiggle between her fingers.

"Don't kick the hive, missy." Bee motions to her Hoppers. "I don't think you can handle this."

"I can certainly handle you," Rahki shoots back. "*Missy.*"

Bee cocks her head. "But can *they?*" She waves at the men and women around us. "Why don't you have a seat and let the grown-ups talk."

Rahki purses her lips, but eventually backs off and steps down from the platform.

"Kinda funny meeting again like this, ain't it?" Bee says, turning to me. "Last time we were on the same side."

"I guess that was my mistake," I say.

"No hard feelings. It's just business." She gestures for the mic. "I'll take that, thank you."

I reluctantly hand it over.

"Allow me to introduce ourselves," she says, voice projecting through the barrels. "We're the Hoppers, and we're here to collect our Hotel tax, if you don't mind. Or even if you do. We don't judge."

The scattered Hoppers aim their slivers at nearby guests.

"I'm the busy Bee, by the way." She performs an awkward curtsy. "My associates and I would appreciate it if you would go ahead and take your valuables out of your pockets, wallets, *et cetera, et cetera*, so that we can relieve you of them with as little fuss as possible."

"What are you doing?" I expected some kind of grand scheme, not . . . this. I thought Nico was above petty thievery.

"What's it look like, boy-o? You said it. I'm a thief. Thieves steal. So here I am. Thieving." She raises the microphone. "Go ahead and remove all those pretty jewels from your necks, too. Oh, and pocketbooks—can't forget the pocketbooks."

"You can't steal from us," one of the ambassadors shouts. "Don't you realize who we are?"

"Oh, I know exactly who you are. A room full of money."

"This isn't the way to get what you want, Bee," I say. "Did Nico put you up to this?"

Before she can answer, another one of the ambassadors makes a dash for the nearest pergola, but the closest Hopper slivers her before she can reach it. I wince at the scream as she vanishes.

"I'd say that no one else should try stepping up like that," Bee crows, "but I do love a good game of Whac-A-Mole."

The audience shifts anxiously as they hand over their necklaces, watches, earrings, and phones to the Hoppers, who shove each item unceremoniously into their bottomless pocks. I could try to get Bee's sliver away from her. If I can manage to sliver her, we might be able to reclaim control. But using slivers is absolutely forbidden for Hotel staff. I'd lose my position quicker than you can say "Have a nice stay."

Bee hops down from the dais and heads straight for Admiral Dare.

"You know why I'm here, Fleet-lady?" Bee asks.

The admiral pulls the chain from her neck, revealing the key I saw aboard the *Roanoke*. The ornate key sparkles like a perfectly cut emerald in the sunlight.

"It seems you found what you were looking for," the admiral says to Bee, just loudly enough for me to hear as she hands the key over. "I hope it helps you in your search."

"I'll take that." Bee snatches the key and tips her hat. "Pleasure to make your acquaintance. And a happy binding day to you, as well."

Why would the admiral give up her key so easily? That key is one of a kind.

Bee turns back to me. "We do what we gotta do, Mr. Cam. Nico did warn you," she says, and gives a wink. "Your donation is much appreciated. Hoppers, grab what you can and let's go!"

They exit through the arches with a resounding *crack*.

19

Garden Variety Disaster

Stillness hangs over the garden like a pin ready to snap. The ambassadors stand like statues scattered across the lawn. Rahki and Sev, even Orban—they're all blank-faced and slack-jawed, staring . . .

. . . at me.

I've failed them. Just when I thought I might be able to pull this whole gala thing off, it goes up in flames. Nico was playing me. All those times I defended him, chose to believe that all these problems were nothing more than petty pranks, and it turns out he really is our enemy. And this . . . this was his declaration of war.

"The arches!" someone yells.

The ambassadors back away from the pergola exits.

"Cam!" Rahki shouts.

"I see it!" The flowers. The black-tipped buds in the lattices over the pergolas are blooming, sprouting shriveled midnight-blue blossoms. The tree roots that frame the arches are growing too, crawling across the grounds, toward the partygoers.

But they're not roots, are they? Roots don't flower like that.

Something else is growing up around the roots. Are they . . . vines?

A lady in a scarlet linen gown steps up onto her chair to get away from the tendrils working their way across the grass. The rest of the ambassadors scatter, but there's nowhere for them to go—the garden is surrounded by a high hedgerow, a safety precaution to protect when we bring the mission kids here. Only now, those hedges have us trapped.

As the vines reach that wall of shrubs, they start grabbing at any ambassadors who come close. So much for making the Kinder Garden safer. Thank the binding that we moved the mission kids back to the Monastery before the party.

"We need to do something," Rahki says. "Quickly."

One of the vines curls up through the trunk of a nearby topiary—the one pruned to look like a life-size giraffe—and the bush begins to move. Slowly at first. The transformation starts in the legs—first the back ones, then the front—and the topiary giraffe steps forward on uncertain hooves. The leafy beast bends its neck and bolts toward the guests.

Plastic chairs fly. An older ambassador in petticoats jumps out of the way, barely avoiding being trampled.

More vines curl through the grass toward the other topiaries—the towering rabbit, an alpaca, a moose, a swan, even an enormous leopard—and bring each to life.

"They are turning the topiaries into icons!" Sev shouts.

Some of the guests flee for the arches, but the vines have grown over the portals and are sprouting more of the black and blue flowers, cutting off our escape. Those shriveled blossoms . . . they're the same as the ones I've been seeing on Nico's lapel. I've seen them somewhere else too, though I can't quite place where.

"Cam!" Rahki calls over the stampeding bushes.

Right. Do something.

The vines are the source of all this chaos—they sprouted when the Hoppers reshaped the bindings on the pergolas—which means the vines are also our key to stopping this.

I call out to Rahki, but she's already directing the guests to stack chairs and tables so that she can bind them into a temporary shelter to guard the guests against the rampaging shrubbery.

Elizabeth, Sev, and Orban answer my call instead.

"We have to plug those pergolas," I tell them. "Break the connection."

They jump into action, each choosing an arch to try to fix this mess.

And what a mess it is. A bushy alpaca trots around the garden wall, leaving root-shaped hoof prints in its wake. The topiary leopard prowls around Rahki's makeshift shelter while Rahki lashes out in careful attempts to bind the leopard's foot or tail to the earth with her duster. The swan splashes wildly in the pond, dark flowers blooming from its beak, the giraffe is barreling across the green, and the topiary bunny is munching on the trees and pooping out flowering mini bushes. Which leaves . . .

The moose. It stands between me and my arch, wagging its antlered head as if to say, *Go ahead. Try me.*

I ready my plug—the spring-loaded mechanism we use to disconnect the doors. The moose paws at the ground like a mama protecting its baby. Only, in this case the baby is the pergola behind it. How does it know what I'm planning to do?

The moose charges, and all I can do is run. I hurtle over dense flowerbeds and short, not-quite-as-murderous shrubs to get away. Branches and leaves scrape across my back as the moose swipes at me with its wooden antlers.

A weight crashes into me from the side, sending me skidding across the slick, cool grass.

I slide to a stop under a calm, cloudless sky.

A hand presses into my chest and holds me down. "Are you okay?" Admiral Dare leans over me, huffing and out of breath. She must have knocked me out of the moose's path before it trampled me. She may be old, but she's still spry.

"I'm okay," I say.

The admiral stands, not bothering to brush the grass and dirt from her taffeta dress. "You have a way to unbind those arches?"

I raise the plug in my clenched fist.

"Get to it, then," she says, and charges off to distract the moose-bush. Maybe she's not so bad after all.

I limp toward the unguarded pergola—the vines grow out from the trellis in a spray like flames—and I struggle to reach through the tangle of overgrowth, but the going is difficult. The tough vines creak and crack; branches snap. My muscles ache as I fight my way through the thickening foliage.

Then I see it—the pin that connects the trellis to the Hotel. I squeeze my arm through the vines to extend the plug, but I can't quite reach the pin. Thorns poke at my skin. Blue flowers bloom and die inches from my face. I stretch as far as my arm can go, breaking what branches I can as the vines curl around my arm, up my leg, my torso. The shoots dig into my belly, as if they're trying to grow through me.

Just a little farther.

Fft-bing!

The pin pops from the hinge, and the vines stop. I take a deep breath, fighting back the tingle of adrenaline coursing through my limbs. One arch down.

I free myself of the tangle and take in the state of the garden. Two of the topiaries—the swan and the moose—have collapsed. Their bond to whatever was controlling them has been broken. Rahki is laying bindings on the rabbit's ears, rooting it to the ground so that it can't go hopping over to trample the guests in their chair-bunker. Admiral Dare has subdued the alpaca, and Elizabeth and Orban are both emerging from their newly plugged pergolas.

Then I spot Sev, lying on the ground.

Under the attacking leopard.

"NO!" I scream, and race toward him. Rahki must see him too, because she leaves her bushy rabbit and takes off in his direction as well. If something happened to him . . .

Elizabeth jumps in my way, her hands outstretched to stop me.

"Move!" I shout.

She grabs my shoulders and forces me to look at her. "Stop, Cam. Stop! You have no weapon, and that monster is not playing around."

Behind her, Rahki takes a flying leap and knocks the flared end of her baton into the topiary leopard's head. The duster sticks firmly, giving her leverage to swing off it and drag the beast off Sev's motionless body.

A twist of her wrist pulls the duster free as she scrambles back to her feet. She's got its attention, but now the icon is turning its ire on her, prowling around Rahki as if looking for an opening to attack. Rahki matches its movements, duster at the ready.

I pull away from Elizabeth's grip. I should be doing something, but she's right—I don't have anything to fight the creature.

Or do I?

The other topiaries lay withered and dead around us, now that the other pergolas are broken. That means . . .

I bolt for the final arch, stripping off my ripped jacket as I go. The fabric will only get caught in the branches.

The vines of the arch engulf me immediately, curling around every part of my body, but I press on. I have to stop that thing. I have to save Sev.

Thorns poke into my skin, scrape my face and arms. One digs deeply into my thigh—and it hurts so, so much—but I'm close now. The pin's head is just under my fingers. I arrange the plug by sense of touch alone, hoping I've got it right, as the overgrowth squeezes the breath out of me.

Ghostly images swim behind my eyelids. Images of Nico, and of Cass, and midnight-blue flowers. As my vision dims, one thought rises to the surface:

Isn't it strange how much these tangled vines look like scribbles?

20

The Empty Chair

I walk the Nightvine in my dreams. It's different tonight, though. More alive.

And it's angry.

The twisting path curls and writhes, trying to buck me off and send me tumbling into that vast emptiness beneath it. All the while Nico's laughter echoes through the air. *You've lost, Cam,* he says. *It's mine now.*

Then I fall. I reach for the vine to catch myself, but my fingers find only loose coins.

I wake to the sound of rain and a choir of chirping birds.

As I blink away sleep, I reach for Nico's coin at my neck, but it's not there. In its place I feel a long, scabbed-over scratch.

The vines. The garden party.

Sev.

I sit up to see where I am, and marvel at the long glass wall that extends before me, fogged with dewdrops. The rain forest jungle beyond teems with life. In the distance a tall, skinny waterfall shimmies as it pours into a rocky pool speckled with rain. A lemur clings to a tree directly in front of my bed, watching me with its huge, curious eyes.

Hospital beds and medical equipment blink and beep all around. I'm in the Apothecarium—the Hotel's equivalent of a nurse's office.

I check out the damage on my arms and legs. My skin is a mess of scrapes and scratches extending all the way up into my cartoon-key-print hospital gown. What happened? Was I able to unbind the pergola and stop the leopard?

Nico's coin rests on the bedside table, along with everything else I had on me, including Mom's key. I feel better once the necklace is tied back around my neck and the topscrew is back in my hand, but then I notice the person in the bed next to mine.

"Sev!" I hop down and stumble over to my friend's side. He's unconscious and doesn't look good—long scrapes crisscross his face, his chest is wrapped with gauze, and there's a cast on his leg—but at least he's breathing.

"I'm sorry," I say. "I should never have convinced myself that Nico was still a good guy, or made Rahki and Cass keep quiet about the letter. I was wrong."

He doesn't answer me.

"Mr. Pronichev is on medication," a voice behind me says in a distinctly Alpine accent. "He won't be waking up for a while." It's the Countess Physiker, head apothecary. Her curly hair is done up in an old-timey nurse's cap.

"Is he going to be all right?" I ask.

She busies herself at her equipment. "Needs rest. Binding will help. Now," she says, shoving me back into my bed, "you rest too. Fixing your face."

"What's wrong with my face?"

She makes a dramatic circle around my entire head with her finger. "Will fix. Lie down."

I obey, trying not to imagine what those thorns did to Oma's "favorite chipmunk cheeks."

Countess Physiker opens a jar and sets it on the bed next to me. "Be still. To screw-up face is not so good." She dips her fingers into the blue substance and smears a glop onto my cheek.

"Is that shaping dye?"

"Quiet, or you will end up with bulbous nose like bird." She motions to a toucan on a branch outside the windows. "Shaping dye is good for healing. Encourages change."

"Are you going to use it on Sev, too?"

"Not yet. To use this soon, I might change too much. Do not worry. He was awake earlier, and told me to remind you that your birthday present is waiting for you in his room." She fakes a smile. "Happy birthday."

Happy birthday, indeed.

"Strange, the way this happened," she says as she works. Her grammar is awkward, like she doesn't quite know how to express what she's saying in English. "The magic that did this . . . it should not. Dangerously close to breaking the Life binding."

"Magics are not allowed to kill," I say, remembering. The fundamental bond of Life prevents even rogue magics from causing lethal harm to people. To violate that rule would have extreme consequences, though I don't know what those consequences might be. "But is that still true if someone is controlling the magics? Then it's the person using the magic that causes it."

The countess frowns. "Even controlled, magics may only harm under special circumstances. They will rarely risk damaging people. The penalties for breaking fundamental bonds are too high. Magics violate the treaty—magics break their binding—magics no longer held together."

She continues slathering my wounds with the dye, and I ponder her words. I knew that Stripe contracted people to do his dirty work because he couldn't do it himself, but I never realized that breaking fundamental bonds could break him, too. Is that what's happening? Is Stripe using Nico to do what Stripe can't, thereby protecting himself from somehow violating the treaty? But Nico was supposed to be immune to Stripe's influence, forever in perpetuity. The only way that Stripe could influence him again is with a new contract.

Unless Nico's doing this on his own.

Eventually the countess stoppers the jar. "It's okay. You can enter," she shouts into the hall. "But only two! The rest wait!"

Rahki and Sana dart through and race toward us—Sana to my bed, Rahki to Sev's. Despite Countess Physiker's warning, Oma lurks in the doorway, hand over her heart.

"Are you okay?" Sana asks me, but her eyes keep darting over to Sev.

"Yes. Sev will be too. Countess said he just needs rest."

She breathes a sigh of relief. "When news reached the Motor Pool, we worried that something had gone wrong with our icons. Thank the binding it wasn't statues."

"Is everyone else okay?" I ask. "The ambassadors?"

"We succeeded," Rahki says. "The ambassadors are still here too. The MC put the Hotel on lockdown; no one in or out. But . . ." They exchange a look.

"But what?"

Rahki glances over at Oma. "She'll tell you. We're just glad you're okay." She takes Sana by the arm. "Come on, *habibi*. Let's give them some space."

The two of them leave me alone with a much-too-serious-looking Oma. Her expression is soft, like the one she wears whenever Cass needs a new surgery.

"Oma," I say, realizing what that look must mean, "where's Cass?" I scan the empty beds. She wasn't in the garden, so she shouldn't have gotten hurt. "Did something happen to her?"

Oma sits on the edge of the bed and hands me a slip of paper folded around a faded wooden coin. Cass's coin.

Dear Everyone,

I'm checking out of the Hotel for a bit to find Nico and join the Hoppers. Don't worry about me, though.

The Museum will take care of me just as well as the Hotel
would.

    And don't be mad, Oma. Cam got to run away last
year. It's my turn.

    See y'all soon,

    Cass

When I look up, Oma's eyes are filled with tears. I sit forward
on the bed and wrap my arms around her. Oma puts her head in
her hands and starts sobbing, and before I even know what's happening, we're both crying.

Cass would know how upset Oma would be by this, adventure
or no adventure. What was she thinking? Now Oma's squeezing
me so hard that I wonder if she's worried I'm going to vanish again
too.

Maybe I *should* vanish. Then at least I couldn't mess up anything else. Did Cass leave because of me and my insistence about
her doing front desk duty? Is this my fault?

"May I come in?" says a new voice.

I press my thumbs into my eyes to wipe them, struggling to
make out the figure of my dad at the threshold.

The sight of him sends a jolt of anger through me. It's not only
my fault that Cass left—it's his, too. He made us like this. We're a
family of people who run, and that started with him. If he'd done
the right thing all those years ago, Mom would still be here, and
Cass would've never met Nico.

"Go away," I tell him, and stare out at the dancing waterfall. "You don't belong here."

"I'm going to bring her back," he says. "Don't you worry."

"Worry?" I clench my teeth. "This is your fault. You encouraged her."

"That's not—"

I let go of Oma, toss the sheet aside, and rush at him to push him back into the hall. He doesn't resist. I knew he wouldn't. Like I know it's not his fault that Cass left. Not really. Even so, once he's through the doorway, I slam the door in his face.

"Cameron!" Oma shouts.

"He doesn't get to be here for this," I say. There's too much going on, and I need to focus on what comes next. Having him around will just complicate things. I can apologize later, once we're all back together.

I brace myself for Oma's anger, but for once she doesn't correct me. Instead she wraps me back up in her arms and sits me back down.

"I'll find her," I promise under my breath, too quietly for anyone but the Hotel to hear me. "*I'll* bring her home."

21

The Intersection of Lost and Found

I flop onto my bed with *The Ledger of Ways*, relieved to finally be home, and anxious to start fulfilling my silent promise to Oma. The book weighs heavily in my lap.

"You should have warned me," I tell it. I don't expect an answer. I just . . . wish someone could have prepared me for this mess.

The days of the Hotel are numbered.

Someone besides Nico.

I settle back into my pillows and run my fingers down the book's pages, watching the paper shimmer to life, recreating the disaster in the Kinder Garden. As if I need a reminder. I'm already angry—at Dad, at Cass, even at myself. Seeing all those Embassy guests running around in a panic makes the back of my neck burn.

"I don't want to see this," I tell the Ledger. "The whole point of you is to show me things I don't know, not to rub my face in my failures."

The page goes blank, and then a single sentence scrawls across the page in what looks like Cass's handwriting.

That's your whole point.

Those are the words she said to me when I was trying to convince her to stick to her front desk duty. I should have listened. When we were in school together, I always got angry at people who treated her differently. They were the enemy. Have I become Cass's enemy?

Light spreads across the paper. It's still showing the garden, but from a different perspective. The drawing shows Cass under one of the pergolas before the attack. That's strange. I never saw her at the party. She's rubbing something onto the pergola's pin. Is that . . . shaping dye?

A burst of energy floods the arch, and she goes through.

My jaw clenches. It was *her*. Cass allowed the Hoppers in.

I flip the page to find her inky figure rolling into a familiar foyer. Checkerboard tile. Angel statue. It's the Museum. Bee gives Cass a bright smile and a pat on the back as if to say *Welcome to the Hoppers*.

The next day I get through my morning responsibilities as quickly as possible, which is a bit easier than usual, thanks to the lockdown. Many of the ambassadors have now been escorted by the Maid Service back to their respective corners of the globe for safety, though a few stayed behind, hoping that the Hotel will return their stolen property to them soon. Good luck on that. Others say they still want to attend the gala, but that will, of course, be canceled now.

One ambassador who didn't leave, however, is Mr. Nagalla.

He's insisting on conducting a full "audit" of our security measures now that we've been breached.

As I busy myself cobbling together a plan to get my sister back, Mr. Nagalla stays a step behind me—or, more often than not, in my way. He's like the world's most annoying shadow. I'm tempted to create a Most Likely to Make Me Want to Punch Someone award if he sticks around much longer.

"Why the sour face?" Elizabeth asks when I come to the front desk window for the daily status report.

"Three guesses," I whisper, eyes darting to my short shadow-man, who is examining the safety pamphlets. "I swear, if he follows me to the bathroom . . ."

Elizabeth covers a laugh. I should know better than to make comments like these to her. Subtlety is not her strong suit. What is it Sev says? *If Elizabeth knows a thing, everyone knows a thing.*

"Leave him to me," she says, and stands to lean over the desk to call out to him. "Mr. Nagalla, have you seen the sorry state of the wood on these counters? It's so grainy . . ." And just like that, Nagalla totters over to examine the poor counters that never did anything to anyone, while I sneak up the stairs to get away from him.

The winds of the Nightvine make me feel at peace. Here, I don't have to worry about people messing with my plans, or taking matters out of my control. This is my domain, if only because there's no one here to challenge me.

I wander the roads—up the rises and down the dips, winding

past hundreds of arches that lead to who knows where. Queenie saunters along beside me, tail swishing back and forth, my ever-present companion whenever I'm here, navigating the roads between piles of forgotten things.

Up ahead I spy an intersection where multiple vine roads connect, and on it another collection of junk from the outside world. It's like the Nightvine collects lost things and builds little shrines out of them for the cats to play on.

Does the magic here feel as lost as I do? Is it gathering lost things because, like me, it doesn't know where it fits?

"I see you've found my hiding place," a voice says from around a junked-out minivan.

I freeze. All this time, I've never encountered another person out here. But I recognize that voice.

"Admiral?" I peek around the minivan to find Admiral Dare perched upon an old box TV set like the one Oma used to have. My mouth hangs open like the koi fish in the fountain. I figured she'd be mobilizing her marines to get her key back.

"Was it you?" she asks as soon as I step into view.

Huh? "I don't—"

"Not you." She puts a fist to her chin in thought. "Your sister, then? Or was it another one of your hotel friends working for Stripe?"

I cross my arms. It's one thing to say that Cass helped the Hoppers, but to suggest that she's with Stripe is going too far. "My sister is *not* working for Stripe."

"Someone in the Hotel is. And yet"—she fixes her gaze on the tea-green sky—"the search brings me here again. I'm not sure why."

"Well, I'm not the one you're looking for, and it's not Cass either." Though, I have to finally admit that it could be Nico. Then a new thought hits me. The trouble at the Hotel, sending out invitations to all those ambassadors, the grand party. . . "Your binding day gala—it was a trap, wasn't it? You were trying to draw out Stripe's agent."

She sits back and folds her hands. "Yes. The gala was my idea, in fact. In a way it worked too, though not quite as I expected."

"Is it even really your binding day?"

"It is, but once you're as old as I am things like that don't matter quite as much. It did provide a fortunate excuse, though. Agapios asked me to track Stripe soon after you evicted him from the Museum. When the key led me to the Hotel, I knew that someone with a strong connection to Stripe had been operating within its walls. Whoever it is, they are very good at staying hidden, and we needed to draw them out." She motions to a boom box nearby. "Have a seat. You make me nervous, lurking like that."

I brush off the old stereo and sit.

The admiral crosses her legs and rests her hands on her knees. "It's been quite some time since I last visited this place. I used to love that wet smell on the air."

"So this really is where you disappeared to," I say. "Your father came to the New World to bind a door for the Embassy, but something went wrong and you escaped by coming here."

"It took four hundred years for someone to learn that secret." She smiles warmly at the sky. "The lost and found of the world."

"Why not tell anyone, though? What happened?"

She scrunches her brow. "The *Commandant* happened; you call him Mr. Stripe. He wanted to take my father's door and use it to add the Americas to his empire. Thankfully, the indigenous people of Roanoke had developed a relationship with a magic of their own." She motions to the verdant sky overhead.

"So they're the ones who created the Nightvine."

"Not created—*cultivated*," she corrects. "They hid us colonists here and pruned the vine safely away from the outside world. She has grown wild ever since."

"She?"

"I don't know what they called this place before we came here. My father called her *Vitis Nocturna Via*, 'the way of the vine of night.' Though, I suppose 'the Nightvine' has a certain ring to it as well. Once those who protected us cut her off from the world, she—and those trapped inside—felt lost and forgotten. She's been reshaped by those feelings. By *my* feelings. The others didn't survive our long imprisonment here, but the vine bonded with me, sustained me. She gave me a place to hide, and her fruit to survive. It wasn't until my father passed that the vine let me use her magic to escape." The admiral pauses. "She gave it to me, you know. The Key of Lost Things—power to seek what's lost, or to lose it entirely."

I toe the dirt with my shoe. "I'm sorry for letting the Hoppers steal it."

"The Nightvine doesn't belong to me, young man, and neither does her key. Magics like that are much too wild to ever be owned. She chose to act kindly toward me. I'm not sure I'll ever know why."

The Key of Lost Things. Was that the Hoppers' target all along? Seems as though something like that would be very helpful right now.

The admiral looks me in the eye. "Don't you worry about that key, keybearer. It was born from the Nightvine's lost state, so it's in the key's nature to be lost as well. The key will find its way back eventually." She stands, dusting the dirt from her uniform. "That's the funny thing I've learned about lost things: the important ones always come back to you."

She starts walking down the path back to the Hotel.

"You're leaving?"

"I have a vengeful magic to hunt," she says. "And I suspect you have one more thing to find as well. A gift from a friend?" The admiral waves, and continues down the vine. "Find your destination, Cameron Kuhn. Find it, and don't let go."

22

Resignation and Determination

One more thing to find.

My topscrew opens the door to Sev's room right up, and the familiar scent of wood shavings and sawdust wafts through.

It's weird entering his room without him—like I'm intruding. Cameron Kuhn, Most Likely to Be Up to No Good. Yeah, right. Nico's the one who deserves that honor. Which raises the question: Why didn't Nico come to the Hotel himself to steal the key? He's a schemer, sure, but he's also prideful—he wouldn't allow Bee to take all the glory unless there was something more important for him to do elsewhere.

Or unless someone was preventing him.

I scan the floor and shelves of Sev's suite, looking for a box or something with my name on it, but I can't find anything. Where else would it—

Then I notice the garment bag on the rack in the closet, a card dangling from the hook with *For Cam* written on it in Sev's neat, blocky handwriting.

Sev got me clothes?

I zip open the bag to reveal a suit—a *fine* suit, tailored in the formal style that Agapios and I wear for our concierge duties. There's a spot of red near the collar, like a tiny drop of blood that couldn't be washed out. I remember that spot. I was wearing this suit when Nico first loosed the cats on the Hotel, and one cat got me square in the face. Sev must have snuck it from the laundry. But why?

I lay the suit on the bed before realizing just how dusty the bedding is—Sev's woodworking projects always leave his room feeling more like a workshop than a bedroom. I quickly yank the suit back off the coverlet to brush loose all the dust off the back, but strangely, there is none. The dust didn't stick.

Curious, I wipe my hand in the dust on a nearby shelf and grip the sleeve. When I release the fabric, it's perfectly clean. The jacket must be coated with something. An anti-binding? After all my complaining about the Laundry Service, Sev made me a suit that won't get dirty. Awesome.

I go ahead and change, anxious to see how the suit looks, but my enthusiasm quickly fizzles when I check the mirror. It doesn't fit anymore. The jacket, the pants . . . it's all much too big, as if Sev resized it to fit him, not me.

I should have known it was too good to be true.

I'm about to take the jacket off and change back into my original suit—filthy now from being dropped on Sev's floor—when I see more words written on the back of the gift tag.

Beshaped Suit (Please read instructions carefully
before using.)
To clean: This Beshaped Suit never needs to be
cleaned. It is shaped and tailored to resist all bindings
beyond the one between it and its wearer.

Ha! Resists bindings? Let's see Rahki try to stick me to a wall now. Though . . . that won't matter if the suit doesn't fit.

To operate, infuse your coin and insert it into the
front jacket pocket.

An infusion: binding a part of yourself to an object for a short time to tap into the binding's magic. We use that whenever we lick the pins and sign our name to our coins with our spit to activate the icons, or the map boards, scattered throughout the Hotel. Does that mean this suit is an icon, too, like the statues, or Cass's chair?

I feel the pocket normally designed for handkerchiefs and pocket squares. This one contains both a normal pocket and a smaller, coin-size inner sleeve.

On first binding, the infused coin will tether you to the
suit, and the suit to you. The suit will then adjust to
fit your needs, and maintain that shape until bound to
another person.
Reminder: like all icon bindings, the magic will only

last as long as the binding infusion remains active. Do
not forget to renew the binding as necessary to use
added functions.
Happy birthday, Cameron. You are a good friend.

Magic? Added functions?

I step in front of Sev's mirror and take in the suit's loose, dumpy appearance. Using a little spittle and a pin from my pin-sleeves, I scribble my name on the coin and slide it into the pocket.

The suit shimmers along its seams. The sleeves draw up to my wrists. The waistcoat cinches around my abdomen, and the slacks rise up on my butt all on their own, tightening around my hips.

When the shimmer dies, I check the mirror again. It's a perfect fit. I admire the cut of it, and am shocked at how sophisticated it makes me look.

I blink, and the reflection in the mirror changes. Nico. Again. Like before, the image isn't the crisp vision you'd expect to find in a mirror, but rather a moving sketch, redrawn frame by frame, like the drawings in the Ledger.

I reach out to touch the glass, and mirror-Nico does the same.

"Can you hear me?" I ask, and the reflection mimes my words perfectly.

Then . . .

"Don't go."

I take a step back. The reflection spoke, in Nico's voice. This time I wasn't saying anything at all.

"If you leave, bad things will happen," he says. "Honor your promise to Rahki. Don't go looking for trouble."

And when I blink again, he's gone.

I march through the Hotel halls with Sev's have-sack over my shoulder, intent on my new goal. I don't know what that was back there in Sev's room, or how Nico keeps managing to appear to me in mirrors, but one thing is clear: he doesn't want me coming to find him.

That's all I need to know. If Nico doesn't want to be found, then I absolutely must find him. But first I have to find Cass. If I'm right, finding her will lead me to Nico.

I rub the face of her Hotel coin under my thumb. She left it behind, and I retrieved it from her room right after the Ledger shared Cass's journey with me. This coin is how I'll find her. There's always that subtle, unstoppable pull between the coin and its owner, and I think I know just how to access it.

"Here, kitty-kitty," I say, adjusting the have-sack and waving Queenie to me in the hall outside the Nightvine. "That's right. . . . Come on."

The little calico prances coyly. She can pretend all she likes, but I know she's been waiting for me to come back, like always.

I strike my hand—wrapped in the Maid Service glove I swiped from Dad's room—down one of my pins and use its dust to attach Cass's coin to Queenie's back. The cat stops rubbing against my knee to lick at the coin, but she must recognize the feeling because she goes back to ignoring it right away.

If I'm right, the coin should draw a cat to the coin's owner as easily as it would a person—better, since animals are more sensitive to the binding than humans. I won't be able to find my way around that maze of vine roads nearly as well as the cats of the Nightvine can, but with the cat's help and the Nightvine's affinity for lost things, I'm really hoping the combination will do the trick.

Of course, the fact that Queenie's still rubbing against my legs nonstop doesn't bode well.

"Go on," I tell her. "Good kitty. Shoo."

Queenie's purring intensifies.

"Cameron? What are you doing?"

I whirl to find Sana creeping down the hall toward me in her Motor Pool coveralls, a suspicious look on her face.

"Oh . . . hi, Sana. Uhh . . . what are you up to?" Way to play it cool, Cam. She's totally going to know something's up.

"Just walking the halls," she says, fidgeting with a hammer in her over-the-shoulder tool-sari. "I like letting my feet wander— helps me figure out particularly tricky problems." She notices Queenie at my feet. "Is that one of the cats that everyone's been looking for?"

I gulp down the panic inflating in my chest. "Uh . . . yeah. Look, I found it!"

Queenie rubs my calf as though I'm her best friend in the world.

Sana places her hands on her hips. "Really? Because it looks as though you bound a coin to that cat in hopes it would lead you somewhere. And if I were to make an educated guess, I'd bet that's Cass's coin."

I'm no Nico when it comes to deception.

"I've got to find her. To find all the Hoppers, and stop them before they strike again—"

She holds up a hand to stop me. "You had me at 'finding Cass.'" Sana bends down and ruffles the scruff on Queenie's neck above the bound coin. "So, why aren't we leaving already?"

"You want to come with me?"

"Duh." Sana examines the coin between Queenie's shoulder blades. "Did you infuse it? I don't sense an infusion. . . ."

I didn't even think of that. Of course. We had to do the same thing when we were searching for Dad.

"You can't come with me, Sana," I tell her. The last thing I want is someone else getting hurt on my watch.

She claps the cat hair from her fingers. "If you want the coin to guide you to Cass, you have to strengthen the binding between you two. The coin connects your will to the cat. It's like the icons, only using something alive instead of a statue. Influence, not control. In order to *influence* the cat, you'll need to add your own binding, so that the magic can read you too." She smirks. "Face it. You need me."

"But—"

Sana searches her tools for a pen. "Here. Lick this and write your name—"

"On the coin. I know."

I do as she says, though my insides buck against the idea of her coming with me. This mission could get me kicked out of the Hotel for good. Will they kick her out as well? And what about the Nightvine? What will Sana think of it? What will *it* think of *her*?

Sana eyes me with suspicion. "What's wrong with you? You look like I spat in your chutney."

"It's nothing," I say as I finish scribbling my name. The crackle of the binding echoes in the back of my mind. "You sure this'll work?"

"I would have tried it myself, but I didn't have her coin. Plus I'm not family-bound. You, on the other hand . . ." Sana trails off as Queenie darts down the hallway and under the veil to the Nightvine. Her jaw drops. "What in the world was that?"

Maybe this'll be fun after all.

"I've got something to show you." I grab the tuft of blossoms in the corner and lift the rippling bricks as easily as I lifted the shower curtain this morning. "This way, before she gets too far."

23

Broken Walls

We step out under the matcha-colored sky of the Nightvine.

Sana stumbles through the veil, gaping in awe. "*Arey*," she says in disbelief, and spins to take it in, arms outstretched like she's dancing in a field of flowers. "What is this place?"

"I call it the Nightvine," I say, and spot the lithe calico scurrying down one of the offshoot paths. "That way."

Sana trails behind me, and I glance back to see her opening and closing her mouth like the koi fish in the Shadedial Fountain. We don't have time to stop and smell the Nightvine blossoms, though—the binding will fall off Queenie eventually, and we have to be there when it does, or risk losing the coin.

"Cam!" Sana calls as I angle down another split in the path. "Do you know the way back? What if we get lost?"

I adjust the have-sack on my shoulder and point to the arrows I've drawn in the dirt over the past few weeks. "It's marked."

She grabs my wrist, dragging me to a stop. "Hold up. Help me understand this."

"We can't. Queenie—"

"The cat will wait, silly boy. That's the whole point of the infusion. She won't go far if you don't want her to."

I glance down the path, and sure enough, Queenie has stopped and is licking her paws.

Sana stoops and runs her fingers through the soil. "What is this place?"

I fill her in on what I know, which admittedly isn't as much as I'd like.

"Fascinating." She wets her finger to feel the direction of the wind. "So, the Nightvine's a House, then. Like the Hotel?"

"I—I think so." I hadn't considered that. "A House of lost things. Though I think . . . I think the House itself is lost too, maybe?"

"If it's lost, how did you find it?"

I point to a cluster of Nightvine blossoms at the foot of a nearby arch. "Those."

She squints at me. "I don't see anything, Cameron."

"Of course you do. These flowers are huge." I push past her and grip the tuft of bright, lime-colored blossoms, and peel up the veil to reveal sunlight beyond.

Sana's eyes widen again. Then she presses a finger to her lips, deep in thought. "You must have bonded with this place's magic."

I drop the veil, and the sunlight fades. "What do you mean?"

"I don't see any blossoms, Cam. That means the Nightvine is revealing more of itself to you than to me. The magics that form great Houses choose who they share themselves with, so the Night-vine must have chosen you."

Like it chose the admiral.

"We must show this place to Agapios," Sana says. "There should never be another House connected directly to the Hotel. It's not safe. When powerful magics intertwine, bad things can happen."

"We'll deal with that later. Right now we need to follow that cat."

Sana bobs her head in what I think is agreement. Though, now that she mentions it, I don't like this idea that the Nightvine might be a threat. Why didn't I think of that?

We track Queenie down the vine's twists and turns until at last she squeezes under a veil and into whatever lies beyond.

"What's through there?" Sana asks as we draw up to the arch.

"Only one way to find out."

I lick a pin from my pin-sleeves and scribble my name on my coin before slipping it into the new suit, hoping its magic delivers on Sev's promise. A shimmer of light ripples through the fabric as the binding renews.

Sana touches the sleeve of my jacket. "Nice. Sev gave you his gift, then?"

"Kinda? I had to pick it up from his room on my own."

"He didn't show you what it can do?"

"Umm," I say, grasping for an answer. "I know it stays clean?" Truth is, I have no idea, but like he says . . . what kind of friend promises bread but gives a stone? Or something like that.

Sana shakes her head. "I'm sure you will figure it out."

We exit the Nightvine into a street lined with gray cinder block buildings. The dingy sky is tinged with dust, and a weirdly familiar aroma stings my nose, almost like . . . french fries? Sana coughs on the thick air.

"Time for Oma's game," I reply. Though it isn't just a game, is it? Oma's where-in-the-world exercise has trained us to orient ourselves whenever we pass through unknown doors—a necessary skill when a door could take you anywhere.

Sana checks her watch. "Time zone combined with the position of the sun puts us somewhere around forty degrees longitude. Anywhere from Russia to South Africa."

"Not Russia." I kick at the dirt. "Somewhere in the Middle East?"

She motions to a series of swooping ruby-red letters spray-painted on a nearby building. "That's Arabic, so maybe you're right."

Rocks shuffle beneath our feet as we venture away from the arch. Hollow concrete buildings line the road, broken and crumbling. Landslides of whitewashed walls pour into the street, bristling with spikes of rebar. Many of the structures are missing their highest floors, as if some giant monster pounded and munched on the buildings as it went.

Working at a place as shiny as the Hotel, it's easy to forget that some places are a little rougher around the edges. It was the same when all I knew was my small Texas town—I'd forget that my experience wasn't necessarily true for everyone. Agapios says every House contains terrors and treasures, but in some places the terrors are hidden, and in others they're out in the open for everyone to see. Like war. War isn't just something found in video games and movies. Real war is a strange, thick cloud that smothers those who breathe it in.

This place smells like war.

Queenie rubs against a wall nearby, and Cass's coin drops to the dirt. The cat gives it a quick sniff, then struts around the corner.

I retrieve it. "This place doesn't look like anywhere Cass would be. Should we try again?"

"No." Sana holds up a finger to test the wind again. "Can you feel that? There's a door nearby."

She leads the way up the broken remains of a building to a flat roof. With the suit reshaping itself with every step, I find myself climbing the rubble faster than I usually would. It's like wearing comfy pajamas. Really fancy pajamas. I wonder what else it can do.

Sana shushes me as we peer through an open crack in the roof into the space below. Inside, a group of women dressed in shades of gray stand around a shorter girl with her back to us. I can't quite get a good look at the girl, though—there are crates blocking my view.

"What do you think they're doing?" I whisper.

"Could be anything," Sana says, "but look at those boxes. I think that's food."

The roof beneath us groans. "Umm, what was that?" I ask.

Sana's eyes grow wide, and she starts to back away.

I glance down to see a spiderweb of cracks spreading out from my palm. Uh-oh.

My equilibrium shifts as the roof begins to crumble and give way. I reach for anything I can find to stop myself from falling, but there's nothing to grab. My world flips as I tumble into the hole.

As I fall—certain I'm about to meet my painful and untimely demise—the bits of mortar and plaster and stone falling around me brighten. The rubble in the air takes on an amber glow, and a strange, tingling sensation runs up my arms, as if something's . . . growing out of them. I feel a sense of weightlessness, and for the briefest moment I wonder if the suit is somehow slowing my fall. But then . . .

Oof. My back smacks into the ground, hard. The force of it knocks the wind out of me. I cough, gazing blearily up through the billowing cloud of dust and into the hole where Sana still stands, tugging on her braid with a worried expression. She's almost two stories above me. That fall should have hurt a lot worse.

I move slowly, testing my legs and arms, noticing the change in my jacket. The sleeves are fringed with strips of fabric, each about three inches wide, dripping down along my sides. I barely have time to notice before the strips roll up into my sleeves and disappear.

Whoa.

"Cam?"

The group of women parts to reveal the girl at their center, dusting off her vest and picking bits of rock out of her braids.

Bee's expression cycles through at least twenty different emotions—confusion, wonder, irritation—before finally settling into a wry grin. "Looks like you found me, mate."

And she bolts.

24

Chasing Bees

I dart after Bee, the seams of my slacks loosening to the point where I can barely feel them swishing around my knees. Sana's footsteps pound across the roof overhead.

The ladies move aside to let me through, allowing me a glimpse of the boxes along the edge of the room. Now that I'm closer, I recognize those symbols. Sana was right; it's food, and medicine. Was Bee stealing from these people too?

I can figure that out later. Right now I can't lose her. Cass's coin led me to Bee, so Bee must be my path to Cass.

I burst out into the street, gripping the strap of Sev's have-sack tightly at my side.

"That way!" Sana calls, dropping the last few feet from a ladder and pointing behind me.

I take off running, arms and legs pumping as hard as they can to catch up. Too bad the suit doesn't make me stronger or faster, but at least it doesn't get in the way. Sana won't be so fortunate—her draped tool belt and coveralls will slow her down significantly. Artificers aren't trained for active missions like this. These types of missions are for the Maid Service, like Rahki.

Rahki, who made me promise not to do exactly what I'm doing.

Bee rounds a crumbling corner, and my right pant leg stiffens around my knee, bracing it to help me make the same turn behind her. The change of direction feels almost effortless. But she's still fast—faster than I am, for sure.

She ducks under the fallen supports of another building and disappears into the rubble.

"Be careful," Sana shouts from farther back. As if I need to be reminded.

I slip into the ruined structure, and pick my way through destroyed cinder blocks and bent rebar. The abandoned building is oddly silent, as if it's holding its breath. Bee is nowhere to be seen. She can't have gotten far, though.

Then I feel it. The slight, almost imperceptible crackle of a door binding. There's something else too . . . something very, very close, and very warm.

The fabric of my coattails lengthens and curls around in front of me. I watch in awe as one of the coattails reaches into my pocket and retrieves my Mom's pearl topscrew. The cloth dangles the key in front of me as if encouraging me to take it.

Huh. That's . . . weird. The key looks different—shinier—and when I hold it, heat radiates off its pearlescent material. My gaze is instantly drawn to the one standing corner of wall. I hurry around the rubble, and there it is. A door.

The shimmer of the key fades as it cools in my hand. Dad said Mom's key could conceal, but he also said there was more than one side to its magic. The key can *reveal*, too. The warmth I felt when I found the Nightvine . . . The key has been doing this all along.

I reach to open the door that Bee went through, but then pause. This could be a trap. I should wait for Sana. But if I do, I might end up losing my chance to find Cass.

I turn the knob and step through.

As soon as I cross the threshold, my sense of gravity shifts, and I quickly realize that this side of the door isn't upright. It's a hole, and I'm tumbling through it.

The fabric along my sleeves stretches as I fall, but before it can finish whatever it's doing, I splash into a pool of cold liquid.

I look up and catch sight of a shadow on a rope ladder, scampering up into the circle of light above me. The place I've fallen into is a shallow stone well in the ground, and Bee is already climbing out.

The water slides off my jacket like rain from a raincoat as I grip the rope rungs and climb after her. "I just want to talk," I yell. Well, talk and strangle her for what she did at the garden party, but she probably won't stop if I'm threatening her.

Bee clambers out of sight over the edge. It's no wonder she, Nico, and Cass are all buddy-buddy. All three of them know how to be both irritating and winsome at the same time.

Bright sunlight attacks my eyes as I pull myself out of the well. A bed of lush, tall grass and satiny, bulb-shaped flowers—tulips— spread away from me in rows of white, red, yellow, and pink.

I shake the water loose from the have-sack and check the time on my watch. Position of the sun, the breezy cool temperature . . . if I were to guess, I'd put us in the Netherlands. I glance back at the door built into the underside of the well's roof. A return trip will be difficult—I'd have to climb upside down to go back through. Who on earth would build a door there? The answer's obvious, of course—someone who doesn't want it to be found.

In the distance, Bee sprints across the field toward a pond sur- rounded by cattails and reeds. I race after her, kicking up tulips, as she disappears under an arbor on the edge of the pond. Yep, this is definitely a trap. I can't afford *not* to follow her, and she knows it.

As that realization hits, I sense another change in the Beshaped Suit. The fabric thickens, hardens, almost like it's . . . armor?

"Calm down," I tell it. "I don't think she wants to hurt me." But the fabric remains leather-tough as if it knows something I don't.

I hurry through the reeds to a windmill at the edge of the small pond, and burst through the door, emerging into deep darkness. Again I fall, only, the drop is shorter this time. I land in a crouch on something soft and squeaky. A bed?

A window nearby shows a clear night sky. I glance up, noticing the door built into the ceiling. This whole chase seems designed as a one-way trip—a series of portals meant to push us forward, but never back.

Bee's footsteps thud down the hall away from me.

I quickly follow her to the first floor of this cabin, and end up in the kitchen. It's quiet. Outside, an owl gives a long, tremulous trill.

Now where'd she go?

I trace my fingers along the wall as I search the room, but I find no doors, no veils, nothing. If there's a crackle of binding in here, I can't hear it over the noisy, archaic-looking refrigerator in the corner. Maybe she went outside?

Think, Cam. What would Nico do? He'd hide his exit in plain sight, so that no one would ever think to look there. The refrigerator—that's in plain sight, and it's exactly the kind of thing Nico would use.

I place a hand on the fridge door, and the key in my pocket warms. *Sneaky, sneaky.* I pull the latch and smile, inhaling the woodsy scent of rain and trees.

The fridge takes me to a high platform built around a tree over-looking an endless forest. All of the limbs above me have been sawn off, leaving a giant, sharp spike of wood to rise above the rest of the canopy below. It's still nighttime here, with a clear, star-strewn sky and warm air that's tacky with humidity. Branches far below wave and rustle in the bright moonlight. A rain forest, somewhere in Central or South America maybe?

To my right, a bamboo bridge dips toward a similar platform built around another limbless tree, and to the left, a cable drops into the moonlit forest below. A wheel mechanism with a triangular handle and a rope loop hangs over the platform.

It's a zip line. Nice.

Bee wouldn't have taken the bridge, because bridges go both ways. She must have taken the zip line. I peek over the platform's edge at the rolling, dark thundercloud of trees below, and my heart leaps into my throat so fast that I almost gag. If I were to fall from this height . . .

The ribbonlike material unfurls from my suit sleeves, only, this time it has time to finish the transformation. The strips bind together into a single sheet that hangs from each arm and joins together with my coattails behind me. Wings. My suit has wings. I'm going to owe Sev big-time for this when I get back.

But right now feels like the wrong time to be learning to fly, so instead I loop the zip line rope around my waist and buckle it tight, then check the strap on the have-sack to make sure I won't lose it.

I grip the handle—no fluff, no feathers—and push off.

Warm, humid wind whips against my body as I whizz down the cable. Beside me, a rainbow-colored bird keeps pace, wings reflecting moonlight.

I drop into the treetop canopy. Branches flick and scrape my cheeks. My coattails reach around to protect me, knocking away the rogue branches as I cling to the zip line handle, gritting my teeth the whole way. I can barely make out where the cable leads now. The roots at the base of a tree have grown together to form an arch—a shadowy hole, ready to gobble me up.

I pull up my knees, close my eyes, and brace for disaster.

There's a splash as if through water, and my breath catches in my throat from the biting chill.

I open my eyes to see snow-covered peaks. An incredible mountain range extends in all directions as I continue to whirr down the zip line, cheeks burning in the cold air. Sun, temp, terrain . . . We're somewhere in the Himalayas, and this cable is stretched between a rocky outcropping and another mountain face.

My collar grows a fur lining to protect my neck against the frigid air, and I can feel the same lining spread down my sleeves and legs, too.

Up ahead, I spot her. At least I think it's Bee—a tiny dot of a person hanging from a pulley like mine, about to enter another portal built into the cliff side. I lift my knees to my chest and charge through the air behind her. The suit's fur collar continues to sprout—black and brown fur whipping around my chin and cheeks—while the rest of the suit compresses against my skin to make me more aerodynamic.

I pass through the hole in the mountain after her, and the world goes black.

The rigging yanks hard as the zip line stops, suddenly. My lungs ache from the cold mountain air mixing with the heavy warmth that surrounds me now as I hang in the stillness.

The lining of my suit retracts, leaving my skin tingling with adrenaline. It's so dark here. No sky, no outside elements, just . . . dark.

A burst of cool wind hits my face. Is that . . . air-conditioning?

I double-check to make sure the suit's wings are still unfurled, then release the clip on the harness, ready to extend my arms and glide if I have to. It's unnecessary, though—as soon as I release, my knees hit plush carpet below. My heart pulses like the final minutes of a fireworks show, making my stomach churn.

When I'm finally sure that I'm not going to puke, I stand on wobbly legs, rubbing the numbness out of my knees and scanning the darkness for any sign of the girl I chased in here.

A bright spotlight flips on, blinding me.

I squint against the ache in my eyeballs. "Hello?"

Boom, boom, boom.

A large shape steps into the light, casting a shadow over me. My vision blurs as I struggle to make out the silhouette—a massive, hulking figure with a hunched back and tree-trunk arms. The suit's fabric hardens again as I realize what it is—a gorilla, twice my height and probably ten times my weight. I doubt there's anything that even Sev's suit could do to protect me against *that*.

I start to back away, but as my eyes adjust, I notice a much smaller something cradled in its arms. No . . . not something.

Some*one*.

My sister gives me her smuggest grin. "About time you got here. We've been waiting forever."

25

A Walk Down Museum Lane

My sister, Cassia Marie Kuhn, Most Likely to Take Up Gorilla Riding as a Hobby.

"Umm . . . ," I say, struggling to comprehend the ridiculousness of the sight before me. "You've got . . . It's a . . ."

"My brother, so eloquent." She gives me a wink as the gorilla lowers her to be eye level with me. "I'm calling her Gogo," Cass says. "You know, like my old gogo. Gogo the Goracious Gorilla."

When we were little, Cass called her wheelchair her "gogo" because it allowed her to "go all the places." This gorilla . . . it's the gorilla statue Sana said went missing. It's an icon.

"Goracious?" I ask. "Is that even a word?"

"It is if I say so."

Gogo leans over to sniff at my hair, then pats my head with her huge sausage-fingers, rattling my brain with each pat.

"It's an awfully cute name for such a vicious-looking thing," I say, wincing, "but . . . it kind of suits you, Cass."

Cass beams. "I've still got my chair for places where gorillas aren't quite up to dress code, but here in the Museum I like to ride in style."

In the Museum. I made it. My brow furrows. After everything that's happened, we're talking about gorilla statues like nothing's wrong? "Why did you leave like that?" I say. "You abandoned the Hotel. Oma. Us."

She leans back into Gogo's biceps and crosses her arms. "Well, *someone* had to go looking for Nico."

"What's that supposed to mean?"

"All in good time, boy-o," Bee says, stepping out from behind the spotlight to join her. "We've got things to discuss."

A twinge of anxiety floods through me when we enter the foyer of Nico's Museum, with its checkerboard tile and twisting staircases.

When Stripe owned this place, it was kept in pristine condition. But this version of the Museum is anything *but* clean. Only a few months have passed since we evicted Mr. Stripe, and yet the Museum looks as if it's been decaying for thirty or forty years. Bits of lumber and sacks of garbage lay strewn about the floor, with soda cans and empty chip bags scattered in between. Even the angel icon that watches over the foyer is draped with cheap, twinkly holiday lights. Deep cracks run along the walls, through the peeling wallpaper, and twisting up the stairs.

And instead of Stripe's docents and suits standing guard, there are kids—a lot of them—all dressed in the same vest and trousers that Bee wears. They pause as we enter.

Cass spreads her arms in a grand gesture as Gogo turns her to face the crowd. "Cam, meet the Hoppers."

Some of the kids take off their flat caps in greeting. Others scowl as if I'm wearing a shirt that insults their mothers. Oh, well. I didn't come here expecting a warm welcome. I came for Cass, and if I can swing it . . . Nico.

"Shoo," Bee says, and the Hoppers scatter.

"So, where is he?" I say.

Cass twists her lips. "That's . . . complicated."

Can't anything be simple? "What do you mean? We don't have time for complicated. I need to talk some sense into him, and then I need to get you back to the Hotel."

Bee steps up onto a platform suspended by a series of pulleys. "Best if we show you."

The lift takes us to an upstairs hall lined with the Curator's "exhibits"—keepsakes from his many conquests. A plaque next to an old Spanish-looking outfit reads DE VACA—DID WHAT HE WAS TOLD—TOO BAD WE LOST THE CITY, AND THE MAN. A red flag with a white circle and a strange, blocky design is inscribed with ALMOST HAD IT. A case full of Civil War relics declares, SHOULD HAVE HAD MORE FRIENDS IN THE NORTH.

I saw some of this stuff before when Stripe was the Curator, but it's been rearranged. Whole sections of carpet have been ripped up from the corners. Silver-and-red wallpaper hangs in torn sheets, with pictures spray-painted on the walls behind it in every color imaginable.

This isn't incidental rubble. This was vandalism.

"Y'all did a number on this place," I say.

Bee snickers. "Nico encouraged us to take our anger out up here. Said the House deserved it, and wanted us to 'put it in its place.'"

Beating a House into submission . . . is that really a good way to make magics obey you?

But there are more important issues to discuss.

I stop and turn to face Cass. "How long have you been working with them?"

She waggles her brow at me.

I clench my teeth, annoyed that she could be so flippant. "You betrayed us. Betrayed the Hotel."

Cass rolls her eyes. "Oh good grief, you're so dramatic. I've been searching for Nico ever since the cats came. He sent the four of clubs to me, and I knew he needed something. It was a message—same card he used in that magic trick the day I first met him."

The four of clubs. I knew that card was familiar. "But you said I shouldn't go looking for him."

She levels an *I can't believe you're that dumb* glare at me. "I said *you* couldn't go looking for him. Rahki was right about that—everyone would have known, and you would've gotten kicked out. That's why *I* had to do it for you."

Cass searched for him so I wouldn't have to. She was trying to help me. "You could have at least told me."

"If I had, you would have taken over and ruined our plan, just like you do everything else."

"I don't 'take over.'"

"You kinda do. You've been all Mr. Important ever since Agapios slapped that cross-keys lapel pin on you. Besides, if you'd known what I was up to, you wouldn't have taken care of the few pieces of the puzzle I needed you to, like the sliver."

"The sliver?"

"Yeah," Bee says. "You never ended up using the one I gave you, so she did."

"Wait, *you* took it?" I say, more than a little flustered. "You went through my stuff?"

Cass gives me a sly smile. "I can always tell when you're hiding something. I found the note and the sliver she gave you in China in your drawer and decided, why not? It brought me here, and Bee filled me in. Then all I had to do was change the date on your gala invites, get the others to plan our birthday party, and ta-da!"

Bee laughs. "See, I told you. Natural Hopper."

"Why, thank you." Gogo does an awkward curtsy for Cass before continuing down the hall.

The weight of everything that's happened presses in on me as we walk. All the ambassadors' stolen items, Sev in the Apothecarium, the topiary attack . . . Cass and Bee act like this is all a big game.

"Cass," I say, "that stuff that happened in the garden—"

"It was fun, yeah?" Bee says, and smiles at me over her shoulder. "Seeing all those rich folks' faces when they lost their stuff? That was prime."

I frown. "I wouldn't call what y'all did 'fun.' People were hurt."

Bee huffs. "Oh, come on. Getting slivered is a little painful, but you probably had those folks found and home safe in under an hour."

"No one's talking to you," I snap. "You stole things that weren't yours to take, and slivering those ambassadors was about the *least* offensive thing y'all did. That thing with the topiaries . . . that's unforgivable."

"Those animal bushes?" Bee gives me a curious look. "We didn't touch your topiaries."

"Tell that to Sev."

"Cam." Gogo holds Cass out to grab my arm. "What do you mean? We didn't do anything to Sev."

"Maybe not while you were there, but after you left, your *friend* here loosed a bunch of angry plants on him. The attack put me in the Apothecarium too. Sev's still there healing, as far as I know."

They exchange a worried look. "Boy-o," Bee says, "our operation ended when I took the key from the admiral lady. We don't know anything about angry bushes."

I cast her a sidelong glance. "Sure, you don't."

"She's telling the truth," Cass says. "The shaping I used on those pins was pretty weak. Once we left the area, it would have failed—there's no way anyone here could have influenced it, and especially not in a way that would hurt anyone."

Gogo huffs in agreement. Cass is many things, but she's not a liar. In fact, she's just about the worst liar I've ever met.

"Well, if it wasn't you, maybe it was Nico?"

"Doubtful," Bee says as we reach the door at the end of the hall.

"You don't know what he's capable of," I say.

She rests her hand on the doorknob. "How about I show you what he's *not* capable of?" she says, and opens the door. "Welcome to Stripe's gallery, or what's left of it."

The room we enter is grand and stately, with vaulted ceilings and a polished floor. Every inch of wall space is covered with murals, shelves full of leather-bound journals, and every war-related item I can imagine.

But it's the odd, viny mass on the far wall that grabs my attention. The wall is completely engulfed in dense foliage that's grown together into a solid, thick shell.

I step forward and run my fingers down the shell, feeling the tough but pliable bark underneath. Dried tufts of what must have been blossoms—greenish ones, like those from the Nightvine—hang in withered clusters at the edges, as fragile as tissue paper. There are other flowers too. Dark, like the ones that came from the arches in the garden. It's as if they've all been cut off from their source and have died, like the topiaries did when we plugged the pergolas.

"What is it?" I ask.

"We're not sure," Bee says. "A couple of months ago Nico and I were supposed to meet here to plan our next few aid operations, but when I got here, he was gone and that thing was here instead. That, and the note I gave you in China."

The one where he said that the Hotel's days were numbered.

Wait a minute. . . . "Aid operations?"

She cocks her head condescendingly. "The Hoppers ain't just thieves, you know. We're like . . . Merry Men. Robin Hood or whatever. We take from people who hoard their fancy jewels and flash their cash, and give it to others who need a little boost to get started."

"Like those ladies I saw you with back there?" I ask.

"We bought those supplies with all the stuff we took from the Hotel job." She holds her head high. "Our mission is every bit as honorable as that fancy Hotel of yours."

"Not really." But at least it's not the attitude of a true enemy. "So . . . you aren't trying to bring the Hotel down?"

Her expression sours. "Of course not. We've got nowhere to put kids when we run across them, which is why I led your maids to those babies in China. You do things your way; we do things ours."

I focus back on the strange wall, gripping Mom's key in hopes that it'll reveal something. But the key is cold. No way through, at least from this side, and I left the Ledger back at the Hotel, so I can't ask it for help.

Then the realization hits me. "You stole the admiral's key in order to find him."

"That was my idea," Cass says, and Gogo grunts in affirmation. "We'd been searching for Nico for a while, and when I heard you ask Djhut about the Key of Lost Things, I thought it might help."

"And?"

She lowers her head in defeat. "We never had the chance to use it."

"Why not?"

Bee hoists her hands to her hips. "My question exactly."

Cass looks everywhere but at me, twisting her fist up in her hair like she does when she's caught doing something she's not supposed to.

"Cass . . . ?"

"I lost it, okay! I don't know what happened. One minute it was in my pocket, and the next . . ." Gogo makes a *poof* sound.

"Maybe it just didn't like you stealing it."

"Isn't that lovely," Bee snarks. "Stolen goods that don't like to be stolen. Puts us right back where we started."

"Not exactly," I say, thinking. Admiral Dare didn't appear concerned about the key—in fact, she seemed to expect it to be lost, and to come back to her on its own. Wild magics do what they want. For all I know, it has returned to her already.

Of course, that doesn't help us find Nico.

I pick one of the withered blossoms loose from the vine wall. There was a binding here at one point. We might not have the admiral's key, but maybe we don't need it. I found Cass after all, and now that I understand the way the icons' magic works, and the Nightvine's connection to lost things . . .

Something is still bugging me, though. Nico appeared to me in the Hotel. He showed up before the garden attack, and he was there in the Arkade, and in the Shaft with the malfunctioning elevator. If Bee's right, all those things happened after he disappeared. And the Nico in the mirror didn't seem like someone who was looking for help.

I won't know for sure until I find him. Yes, I gave my word to Rahki that I wouldn't go searching for him, and yes, he's probably Stripe's agent that the admiral's been looking for, but he's missing, and the connection we share means I'm the only one who can track him down and uncover the truth. I'll just have to face the consequences later.

Whatever it takes, forever in perpetuity.

"You going to help us, hotel-boy?"

"Yeah," I reply. "Let's find him."

26

The Land of Lost Things

Y ou'll have to leave the gorilla," I tell Cass. Again. For about
the twentieth time.

We're back in the Museum foyer, and one of the Hoppers is rolling Cass's wheelchair back from wherever it was stored.
We'll have to head back through the Hotel if we want to reach the
Nightvine and see if it can lead us to Nico. Of course that means
no gorillas.

"But why?" she whines, running a hand through the hair on
Gogo's forearm.

"The Maid Commander would have a fit if you rode that stolen
monstrosity through the Hotel," I tell her. "We're supposed to be
sneaking you in, not barging in with Miss Bam-Bam Gorilla Fists—"

She huffs and pets Gogo on the head. "I'm sorry, girl, but Mr.
Worrypants might actually be right"—she shoots me an irritated
look—"for once."

Gogo rolls a pouty lip and lowers Cass into her chair. Cass slips
her coin out of the slot on the gorilla's arm, transforming the beast
into stone with a sparkling wave of golden light.

"You can be such a joy-suck sometimes," Cass says as she switches her coin into the arm on her chair. There's an almost green-ish tint to the light as it flows from her wheels to her handlebars.

"That's my job," I reply, puffing out my chest.

"Only, it's not," she continues, and her face is serious. "You're not responsible for always making sure everything is perfect and safe."

"But someone—"

"I mean it, Cam. It was one thing to worry when I had surgeries all the time." She raises her arms and spins in her binding-driven chair. "I can control my chair with my *mind*. We both work in the Hotel, equally. Alongside everyone else. We're all just as import-ant as you."

She's right. I am always trying to take responsibility for every-one, especially her. It's not even about *her*; I just hate feeling like I'm not in control. *I'm* the one who's afraid that everything's going to fall apart if I don't manage it all perfectly.

So how do I stop doing that?

One of the Museum doors leads us to the back of the 7-Eleven near Oma's house, where I met Nico all those months ago. The Dallas Door lies across the parking lot, still as shiny and out-of-place as when I first discovered it. Bee stays behind, of course. Sneaking an actual Hopper into the Hotel would probably result in permanent expulsion.

I pull out Mom's key. No sense in knocking—that would only draw attention to Cass and me coming back, and we need to slip through as unnoticed as possible.

"Does it seem extra quiet in here to you?" Cass asks as we enter the North American Lobby. The lobby is emptier than I've ever seen it. I half expect to see a tumbleweed roll by. "Where is everyone?"

"The MC was livid after the garden party fiasco," I tell her. "She put us on lockdown—no one in or out unless escorted by the Maid Service—and instituted a curfew. I'm sure it's nothing." Though, I'm not sure whether I'm saying that more to convince Cass or myself. "Let's move."

Something else is bothering me too. Cass broke her contract when she used the sliver, but now she's able to roll right in. And where are Rahki's additional security measures?

Cass stays a little ways ahead of me all the way back to the hall where I first lost Queenie, looking back every once in a while to make sure she's heading in the right direction. When she reaches the veil, she runs her fingers along the stones that separate the Hotel from the Nightvine. "This is it?"

I grip the cluster of blossoms and lift, revealing the path beyond.

Cass gapes. "Okay, you're definitely going to have to show me how to do that."

As I motion her through, I notice the shadow of vines stretching along the walls, curling through in long, crooked fingers. They look almost like the cracks in the hall leading to Stripe's gallery. Strange. . . . They're not headed away from the veil. They're heading toward it.

When Cass crosses the threshold, she lets out an audible gasp. "Cam, this is amazing."

"I know," I say, swallowing my worry and scanning the road ahead.

"How do you plan on finding him?" she asks.

I untie Nico's coin from my neck and unstring it from the necklace, tucking the string into the unbound pocket of the have-sack. "Now that I understand how to follow bonds with an icon better, I can use his coin and the suit together to guide me to him. The bond between us should draw the suit to him, the same way your coin drew Queenie to find you. And the admiral said this place's magic is connected to lost things. It's like . . . the lost and found of the world, so I think that'll help."

"You're using different magics together."

"Something like that." I infuse Nico's coin and pop it into the suit's breast pocket alongside mine. The suit crackles, and sure enough, I can feel a magnetic tug pulling me down the road. "It's that way."

Cass turns the back of her chair toward me. "Hop on then."

"Huh?"

"We're in a hurry, right?" She flicks a lever on her chair, and a small, foot-wide platform drops down from the rear. "Grab on and hold tight."

Cass's icon-bound chair zooms—hair-raisingly, eye-wateringly fast—down the twisting roads of the Nightvine, just barely managing to dodge the massive mounds of junk scattered sporadically throughout. I clutch the have-sack tightly under my arm to keep from losing it. Any minute now I expect to go flying because Cass's wheel hit an unfortunately placed pile of car keys.

The bits of the Nightvine I've explored zip by in a blur as I cling tight to the handles, feet planted on the platform. In mere minutes we leave the last of my arrows behind, and with them, all sense of familiarity. It gives me a new perspective on how wild and expansive the place is. This massive plant has been growing for centuries in this hazy, green twilight.

We round a bend in the vine, and her chair lifts up on two wheels.

I jerk in the opposite direction to counterbalance us back to the road. "Slow down!" I shout over the wind roaring in my ears.

"Why?" She weaves to avoid hitting a half-buried Volkswagen. "Did you get a new direction from the coin?"

"No, but if you're not careful, we're going to get blown off the edge!"

"We'll be fine!"

I focus on the sensations in the suit, anticipating the next few branching paths, letting Nico's coin guide us. The vine is thicker here, and the path is wider than before, clearer, and just as endless. Thank goodness Cass's chair doesn't require fuel, or we'd probably run out of gas soon.

"Turn," I direct, and Cass angles the chair down the next slope.

She motions to something up ahead. "What is *that*?"

A thick, spherical mass about ten feet in diameter hangs off the edge of the Nightvine. It's surface is rough and wrinkly, like a coconut, or an avocado.

Or like the wall in Stripe's gallery.

"I think it's a fruit," I guess. A couple of stray cats lie sleeping next to the stem sprouting from its top.

"Actually," Cass says, "I'm pretty sure it's a drupe."

"What's a drupe?"

"A kind of fruit with a skin and a fleshy part and a pit in the center. Like peaches, and coconuts. Think it's important?"

Admiral Dare said the Nightvine's fruit sustained her when she was lost here. These must be what she meant. I don't feel a tug toward this giant coconut thing—just the draw of the binding to continue down the vine.

"No," I say, "but I think we're getting closer."

The farther we ride, the more the vines around us change. Those here aren't as green as the ones closer to the Hotel. Dark brown tendrils curl through them. Even the sky has a sickly, grayish cast to it.

Then I notice the buds. Not the bright, lime-colored clusters that grow at the veils. No, these blossoms all bloom a deep indigo, like the flower in mirror-Nico's lapel, and at the garden party, and the one the MC wore on the trip to the EFS *Roanoke*. They're choking out the Nightvine, leaving the green blossoms withered, same as in the gallery.

The tug on my suit draws us to one of the larger drupes—a misshapen, barn-size monstrosity hanging from an overhead vine to rest on the road. There's no mistaking it; the pull is like a magnet ready to snap into place.

I hop off Cass's chair, legs wobbly and numb from our bouncy ride, and rest my palm on the fibrous hull of the drupe.

"Is he inside that thing?" Cass asks.

I walk around it, taking it in from every angle. "I'm not sure. If he is, I don't know how we'll get him out." The vines here are almost exclusively the dark brown ones. Thick clusters of deep blue flowers bloom across the ground, the tips of their petals black as if singed by fire.

The drupe's not a perfect ball—more oblong, like some misshapen eggplant-coconut hybrid that deformed as it grew against the road. A smattering of junk lies scattered beneath it. Some of the half-buried items catch my eye—a dusty oil painting of some old white guy on a horse, and . . . is that a medieval gauntlet?

"Oh, wow." I drop to my knees and pick through the junk, lifting each item to examine it. "A rusty sword, a cracked vase, and these journals . . . You know what this is?"

Cass nods gravely. "This stuff came from the gallery."

"This thing is connected to that wall where Nico disappeared. Which means there's a veil here. Or maybe . . ." I scan the dozens of other drupes hanging in the distance. "Maybe the drupes are all veils, growing on the vine. The veils are how the Nightvine finds lost things and claims them as its own."

"Okay," Cass says, "does that mean the Nightvine used this drupe to collect Nico, too?"

"Let's break into it and find out."

Of course, finding a way into the drupe turns out to be a lot harder than it sounds. I don the metal gauntlet we found in the dirt and try digging my fingers into the fruit's woody surface, but I can't get any leverage. I even try piercing the skin with the sword, but the blade breaks—actually snaps in two—when I put my weight into it.

"Calm down there, muscle man," Cass says, and laughs.

"Something's not right," I say, still piecing it all together. "Nico's been missing a couple of months, but he's been sending messages out somehow. How does that work?"

"The cats," she replies. "They can pass through those veil things, right?"

"But how did they get to him in the first place? They came to us through the blossom clusters, but these blue flowers aren't tied to the veils. I'd need Nightvine blooms to get inside, if there even is an inside. Unless . . ." I search for a handhold in the drupe's rough surface and try lifting myself up. The ridges seem strong enough to support my weight. "I need to climb up top. Stay here."

When I reach the top of the drupe, I find what I'm looking for—a large patch of yellow-green blossoms, bursting forth at the stem. And lying in the midst of the flowers is Queenie, stretching a full-force yawn.

"Hey, kitty-kitty," I say, rubbing the scruff between her shoulder blades. She flares her toes and rolls onto her back to nuzzle my hand. "How'd you get here?" Then I realize. "You've just been waiting for me to find him, haven't you?"

She gives me a questioning look.

"I don't know what happened to Sana," I tell her. "Though, knowing her, she's probably safely back at the Hotel by now, telling Agapios everything."

Queenie lays her head on the drupe, purring loudly. It's almost as if she understands me.

"Who are you talking to up there?" Cass calls up.

"No one." I grip the stem near the flowers, and the seam between the stem and the drupe peels free just like the veils, revealing pale green light inside. "I found a way in."

"Be careful!" she shouts back, and I know she means it. We may tease each other and fight, but deep down we both care about the other a lot. We always will.

I lift the veil and drop inside.

27

The Bonds of Friendship

I land in a crouch on the squishy, luminescent floor and look up to find myself face-to-face with none other than my blood-brother, Nico Flores.

At least, I think it's him. The boy before me looks so different in this hazy, lime-colored light. He's hunched, skinny—malnourished, even—with dark, sunken eyes a little too wild to belong to my friend.

"You're here," I say, wiping my hands and taking a step toward him. He's dressed like the rest of the Hoppers—tweed vest, white button-up, brown pants with suspenders—only, the clothes are filthy and hang off him like he's a kid playing dress-up. His lips are chapped and peeling, and his hair is longer, slicked and shiny and curling off his neck. "What happened to you?"

The wall behind him matches the ones in the Museum gallery, a gaudy display of Stripe's trophies. The look in Nico's eyes is similar to those trophies. Worn. Tarnished.

He shuffles back, stumbling as if it's all he can do to stay upright. "You should have come sooner," he says.

I adjust the have-sack on my shoulder and take in the rest of our surroundings. While the wall behind him matches the missing portion of Stripe's gallery, the rest of the wall curves around us like the interior of an oblong globe. It has a smooth, wet texture, the color of a kiwi. The flesh inside the fruit glows softly, illuminating the small space.

Black veins have wound from the Museum wall into the drupe's pale flesh where the two meet, leaving the seam between them rotten and oozing. A bookcase that was once filled with leather-bound journals has been emptied, and the journals are strewn across the bit of carpet that fades into the glowing husk.

"You should have come sooner," Nico says again, this time with more urgency. His voice is dry, like he hasn't spoken in weeks.

It's only then that I notice the thing clenched in his fist. A sliver. He grips the wooden spike like a dagger, flexing his fingers around the pommel. His hands are covered with tiny red pinpricks.

"A lot could've been different if you'd come when I called," he says. "If you'd listened. But I can't count on anyone but myself. I know that now."

This isn't the Nico I know. There's a cynical sneer in his voice that reminds me of Stripe. But still . . . he seems to remember *something* about me.

I take a step closer. "Nico, do you know who I am?"

"You're the one who abandoned me."

He brandishes the sliver and jabs it in my direction. It's a quick motion for someone who looks so weak, and catches me off guard, but I manage to jump back just in time.

"Wait. It's me," I plead. "It's Cam. I didn't abandon you."

"You're the one I'm bound to," he breathes, and swipes again. My waistcoat tugs my torso to the side, out of the path of his sliver. "I waited for you. I was supposed to be able to depend on you. You must not be a very good brother."

I back away, struggling to understand. If he's been here all this time, waiting for someone to find him, why send all the pranks?

The cats *weren't* a prank though; they were a cry for help. Cass figured that much out. Those pricks on his hands . . . He used our blood bond to send the cats to the Hotel—the four of clubs for Cass, the queen of hearts for me. But why make us guess? Why not just tell us where he was?

I'm missing something. Nico couldn't pass through the veils— that much is clear. But *I* can. I see the blossoms because the Night-vine bonded to me. He's been here, so why didn't it bond to him too? And what about all the other hotel fiascos? The chef's pans, the oozing fountain, the broken elevators . . . and that taunting reflection . . .

"Nico, we need to get you out of here," I say. "You need food, water. I don't know what's going on, but we'll figure this out. It's going to be okay."

"It's not okay!" he roars. "We're too late. We lost. *You* lost."

It's as if he's talking around what he really wants to say. As if . . .

As if there's a secret that's protecting itself.

And then I feel it, lurking on the edge of my awareness, lingering like an afterimage from a camera flash—the remnants of a bond.

Stripe. He's here, listening. Watching us.

I circle the room, pulling out Mom's key, willing it to help me see what I'm missing. The key warms, drawing my gaze to a nearby glass case, and the object inside it.

It's a stick—no, a *branch*—nearly four feet long, displayed like an ancient sword in an exhibit. Caustic oil dribbles from the wood. I know that oily substance; it's the same sickness that's been affecting the Vesima tree. Diseased vines coil around the pedestal, joining with the stick and blooming with wilted indigo flowers. I can sense its magic, like the magnetic tug that drew me to Nico, only in reverse. I want to get away from it as fast as I can.

"Stripe left something behind," Nico hisses, angling the sliver toward my chest.

"What is it?" I whisper.

"The Blight. It was the heart of Stripe's House. Not like other House hearts, though. A bit of magic that Stripe broke off from himself." He stares into its streams of tar. "I thought I could contain it. When I realized what it was doing, it was too late. I tried to get rid of it, but the magic backfired and I ended up here."

He was trying to fight back.

"I understand it better now, though." There's a storm in Nico's eyes as he raises the sliver toward me. "The Blight is the heart of *my* House now. I won't let you take it away from me."

He races for me, sliver raised.

My suit tightens around my limbs, pulling me out of the way.

"Stop," I shout. "I'm here to help!"

"You don't care about us," he snarls. "The Blight was right—you want to own the Museum *and* the Hotel. You want to control everything."

He strikes again, and this time my coattails reach around to block him, and knock his sliver off its mark.

I scurry around the glass case, putting his precious branch between us. I've never seen him angry like this. "I'm only here for you, Nico. I promise. I don't want your house. I'm here to save you."

"I don't need saving. Not anymore."

The suit bends and dodges and blocks, keeping me just out of his reach as he attacks again and again. His scowl grows deeper with each miss.

"Stripe's influencing you! You're not yourself."

Nico wheezes, struggling for breath. "Stripe . . . has . . . no hold . . . on me."

"It's this place," I say, taking an unnaturally long step out of the way. "The Blight is changing you. Shaping you."

"Making me stronger," he growls. "The Blight gives me what I need."

"And what is that you need? To hurt me?"

"To own it all," he screams, "before *he* takes it from us!"

With his next strike he stumbles, gulping air and clutching his side.

He motions to the pile of journals at the foot of the bookshelf. "See those?" he huffs. "They're his. A catalogue of his deeds. I've read every word. All the civilizations that Stripe has brought to their knees, all the powerful people he's humbled . . . he's magnificent, Cam. My father, the Conqueror of Nations."

Hearing him call Stripe his father forms a lump in my throat. "Nico—"

"He's going to possess it all. Soon he's going to take the world away from us because he thinks we don't deserve it. He'll beat everyone in the end." Nico pushes to his feet, eyes glistening with hunger. "Everyone except us. You and me, brother, forever in perpetuity. We beat him once—think what we could do together."

My eyes widen. Part of him *does* remember. The memories are in there. Only, they're hidden. *Concealed.*

That means I can still reach him.

"We can take Stripe's plans and make them our own," Nico continues. "We can have the Hotel *and* the Museum. All the great Houses. We could break the fundamental bonds, and become whatever we want to be. Stripe won't be able to own the world if we take it for ourselves first."

I shake my head. "The Nico I met last year knew better than that. That Nico beat Stripe because he found compassion to balance out his ambition. He trusted people—trusted me—and we saved each other."

"Don't you see?" Nico urges. "We could be powerful together."

I pull Nico's coin from my breast pocket, and the binding on my suit fades. If I'm right, and the sliver pricks on Nico's hands mean what I think they mean, there's still one thing I can do.

"Maybe you're right," I tell him. "Or maybe I should just take it all for myself instead."

Nico snarls and lunges, rage in his eyes.

And this time, I let him.

His sliver pierces my shoulder, and the world inside the drupe stills. But there's no scream, no magical weight crumpling me up like a sheet of paper. I was right. The sliver's magic doesn't work here.

But the coin's magic does.

I grab Nico's wrist, wrench the sliver out of his grip, and force his hand into a handshake, the coin pressed between our palms.

He tries to pull away, but I hold tight as Nico's memories flow back into him. The memories I made while carrying it are transferred too.

There's something else hiding on the edge of his mind. A scribbled shadow haunts him, fogging his thoughts, concealing pieces of him from himself. No, I won't let what Stripe left behind hurt the real Nico.

Still gripping his palm—the coin clasped between us—I pull out Mom's topscrew and instinctively drive it toward the back of Nico's hand. As key meets skin, a keyhole forms there on his hand. A magical flash of silvery foam oozes out, allowing the key to push through his hand, right through the center of the coin, and pass painlessly through my palm and out the other side.

A buzz of electric current races up my arm. Every hair stands on end as the key's magic binds us with the coin.

Nico's eyes lock on mine. There's fear in that look.

And then—the coin between us, the key connecting us—I turn the topscrew.

A shock of energy bursts from the coin. Our handshake breaks as I stumble and fall onto the drupe's wet floor. Nico smashes into the case with the blighted branch—shattering the glass—then slides to the carpet, gripping his head in pain.

The coin drops to the ground, Mom's key still piercing it.

Nico examines his hand as if amazed by what he sees. I glance at my own too. There's no evidence that I just rammed a key through us both and used the two magics—two *separate* magics—together. A coin that had locked away Nico's memories, and a key that can reveal what's hidden. The only question is, did it work?

After a long moment, Nico looks up, slick hair dangling in messy strings in front of his face.

"Hey, kiddo," he says. "Thanks for finally showing up."

28

The Ties That Bind

I can't believe Sev *made* this suit," Nico says, swallowing another bite of the sandwich I thankfully thought to pack in the havesack. He holds up the jacket, inspecting it. "I mean, I know he's always making stuff, but this . . . this is his coolest yet."

I pull Nico's brown vest on over my button-down. The vest reeks of two months' worth of BO—a smell that even Mom's key won't be able to conceal—but it's cold in here without my coat. "The suit was my birthday present," I say. "Though, I still don't know everything it does."

Trading clothes was my idea. Nico was so weak after I broke the Blight's hold on him that he could barely stand, much less make it out of here. If the way the suit worked for me is any indication, it should help him enough to get us home.

Nico inserts his infused coin into the pocket—now separate from Mom's key—and the fabric shimmers. The stitching doesn't have to adjust much—mainly just drawing up the hems, since he's a few inches shorter than me. I can tell the difference in his posture right away.

"Better?" I ask, buttoning his Hopper vest over my shirt.

"Better," he agrees, admiring the spotless sleeves. His face still looks worn and tired and not at all healthy, but at least I won't have to carry him. "Sev's really outdone himself."

"Don't get used to it. I'm only loaning it to you."

He watches me, head held high. "Hey, remember when I had to teach you how to wear a suit, and you never would stand up to me? Now you're literally standing me up." He motions to the suit and wipes a pretend tear. "My little brother's come so far."

"Shut up."

I'm glad to have him back, but as I watch him straighten his sleeves, the worry starts to creep in again. The fact that Stripe—or the Blight, rather—managed to influence him concerns me. Maybe we're never really in control like we think we are.

Nico retrieves his sliver and turns it over in his hand. "How did you know the sliver wouldn't work?"

I grab the have-sack off the floor. "Those marks on your hands—you'd been pricking yourself a ton before I got here. If you could have slivered your way out of this overgrown fruit, you would have."

"Smart." He scans the room. "So these blossom things will get us out of here?"

I point to one of the few clusters that isn't wilted on the gallery wall. The blue-blossomed Blight vines have choked the others out. "I bet those will take us back to the Museum. But we should get Cass first before we head back. She's waiting outside. We'll have to pile all this junk up and climb out to bring her in here, and then we'll take that wall back to the Museum."

"Sounds good," he wheezes, and then reaches to take the havesack from me. "Here, I can carry that for you."

"You shouldn't be carrying anything in your condition."

"It's the least I can do, since you're the one who has to prepare for war."

"War?"

He gives me a long look, then takes the sack from me. "Get Cass. Then we'll talk."

Once we've retrieved Cass and started on our way, Nico explains what I've already started to suspect: those "pranks" weren't him at all. The smells, the fountain sludge, the collapsing air ducts and mis-moving elevators . . . those have all been the work of the Blight.

Then he confirms my biggest fear. The Blight has infected the Vesima tree. Stripe left the infection behind when we kicked him out of the Museum, and it's been slowly creeping through our corridors, wrapping itself into the elevators, and snaking through our plumbing. It's the sickness we've been trying to cure, the agent Admiral Dare has been searching for, and it's been working hard to take our Hotel away from us.

It's smart too—smart enough to mimic Nico and make everyone believe he was the one causing the Hotel's problems while it spread to every corner of the Hotel. And now Nico says the

Blight's ready to enact the final part of its plan—welcoming Stripe into the Hotel so that he can claim it as his new home.

So here we are—Cass, Bee, Nico, and me—crouched next to the 7-Eleven dumpster across from the Dallas Door. I'll have to find Agapios, save our family, evacuate the remaining guests and ambassadors, and cleanse the Blight.

Just a touch.

"We'll follow as soon as you send word," Nico says, and hands me his coin. "Get in, figure out what's happening, and let us know what we should do." He gives my shoulder another pat. "Stay rooted, my friend."

I leave the relative safety of the dumpster and head across the parking lot, but before I can even ready my topscrew, the Dallas Door swings open and a hand grabs my collar.

"Get your scrawny concierge butt in here," Elizabeth says. "We've got a problem."

She drags me quickly through the lobby and into the front office, before shoving me under one of the desks. "Hide."

"What's going on?"

"Quiet," she shushes. "Maids are monitoring the knockers."

Feet march past the counter window. Well, that answers one question. The Blight has indeed seized control of the Hotel's main defenders. Wonderful.

"What if they come in here?" I whisper.

Elizabeth presses a finger to her lips as the feet pass by and continue on. "They haven't been paying the office much mind," she says once they're gone. "So far I've remained undetected."

"Well, at least that's something."

"Where did you get those clothes?" she asks, curling her nose. "You smell like a toilet."

Nico's clothes. "It's a long story."

Elizabeth fills me in. Strange icon activity, power outages, unbound halls. "The maids have been rounding up the guests and ambassadors, and are holding them aboard the *Accommodation*," she says. "Elevators have turned hostile too, takin' folks straight to the ship. Oh, and the cats are back."

"What about Agapios?"

"Haven't seen him. Reports don't mention him either."

That's not good. "We should call the Concierge Retreat."

"Don't you think I already tried that?" Elizabeth draws her lips into a thin line. "You always do that, thinking you are the only one who knows how to do everyone else's job. You should trust us by now."

I swallow. This is exactly what Cass was talking about.

"I'm sorry," I say. "I'm not thinking straight. Thank you. You've done a great job."

She gives a curt nod. "Anyway, I went to find the Old Man when things started gettin' weird. Found this instead." She pulls an envelope from her inner jacket pocket.

"It's addressed to me," I say, reading my name in Agapios's flowing script.

I open the letter and scan the page.

Mr. Cameron,

I must offer you my sincerest apology. I made an agreement with you that I would train you for this position and would not force you to do anything you did not wish, but an unfortunate turn of events prevents me from keeping my promise. I must now leave the Hotel in your hands, where it is safest, whether you are ready or not.

I make this decision with full knowledge that it breaks our contract, which clearly stated that you could leave your duties at any time. In accordance with the bond of Law, breaking such a contract puts me in great debt to you. I therefore offer up the deed to The Hotel Between as collateral—a loan, if you will—until I can repay that debt.

The Hotel Between belongs to you now, Cameron Kuhn, Interim Grand Concierge, until such time as my debt is repaid. This notice shall serve as the deed to the Hotel, and grants you the right to make whatever decisions you deem necessary for its protection and security.

Signed and sealed,
Agapios Panotierri, former Grand Concierge of The Hotel Between

P.S. Remember, Cameron. Knowledge and truth are among the sharpest blades in the world.

Elizabeth reads over my shoulder. "Does that mean what I think it means?"

"He's gone." I stare at the page in shock. "The Hotel is mine."

"Sounds more like a loan to me."

What am I supposed to do with it? Did he know that something bad was coming? Was leaving his way of getting out before things got bad? Did he just . . . abandon us when we needed him most?

No. The deed is the contract of ownership between a person and the magic of a great House. If the Blight gained command of the maids because of their trust in the Hotel, the same could have happened with Agapios. The Blight could have forced him to sign the deed over to Stripe instead, and I shudder to think what Stripe would do if he got his hands on this place. There are too many secrets here. Too much power.

The Old Man didn't abandon the Hotel—he left it in my care to keep it safe. He knew that my contract with Stripe prevents him from gaining control over me. But is the Hotel really safe? The Blight got influence over Nico, so couldn't it do the same with me?

"What do we do now?" Elizabeth asks.

I slide the deed into the interior pocket of Nico's vest, which is about as secure as I can make this priceless slip of paper in the moment. "I have to get to my room. There's something up there that might show me how to reverse this process before it's too late."

"Okay," Elizabeth says. "What about me?"

I scrunch my brow. "What about you?"

"Yah. What should I do?"

I'm not sure how to respond to that. "I thought . . . I mean, weren't you just telling me that I should trust you to do things on your own?"

Elizabeth sighs, long and hard. "Sure, trust me to do my job. You're Grand Concierge now, and that means you're the one leading us. That's how this works. I trust that your decisions won't get me killed or bound, and you trust that I'm smart enough and good enough at my job to carry out my part." She cocks an eyebrow. "This leadership stuff isn't hard."

"Okay," I say. "I'll send a message to Nico. I need you to let him in when he knocks. Help him free the guests and the ambassadors aboard the *Accommodation*. Cass and Bee will take care of the mission kids and everyone in the Apothecarium."

She narrows her eyes. "You really trust that girl?"

"Yes," I say, and for once I mean it. "I'm choosing to trust them, just like I trust you." I start to head for the stairs, but an idea stops me. "See if you can track down Admiral Dare as well. She may have something I need."

First stop, home. Cass made me promise to warn Oma and Dad before anything else, and the Ledger is in my bedroom anyway. It might hold the solution to fixing this mess. If it doesn't give me an answer, I hope the admiral has found her key, at least. That topscrew could end up being our last chance to keep the Hotel out of Stripe's hands.

I just hope we don't have to use it.

With the Blight in control of the elevators and me on the Blight's naughty list, I'm forced to take the stairs. In between all my huffing and puffing on my way to the seventeenth floor, I'm struck by the sheer number of cats that have invaded the Hotel in just the past few hours. It's like they've decided to throw their own gala. I spy dozens of new Nightvine clusters growing in the stairwell too, intertwined with other vines bearing the darker, indigo blossoms. The Blight's vines.

Every time I used Mom's key to conceal all the issues that have been plaguing the Hotel, I was unwittingly helping the Blight cover its tracks. My need to convince everyone that I could keep this place under control is what allowed the Blight to spread as far as it has. Now it's in the Nightvine, too. Djhut said that we shape the magics, and the magics shape us. But the way the Blight is mirroring the Nightvine and tangling itself up with the Vesima makes me wonder: Do magics shape other magics, too? Is the Blight mimicking them, or is it *becoming* them? And if it's the latter, what does that mean for us?

When I reach the stairwell door to the seventeenth floor, I'm ready to collapse from exhaustion. Part of me wishes I hadn't loaned Nico the suit, but then we'd be down a person, and right now we need all the help we can get.

I open the door.

And there's Rahki, waiting for me—duster in hand, scowl on her forehead. She must have known I'd come for Oma and Dad.

THE KEY OF LOST THINGS

"Step back," she says, her tone dull and gravelly. "Hands up."

"Rahki," I say, "are you—"

"You're too late," she says. "He's coming."

My gaze falls to the blue blossom on her lapel. This isn't her. She's being influenced. Her unwavering trust in the Hotel's mission gave the Blight a loophole to manipulate her, and this time I don't have a coin to remind her who she is.

I swing the have-sack around behind my back, readying myself in case she attacks me the way Nico did.

The Blight's words hiss through her voice. "My master will reward me for my loyalty. Together we will uncover the secret bonds hidden in this place. We will—"

A gloved hand claps around Rahki's mouth from behind, shimmering amber. When it pulls away, it leaves behind a thick strip of leather binding Rahki's lips.

Rahki whirls, revealing Sana behind her, a duster in one hand, a glove on the other. Her fingers still sparkle with the binding dust.

"Watch out!" I say. "She's not herself."

"I know." Sana settles into an attack pose. "This stupid Hotel is turning against us."

Rahki strikes her own duster and lashes out, but Sana dodges. Sana did well to silence the Blight, but there's no way she'll be able to keep up with Rahki's Maid Service training. Their dusters clash, and the weapons repel each other in a burst of colorful energy.

I've got to help, but how?

Behind them, I notice a small cluster of Nightvine buds growing together with some of the wilted blue flowers. I dart for the flowers—past Sana, who's barely deflecting Rahki's blows in mini sonic booms—and grip the cluster.

The veil lifts.

"Sana, here!"

Rahki strikes out with a sparkling glove. Sana drops her duster and lets Rahki stick her arm to the wall. Then, in one awkward, jerky motion, Sana grips Rahki's elbow and pivots, redirecting Rahki's momentum and sending her stumbling toward me.

Rahki grabs for the wall to stop herself, dropping her own duster in the process, but I give her one last shove to send her sprawling into the Nightvine.

The veil falls behind her.

I bend over, breathing hard. "That's one way to do it."

"Will she be all right?"

"She'll be fine." I pick up Rahki's duster to free Sana from the wall. "I'll find her once all this is over. Hopefully by then we'll have conquered the Blight."

"The Blight?" Sana asks.

"I'll explain on the way."

29

In Deed and Purpose

Hello?" I say as I enter our house from the seventeenth-floor hall.

"There he is!" Oma's voice calls as she rounds the corner from the kitchen and runs for me. She wraps me in a gruntingly painful hug. Sana chuckles when I look to her for help.

"What did I tell you, boy?" Oma says, releasing me from her death-grip. "You don't—"

"Leave, lock doors, or look for trouble. I know, I know. I'm sorry."

Dad appears in the kitchen doorway, concern all over his face. The last time I saw him, I was pushing him away. I'm starting to realize that keeping him at a distance isn't the way to solve our issues. I'm going to have a lot of apologizing to do.

"Oh, Cammy." Oma waves her hand in front of her nose. "You stink something awful. Where have you been?"

I give them the short version—Cass is okay, Nico's one of the good guys, Stripe's coming to steal the Hotel. "We're closing the Hotel down, just in case I can't solve this problem," I tell them, wrapping up. "I need y'all to get out of here while Sana and I go back."

"No." Oma says. "You are absolutely *not* going back in there."

"I have to. Cass is in there, and I've got to at least *try* to cleanse the Blight from the Vesima."

Dad steps forward, forehead creased. I brace myself for another argument, but instead he says, "I'm coming with you."

"What?" Oma and I exclaim together.

"Melissa gave up everything to prevent this; we have to be willing to do the same," he says. "If there's a way to keep the Hotel out of Stripe's hands, we have to find it."

The mention of Mom drops a brick into my stomach. Mom's bound to the Vesima, which means the Blight is in her, too. Is that why she stopped appearing to me in the Ledger?

"Are you willing to let that monster get your son, too?" Oma snaps. "It's one thing for you to go; you're a grown man who's already made his mistakes. Cam's just a boy. If Mr. Stripe comes for him—"

"Stripe won't get me," I say. "Or Cass. We're immune because the contract I made with Stripe says so. Nico, too." I look to Dad. "And you. That's why we have to be the ones to stop him."

I don't mention the danger the Blight poses on its own. The fact that it had any influence on Nico at all proves we're not safe.

"Besides," I continue, "there are things that only I can do to stop him. Agapios made me CiT for a reason, and now I have to see that through."

Oma hoists her hands to her hips. "I won't allow it."

Dad places a hand on her arm. "It's not your choice, Mom." He looks over at me. "Decisions like these shape us. When I had shaping choices, I made poor ones. I won't prevent him from making better ones."

I never thought I'd have my dad stand up for me like this. Maybe there's hope for us yet.

"When we leave," I tell her, "unbind our front door from the Hotel. We can't leave Stripe any foothold."

"No." Oma's cheeks are red with frustration. "Not as long as my family is in that blasted place. I'll be guarding this door until you come back. So you *have to* come back, ya hear me? All of you."

"We'll hurry," Dad tells her. "Love you, Mom."

Oma throws her arms around us both.

This time I don't mind my ribs being crushed quite as much.

After a short discussion Sana heads off to complete her piece of the plan. If we fail to cleanse the Hotel, I'll need her knowledge of shaping dye and binding to keep Stripe out. Like Elizabeth said, I have to trust everyone to do their job. My idea is still a long shot, but if anyone can make it happen, it's Sana.

"Where's your sister now?" Dad asks as he and I burst through the crash bars into the odd half-light of the Mezz.

"She's making sure the mission kids get to safety. Then they're evacuating the third and fourth floors."

"The Apothecarium," he says. "Your friend Sev?"

I nod, but truth is, I don't know what state Sev's in. That's another area where I'll have to trust Cass to do what I can't.

The Mezzanine feels unusually empty for this time of day. These grounds are typically packed with people tossing Frisbees, or taking in the view of the Sundial Courtyard, or basking in the sun-windows that shine like stadium lights across the potted trees that make up the Mezz's fake woods.

The Blight has changed all of that. The once vibrant grass is dried out and brown. The water that babbled through the stream is murky. Blighted roots even climb the posts that support the sun-windows, dimming our view of the outside world. Seeing the Mezz like this—darkened and decaying—makes me start to sweat, even with the cool breeze.

Dad stops me a few feet from the arch that leads to the Greenhouse. "I need to tell you something."

"Can you tell me later? We don't have time—"

"No. This is important." He grips my shoulders and pauses, choosing his words carefully. "I know I'm supposed to say it more—and I probably haven't said it at all yet—but . . . I'm proud of you. The way you take your job seriously and want to help other people . . . you remind me so much of your Mom. You are becoming a good man—you *are* a good man—and, I'm proud, Son."

I don't know what to say. A million different emotions flood through me: joy, that my dad—my *dad*—sees something in me to be proud of, frustration that he would wait until everything's falling apart to tell me so, and guilt for all the ways I've failed every-one. The way I failed *him* by not giving him enough of a chance to be the kind of dad he wants to be.

"You're stronger than you think you are," he says. "But you're smart, too. Smart enough to know when to let go."

There's an unexpected heaviness to those words, as if he's just shoved a bag full of squirming cats into my arms.

"Sometimes you can't control it, Son. Sometimes you fight as hard as you're able, and life still doesn't turn out how you want it to."

Like him. Dad did everything he thought was right for us when we were little, and he still ended up failing. Yeah, he made mis-takes, but he's here. He's trying.

"We do what we can, Dad," I say, and I hope these words are enough—that he knows I forgive him.

When I turn Mom's key in the Greenhouse doors this time, I wish for the key to reveal everything. No more hiding, no more controlling—it's time to face the unconcealed, terrible truth.

The path to the Vesima tree is blackened and withered, with scorched grass and rotten fruit scattered across the hill. The tree looks worse than when it was attached to the Museum. The Blight vine wraps all around it now, all the way up in the branches, its rot-ten goop coating the trunk with sticky brown sap. The rot has been spreading for months, even as Agapios and everyone else thought the Vesima was healing. It was using me, and Mom's key.

I hurry to one of the herb tables and pull the Ledger from the have-sack. I don't know if Sana has made it down to the glowworm caves yet, but there might still be time to save this place. There's got to be a solution in here. Something that can cure the Blight so that we don't have to flee the Hotel, something that will save Mom and protect everyone else.

But as I search the Ledger, I find nothing but scribbles.

"It's not working," I say as I frantically turn page after page, searching for a clue—searching for her. I'd hoped that being closer to the Vesima would strengthen the bond between the Ledger and the Hotel, but the Blight is interfering. If this book has an answer, it's not sharing it with me.

The next page confirms my fears. I watch as the ink scratches words onto the page in uneven, crooked letters: *Would you like to make a deal now?*

I rip out the page and hurl it to the ground.

"It's not over yet!" I shout at the tree covered in midnight-blue blooms. "We're going to save her! We'll stop you, and we'll stop Stripe. You can't have her!"

The Greenhouse doors open behind us.

I wipe my eyes and spin around.

"Nico," I say, "I'm glad you're—" But then I notice his suit. It's not Sev's suit but instead the gray pin-striped one he wore when he was with Stripe. The outer edges of his figure keep moving, those familiar lines redrawn over and over again.

"Your fight is over, boy," the figure says, its words rustling the dying limbs of the Vesima above us. "We possess the Hotel now."

That's not Nico at all. This *thing* is the Blight.

Dad grabs a long-handled gardening hoe from one of the herb tables and steps in front of me.

The Blight cocks its head to look at him. "You can't fight me, Reinhart." Its voice rumbles like gravel. "I have this whole place, all these people under my influence. It's so roomy in here. And what grand secrets it hides."

"The Hotel's not yours yet," I reply.

The shadow and the tree laugh in unison. "All that's left is to transfer the deed."

Agapios's letter weighs heavily in my pocket.

A sneer appears on the Blight's sketched face. "My master will be so pleased when he finds out all I've done for him," it says. "We'll break the locks on these chains yet. Everything will be ours again."

When he finds out. "Stripe doesn't know," I whisper.

Dad flashes me a confused look.

"We may not be able to cleanse the Blight, but we can at least keep Stripe out," I tell him.

I swipe the have-sack off the ground and check my pocket watch, silently sending out a hope that Sana has finished her task. Either way, we're out of time.

The binding takes hold as I insert the pin that Sana gave me into the strap, sending a wave of gold across the mouth of the have-sack. The glow of a million blue lights appears on the other side. The glowworm cave—an underground sea of shaping dye—right there for the using.

It was the Old Man's gardening that gave me the idea. The roots of the Vesima drank the water right up when he poured it onto them. Sev said the shaping dye is made of water. The Vesima's roots wind throughout the whole Hotel, so if those roots can soak up the shaping dye, they'll carry its magic to every door, every room and corridor. And Djhut said a magic that penetrates to the heart of a thing can reshape every part. If that's true, I might be able to reshape all the doors, all at once.

That's only half of the solution, though. Admiral Dare still has the other half. At least, I hope she does, and that Elizabeth can find her.

Sana peeks into view in the have-sack opening. "All ready, boss."

The Blight growls, baring its inky teeth. The branches of the Vesima groan with it.

Dad raises his hoe. "Cameron?"

"Do it, Sana!" I shout.

The view in the have-sack portal wobbles as Sana gives the makeshift door she slapped together in the caves a strong push. The frame leans, falling . . .

Into the lake of dye.

I aim the sack at the foot of the tree as a rush of glowing water explodes from the opening, pouring from Sana's now-submerged frame and out through the mouth of the have-sack.

When I asked Sana to build a door, bind it to the have-sack, and drop it into the lake in the glowworm caves, I wasn't sure my plan would even work. But now, as the sticky blue substance from the underground pool floods the Vesima's roots, I've never been happier to be right. I drop the have-sack and let the stream pour forth on its own. We might just pull this off after all.

But when I look back up at the Blight, it's smirking. Oh no.

The eastern and western Greenhouse doors burst open, revealing half a dozen maids wearing midnight-blue boutonnieres, and one very imposing Maid Commander at their lead.

No.

The bond of Life prevents the Blight from harming us directly, but those restrictions won't prevent the maids from attacking us. It's in the maids' contracts to do whatever's necessary to protect the Hotel. And now that the Blight has spread throughout the Hotel—now that it and the Hotel are becoming one—the maids' own commitment to serve the Hotel has been twisted into a call to serve whatever's infecting it. The magic of their contracts can't distinguish between the two, which means that right now the maids' job includes protecting the Blight . . . from us.

The MC unsheathes her sword; her maids raise their dusters. There's no way that Dad and I can fight them on our own, no matter how sharp Dad's garden hoe is. And the dye's flowing, but it's piling up and sliding off the roots. Shouldn't the tree be absorbing it by now?

"Any other ideas, son of mine?" Dad says as the maids advance.

And then, with a resounding *boom*, the southern door explodes.

30

The Decisions That Shape Us

"Get back. Get back! GET BACK!" Nico shouts as he comes running into the Greenhouse. The *real* Nico.

A second later a ten-foot-tall lion bursts through the doors behind him, biting at his heels. Nico dodges around one of the herb tables, putting it between him and the enormous Chinese lion that until recently was a statue standing guard over the Asiatic Lobby. Veins of Blight curl up its legs, just like with the topiaries.

I glance back to where the manifestation of the Blight stood only moments ago, but it's gone.

Nico ducks out of the lion's reach, the suit constricting around him to dodge the lion's paws. "I do *not* like this Hotel anymore!"

"Did you ever like it?" I call back.

"Not really." He spots the blighted maids, the blue goo everywhere, Dad wielding a garden hoe like a battle-ax. "Cass, get in here!"

A thunderous thump rattles the Greenhouse as a massive gorilla plows through the doorway, cracking the glass around it.

Gogo beats her chest with a loud roar. Cass clings to Gogo's back, beaming like a kid at Christmas.

"Here, kitty-kitty!" Cass calls to the lion. "You leave our Hopper King alone."

Gogo leaps for the lion, wraps her considerable hands around its neck, and tosses it back through the Greenhouse doors.

"Are y'all done yet?" Cass calls. "It's getting hairy out there."

"The maids!" I yell. "Stop them, but don't hurt them!"

Cass rolls her eyes and holds tight as Gogo barrels toward the advancing maids.

I rush back to the foot of the Vesima, sloshing through the growing mound of dye as it slides across the grass. My pants absorb the stuff instantly, so why won't these roots? If the dye doesn't sink in, it'll never make its way through the Hotel, and I won't be able to follow through with the next step in my plan—reshaping the doors.

Nico crouches next to me. "We have to leave, Cam. The Hotel's fighting back. You should see the Mezz. The icons are attacking, and the Maid Service is all *grrr*, and—"

"We can't go," I say. "Not yet."

Nico looks the tree up and down, touches the sticky brown sap that coats the bark, and gives me a pitying look.

"You'll never succeed," another voice says.

I turn to find the Blight's image crouched on the opposite side of me, still etched with Nico's face.

The real Nico jumps back. "Whoa! What is that?"

"I know how you feel, Cameron," the Blight says, leaning closer to me. "You try so hard, but the truth is, you're not strong enough to do what's been asked of you."

The truth? What does the Blight know about truth?

"You were never going to live up to your mother's legacy," it continues. "You're only a boy, lost in all those expectations. Give up, before you make anything worse."

No. It's not that I wasn't good enough. The *truth* was that Agapios never meant for me to do this job alone—it just took me until the past few hours to figure that out. He and the Hotel were trying to teach me that when they assigned me the gala project, and the end-of-summer staff awards. Agapios kept telling me there were plenty of people who knew things I didn't, who could do things I couldn't.

I felt lost because I was trying to do it alone. The Hotel wanted me to learn to rely on my friends, so that we could succeed together.

"You don't have to keep fighting," the Blight whispers. "You could run away again. Run back home where it's safe, and you can keep everything under control."

Safe.

I turn to see Cass and Gogo, holding back the maids all on their own. Without her adventurousness, Cass wouldn't be able to protect us right now. And what about Nico's scheming? His cats started us on this path. Same with the others. Without Sana's brilliance and Rahki's tenacity, without Sev's creativity and Orban's fun spirit and Elizabeth's willingness to challenge people, I couldn't have made it this far.

"It's not about control," I say, standing to face the Blight. "Control is what Stripe wants, and I'm not him. The truth is that we work best when we depend on one another."

There's something else, though. Something I've been missing. A secret that the Old Man couldn't tell me outright but that he hinted at all the same.

I slosh through the rising mound of dye to where I cast the Ledger aside. I pick it up and examine the inscription on its front.

> *Knowledge and truth are among the sharpest blades*
> *in the world. When used together they are a double-*
> *edged sword, able to cut deeper than any other.*

Agapios said I wouldn't be able to use the Ledger to its fullest until I figured out what it was trying to teach me. This is it. I can't control everything. I'm not supposed to do everything on my own. The Hotel succeeds because everyone in it does their part. Even Nico said it in the Nightvine. *We could be powerful. Together.* That's the knowledge that the Hotel wanted me to have, and if the Ledger provides knowledge, then the truth . . .

It's Mom's key.

I pull the topscrew from my pocket, and it's already radiating heat like a campfire. I used the key to hide things that were going wrong, sure, but it also showed me the reality of things I had missed. It revealed the path to the Nightvine, uncovered hidden doors, and in the drupe it helped to remind Nico of everything that he had forgotten. Even back when I first got the key from Agapios, it showed me the door to this very Greenhouse that had been concealed for so long.

If the admiral's topscrew is the Key of Lost Things, then Mom's . . . It's not an illusion key at all. It's more like . . . a Key of Truth. And just like the Key of Lost Things has the power both to lose and to find, Mom's key has the power to reveal truth or to conceal it altogether.

A keyhole begins to shine in the leather directly under the Ledger's inscription.

"What's it doing?" Nico asks, face illuminated in the light.

The Ledger of Ways holds all of the Hotel's knowledge. Mom's topscrew is the Key of Truth. *Knowledge and truth are among the sharpest blades in the world. When combined . . .*

"Hold this," I say, and shove the Ledger into Nico's hands. "Here goes."

I insert the key into the keyhole, and turn.

Beams of golden light frame the Ledger's binding, so bright that I'm forced to look away. When the light fades, it leaves behind a glistening golden sword in Nico's hands.

"Okay," Nico says. "Now, that's cool."

I take the sword and examine it in the light. It's so shiny and perfect. The hilt looks as if it's made entirely of the same pearlescent material as Mom's key, but the blade is polished gold—with an uneven edge of drawn lines that reminds me of the sketches in the Ledger.

Etched along the length of the blade in swirling letters is one word:

Together

But . . . what do I do with a sword?

I scan the grounds. Gogo's managed to dodge most of the maids' strikes, but one of her massive hands is now stuck to her chest, and Cass is holding on for dear life as the gorilla scrambles away. Meanwhile, Dad's occupied by two more maids and is doing a pretty good job of holding them off. He's yelling something, though I can't tell what.

Wait a minute—where's the MC?

"Look out!"

I duck, barely avoiding the sharp end of the Maid Commander's sword. The blade slices deep into the wood of the Vesima tree just above my head.

"Mom!" I scream.

The Maid Commander pulls her blade loose, and a large chunk of the tree falls free. She grips her sword tightly, aiming it directly at me. It shines in the sunlight, the French word HONNEUR emblazoned across the flat of the blade. Are these two weapons alike?

I lift my sword and attempt to point it at her, but it's so heavy. How am I supposed to fight with this thing?

She lunges, and I jump back, tripping over the enormous roots to land in a mounding wave of dye. Again, the MC's sword slices into the wood, and embeds itself deep in roots near my hands. She rips it loose and raises it to strike again.

This time a thick ribbon of silky, black fabric sweeps in front of her and wraps around her wrist.

"Whoa," Nico says as one of the suit's coattails holds the MC's sword arm up over her head. The coattails are longer than I've seen them, but then again he's also standing in a pool of shaping dye.

I scramble to my feet and raise the Ledger sword alongside Nico.

The MC charges, but this time we're both ready. Nico's tails redirect her blade to meet my own, and the force of the two magics colliding knocks her a step back. The MC yanks her wrist free and strikes again, but my sword and Nico's suit work together to divert her swing, forcing her to drive her blade deep into the tree. Very deep. I didn't know she was that strong.

Her lip curls as she yanks the sword free, readying for another attack.

But before she can strike again, a figure plows into her from the side, tackling her to the ground. Dad. He wrestles the blade from her grasp. Maybe she's not that strong after all.

Maybe the blade is that *sharp*.

I glance back to the cuts she's made in the Vesima's trunk. The flood of dye seems to be shifting toward it, as if the glowing liquid is drawn to the wound. A trickle runs in a reverse glimmering rivulet up the bark, and sinks into the cut.

A horn blares across the grounds, shaking the Vesima's

branches and piercing my eardrums. The lion is back, but now the admiral's marines are pouring through the southern door in a wave of turquoise uniforms.

The soldiers raise their sandstone sabers to attack.

The admiral herself leads the charge. "All right, you big stone beastie," she booms. "Why don't you prowl over here and get a taste of the Fleet Marines!"

Elizabeth found her. Hopefully Admiral Dare has the last puzzle piece I need to shut the Hotel down and keep Mr. Stripe from steal-ing its secrets.

I look between the sword in my hand and the tree's wounds that are drinking in the shaping dye. There's so much dye though, and it's moving so slowly. At this rate it will take too long for the dye to spread. I see what I must do, but . . .

"Dear boy," the Blight says into my ear, "you're not thinking of harming your mother just to hurt me, are you? What kind of person would even consider something like that? And besides, what good would it do? Soon my master will be here, and such a sacrifice will be for nothing."

Not for nothing. It'll be for them. To help everyone escape. For the maids, and the ambassadors, all the people that Stripe would harm if he got his hands on this place. For the mission kids, and the staff. For my family.

"Your plan won't work," the Blight whispers. "You can't con-trol this. You'll try. You'll fail. And then where will you be? Forgot-ten. Abandoned. Alone."

I look the shadowy image dead in the eye. "You're a liar," I say. "And I'm never alone."

A sword, glimmering and sharp and bearing the word HONNEUR down its flat rips through the inky Nico. The drawing stutters, and pen strokes unspool from its edges and pile into a heap of scribble on the dye-soaked ground.

The real Nico hoists the Maid Commander's sword over his shoulder. "That thing didn't look a bit like me. I'm not *that* short."

"That won't have killed it," I tell him.

I turn to face the tree. To face my choice.

Thirteen years ago Mom sacrificed herself to save the Hotel and its people. She would want me to take the risk to save those people again—I know that—but can I do it? Can I really harm this tree that's bound so tightly to my mother's spirit, just for a chance to keep Stripe out? I could be giving up my last hope of ever getting her back, and I'm not sure that's something I can do.

At least, not alone.

"I need your help," I say, though I can't bring myself to look Nico in the eye as I do. I don't want him—or anyone—to see my tears when I tell him what I know must happen next. "These swords can cut deep into the tree—deep enough to let the tree drink up all this dye and spread it throughout the Hotel."

"Cam," he says, his voice uncharacteristically solemn.

"I can't do this on my own," I say, wiping my eyes. "Will you help me?"

31

Stay Rooted

My eyes are bleary as Nico and I hack away at the massive trunk of the Vesima tree. The Ledger sword slices through the wood far more easily than I would have expected. Like other magics, it seems to know what I intend and feed on my emotions to make it happen.

On the other side of the tree, Nico slices more quickly and decisively, cutting deeply with each blow of the MC's blade.

I close my eyes and swing again, and feel the sword pass smoothly through the trunk. "I'm sorry, Mom," I whisper. "I love you, but I know this is what you'd want."

It is.

I pause. Did she . . .

I raise the sword once more, struggling against its weight, and swoosh the blade through the trunk.

You've done well, my sweet, sweet boy. I love you too.

"I wanted to know you," I say, tears choking my voice.

You already know me. All of me is in you, and so much more. And you have others to be with you now.

I glance back at the chaos unraveling around us. Cass, pressing Gogo's foot into the lion icon's throat as a wave of gold transforms the lion back into jade. Dad, wielding garden tools alongside the admiral's marines to hold back the maids. Even Bee is here now, buzzing through everyone with her sliver.

"I don't want to lose you again," I tell her.

A person alone is lost, but a person rooted in their friends always knows exactly where they are. They are your family too. Know them. Listen to the truths they tell. They have far more to offer than a mother stuck in a tree. But there is one thing I can still do for you.

Crack!

I jump back as the enormous trunk groans. Branches shift and moan. Leaves flutter in the air.

The fighting at the base of the hill pauses. Even the corrupted maids hold their breath as the Vesima shifts, the wood creaking loudly.

"It's coming down!" Nico shouts.

"Over here!" Cass waves. Gogo grabs one of the herb tables and lifts it over her head, sending potted plants flying. "Take shelter under her!"

The Fleet Marines and Admiral Dare race for the gorilla as Cass removes her coin to transform Gogo into its statue form, still bearing the table over its head.

The trunk leans as gravity starts to take hold.

"Maids, too!" Cass yells, beckoning them to her. "We can get back to beating each other up in a minute."

The remaining maids who haven't yet been whisked away by Bee's sliver quickly join the others under Gogo's protection. The Blight's influence can't bend their fundamental bonds of Life and Nature so far that the maids won't protect themselves from falling trees.

The trunk splits with a sickening groan, and Nico and I scramble out of the way as the once grand, powerful Vesima—the heart of the magnificent House known as The Hotel Between— comes crashing to the ground.

Branches snap and crack as they drive into the earth, shooting splinters and twigs out in a deafening explosion of broken wood. And then, the Greenhouse stills, save for the quiet flutter of dead leaves swirling through the air.

I step up onto the stump of the Vesima, amazed at how wide it is. The swords aren't that long at all, yet those blades sliced through nearly twenty feet of wood on all sides, leaving only a splintery, broken outcropping at its center.

The shaping dye creeps up the sides of the stump, streaming slowly alongside me as I head for the tree's center. One last thing to do to make sure the dye can travel to every part of the Hotel network as quickly as possible. The magic shapes the wielder. The wielder shapes the magic. And when it penetrates deep into the heart, that magic can shape every part.

I lift the Hotel sword—*my* sword, *my* magic—and drive it into the heart of the Vesima.

The ground quakes. Dye rises in a swirl of blue molecules

around the shimmering sword. It spins together with the fallen leaves and hovers in the air before plunging into the stump where blade meets wood. My heart aches as I grab the still-flowing havesack and hang it upside down from the sword's hilt to pour what remains of the underground pool into the tree's open wound.

"Good-bye, Mom."

When I turn to face the Greenhouse, everyone is staring. Nico's mouth hangs open. Dad watches with a white-knuckled grip on his garden hoe. Cass and Gogo, who is bound and flesh once more, are both crying. Gogo wipes sloppy tears with the back of her furry hand.

"Where are the maids?" I ask.

Cass shoots Bee a dirty look. "*Someone* slivered them when they ran for cover."

Bee shrugs. "Hey, I got them to safety. I just did it my way. They're enjoying a nice, refreshing dip in a mountain lake right about now."

"And the Maid Commander?"

"I took care of her," Dad says, sliding the sharpened pin he showed me in Germany into his pin-sleeve. He turns to face the admiral. "What now?"

Admiral Dare defers to me. "It's your House, Cameron. We're only here to help."

My House.

I glance back at the stump and the sword, which is completely engulfed now in the flow of shaping dye. "We need to leave. This won't have killed off the Blight. Not yet, at least—it's spread too far. Stripe's still coming, which means we have to close the Hotel. All of us. Together."

A cool wind gusts through the Greenhouse door as we cross back into the Mezz. Nico carries the MC's sword slung over his shoulder. That, combined with my pristine suit, makes him look large and in charge.

Meanwhile, I'm dressed in his dirty clothes and soaked in blue goop and look like a hobo.

The chaos that started in the Greenhouse has spilled into the Mezzanine, ranging all the way from the potted grove to the bouldering cliffs and the Mezz waterfalls. Only, it's not people fighting off the blighted maids—it's statues. Dozens of terra-cotta warriors attempt to subdue the maids with clay fists, while the maids strike and bind as many of the icon soldiers as they can.

Sana stands away from the fighting, her attention focused on her terra-cotta force. She must have swung by the Motor Pool on her way up from the Shaft.

"Looks like a party," Nico says.

"The Blight's fighting back," I reply, noting the blackened roots climbing the sun-windows and wrapping through the potted grove.

"Yeah," Cass says, "but look down there!"

She and Gogo are leaning over the balustrade overlooking the Courtyard, pointing together at the Shadedial Fountain. The fountain is overflowing again, but this time it's not with sickly, stinky sludge. It's the dye. Glowing, icy-blue liquid now flows from the marble tree's white branches, spilling onto the ground, and spreading out across the Courtyard.

"It's in the arches, too," Dad says, motioning to the Greenhouse doors. The tangled roots glimmer as the dye flows through them, seeping all the way out to the knotted tips.

"The plan's working," I say, relieved. Wait. . . . We're missing people. "Where's Sev? Elizabeth, and the others?"

"We are here," Sev's voice calls. He, Elizabeth, and Orban emerge from the fake rocks near the bouldering wall. Sev's riding in Cass's wheelchair. I hope that just means he's still healing, and not that he's permanently injured.

Admiral Dare joins us too. "It appears that despite our best efforts, we are going to lose the Hotel."

"Didn't you say you had a plan?" Nico asks me.

"Yes," I say, and face the admiral, "but that kind of depends on you."

She cocks an eyebrow.

"In the Nightvine, you said the Key of Lost Things might make its way back to you." I take a deep breath. This is the last piece I need to make sure Stripe never steps foot into our Hotel. "Do you have it back?"

Her disappointed brow tells me all I need to know.

She looks to Bee. "It was you who took it, was it not?"

"Yeah," Bee says, "but Cass had it last."

Gogo pulls Cass closer and glowers defensively.

"I don't know what happened to it," Cass says, giving her gorilla a pat on the arm. "It just vanished from my pocket."

The admiral sighs. "That's something that key does. It enjoys being lost. I lose it all the time at home. Most often I find it in the couch cushions."

Out of my pocket. In the cushions.

I turn to Sev, seated in Cass's wheelchair. "Look underneath you."

"What?" he says, still drowsy from Countess Physiker's medicine.

"In the chair," I say. "Look in the cracks, next to the cushion."

He runs his fingers along the edge of the seat and pulls out a glittering emerald key.

"Oh my gosh," Cass says. Gogo facepalms dramatically.

"Admiral," I say, taking the key from Sev, "I know this belongs to you, but do you mind if I borrow it for a little while longer?"

She smiles. "Please do. But be careful you don't lose it again." She pauses, considering. "Or if you do, that's okay too. Maybe it's time that the key found its way into some new hands."

"Uh, also," Nico says, raising a hand, "you have a fleet, right?"

The admiral looks him over. "Yes."

"I . . . may have severed the *Accommodation* from the Hotel with all the ambassadors aboard, so I'm pretty sure they're out there floating in the ocean somewhere." He grins. "Some guy named Nagalla made a big fuss about us leaving them, and how when he was event coordinator, blah, blah, blah. I stopped listening. Anyway, you might find him in a lifeboat somewhere else."

"Duly noted. We will find them." She looks to me. "Am I to understand that a speedy escape is in order?"

"As soon as the dye makes its way through, I'm closing the Hotel," I tell her. "We're going to lock this place down and make sure Stripe can't find it."

"I see." She pauses, considering. "Are you sure you want to do this? Those who locked us in the Nightvine weren't able to find us again. I wouldn't suggest doing this lightly."

The letter from Agapios weighs like a boulder in my vest pocket. "It's our best option. The tree may be gone, but there are still too many secrets here to let Stripe have access to any of it. Losing the Hotel is the only way I know to keep him out."

"Then this is where we part ways, Mr. Kuhn."

"What will you do?" Cass asks her.

"My hunt for Stripe has only begun, I think." She gives me a salute. "Happy to have served with you all, no matter the outcome."

"Likewise," I say. "And, Admiral, stay safe. Now that the Blight is in the Nightvine . . ."

"Stripe will be looking for a friend of the Nightvine to invite him into it," she says. "Rest assured he will not find one with me. Use the key. Lose this place as completely as you can."

She places a fist to her heart and bows, then jogs away after her soldiers.

"I'm afraid I have to say good-bye for now as well," Dad says, gripping my shoulder.

I spin to face him. "What?"

"Someone has to stay behind and care for those who remain. Someone who knows Stripe, and can keep things going without the Blight's magic gaining hold over them. I can do that."

"But we just got you back," I say. "Let me stay instead."

He places his callused hand on my cheek. "My boy," he says, and my vision blurs. "We both know you can't be the one. I know the responsibility that Agapios tasked you with. It can't stay in this House."

He means the deed. I have to leave in order to ensure that the deed, and the person who owns it, never fall into Stripe's hands. "But there's no telling what the Blight might do to you," I say. "And there are so many maids, and the icons . . ."

"If you're to find this place again, you'll need an anchor. The Blight will prevent the Hotel from drawing you like it used to. Someone has to be your light here to guide you back."

"You can't," I plead. "Cass, tell him he can't."

She sits tall and grabs Dad's hand. "We'll find you again," she says. "We're family. That's what we do."

He pulls us both in for a hug. "I am so proud of you both," he says. "Stay rooted in your friends. They will take care of you. Now go. Find a way to cleanse this Blight. When you knock, I'll be here."

32

A Turn of the Screw

I direct our crew all the way back to Queenie's hall. Cass blazes the trail on her Gogo, knocking aside any blighted icons, while Sana's icon soldiers cut back the corrupted vines. Nico scouts ahead, the MC's sword slung over his shoulder, checking to make sure we don't cross paths with any maids. It isn't easy, but with everyone doing their jobs, we're able to push through.

Once everyone's standing safely under the Nightvine's pistachio sky, I turn to face the veil that connects back to the Hotel.

"How's this supposed to work?" Nico asks.

"I'm not sure." I place my hand on the wall, and I can feel the whole Hotel at once, just like at the bluestones, only stronger now that I understand the vine's desire to connect everything.

What I sense through the veil saddens me, though. The Hotel is dying. I can feel it wheezing, barely clinging to its last breaths. I picture the admiral and her marines passing through the McMurdo Door, and Dad doing what he can to corral the maids and anyone else still inside. I can't be certain, but I think I sense Mom, too, sending us her love.

But I also feel the Blight, gathering the Hotel close, like a dragon hoarding gold. *Mine*, it says. *This place is mine. You can't take it from me.*

Maybe not yet, but one day we'll be back.

I place my other hand against the wall, reaching out for the Hotel sword with my thoughts. The dye flows through the Vesima's roots—I can feel it as clearly as I feel the warmth in my veins.

With my will connected to the sword, my clothes dripping with dye, I focus my intent. It's like controlling an icon, or my suit. Only, empowered with all these magics at once, I feel so much stronger. We will protect the Hotel's secrets.

In my mind I gather the Hotel knockers scattered all over the world. The veils of the Nightvine too, intertwined with the roots of the Vesima. I bring them all together into one knotted bunch—one flowering cluster—and yank as though I'm ripping a weed from Oma's garden.

The road shudders beneath us as the Hotel knockers pull free from the world to join with the Nightvine instead.

It's done. Every knocker in the Hotel network has been re-bound. All, that is, except one. One last door, tucked away on the seventeenth floor, where the dye hadn't quite reached yet. I couldn't get to it to pull it free.

But I don't tell the others that. Not yet.

"The Hotel is closed," I tell them. "Let's get out of here."

• • •

The Nightvine has changed. The Blight spreads more quickly now, its rancid indigo blossoms choking out the Nightvine's pale green ones. The cats of the vine race past, yowling and hissing at the dreadful blooms that have invaded their home. Even the emerald sky seems duller, drearier.

A little ways down the road, we find Rahki nursing a headache, back to her senses now that she's out of the Hotel.

"My coin was leading me home, then suddenly it wanted to lead me everywhere," she says.

"It's good to have you back," I tell her after explaining what I've done. "I'm sorry I broke my word."

She frowns. After all that's happened, I'm sure she'll have a few words for me later, but right now it doesn't seem quite that important.

The next veil we find lands us in a circle of ancient stones standing in a wide-open field. I hold the veil open for everyone to leave the green glow of the Nightvine behind and step out under the starry English sky.

The bluestones of Stonehenge seem to glow in the moonlight.

"How'd we end up back here?" Cass asks. "And why Stonehenge?"

"Djhut said these stones have a lot of old binding left in them," I tell them. "When I reshaped the Hotel and the Night-vine together, I bound all of the leftover veils back to this place. That way we'd only have one final door to lock." I only wish it had worked out that way.

I face the bluestone arch and pull out the Key of Lost Things.

The space in the arch ripples as a keyhole forms between the stones.

"Whoa," Elizabeth says.

I focus my intent, hoping the magic will know what to do, and turn the key. The veil vanishes in a flash of green.

Nico waves a hand through the empty arch. "Is it . . . ?"

"It's gone," I say, and lean against the stone. "It's over."

Cass groans. "You say that like it's a bad thing. We kept Stripe from getting what he wants. This is a win."

I stare at the grass.

"Cameron," Sana says, "what aren't you telling us?"

"The dye didn't reach everywhere like I'd hoped," I say. "When it was time to reshape the pins, I . . . I couldn't reach them all. There's still one root—one door bound to the Hotel that Stripe can use to get inside." I look up at Cass. "On the seventeenth floor."

Her eyes glaze, and she clutches Gogo's fur as she realizes what that means. "Oma's house."

"Are you sure?" Sev asks.

"I felt it. The Blight's already using it to reach out to Stripe. It won't take him long."

"We should call her," Sana says. "Anyone have a phone?"

"His Oma cannot simply unpin the door," Sev agreed. "The plan only works if we eliminate all routes that Stripe could use to get into the Hotel. To unpin the door from this side would leave that pin in Oma's possession. All it would take is for Stripe to take that pin from her, and the Blight will be there to welcome him in.

The only way to be certain that Stripe cannot reach the Hotel is to use the admiral's key on the last remaining entrance." He groans. "*Vidit oko, da zub neymyot.*"

"Our solution is just out of reach," Rahki interprets.

"It's a touch," Nico says. "We'll take a sliver back to the Museum, and we can get to your house from there. I lost my sliver in the Hotel, but I'm sure Bee still has hers."

Bee shakes her head. "That maid lady took mine."

"No more talk of slivers," Rahki says, glowering. "They are forbidden."

Silence falls over our motley bunch. That's it. All that work, and Stripe is still going to get in.

I look them over, each in turn. Nico in my suit, leaning on the MC's sword. Cass in Gogo's arms, Sev in her wheelchair. Rahki and Orban, Sana, Elizabeth, even Bee—they all did everything they were supposed to, and still . . .

Sev rolls forward. "Cameron, do you have the pin I made for you last year?"

A pin? The pin! The one Sev bound to my bedroom. It's not Hotel-bound, so I didn't even think about it.

I feel for my pin-sleeves, but they're not there. Of course not, because Nico's wearing my suit. I grab him by the lapels and yank him to the side—Nico yelps in surprise—and see the row of pin-sleeves in place of a normal breast pocket. Right on top sits the pin that leads to my bedroom.

"Here!" I say, holding it high and ignoring Nico's grumbling.

But a second revelation sucks the air out of my lungs. We're standing in a field of giant rocks in the middle of nowhere. There's not a hinge around for miles.

"Give it to me," Sev says.

I do as he asks, and watch as he carefully removes a whittling knife from his pocket.

"I had Rahki bring my kit when I woke in the Apothecarium. I was bored," he says with a shrug, and begins shaving off bits of the pin with his knife.

"What are you doing?" I shout as Sev utterly ruins the perfectly formed pin. "We need that."

"Trust me." A few more scrapes shave the tip down to a fine point, and he holds it out to me. "Here."

I take the pin in my palm. It's sharp, like the one Dad had. "What did you do to it?"

Bee scoffs. "You don't know a sliver when you see one?"

A . . . sliver?

"Slivers are cruder and less predictable than pins," Sev says. "That also makes them easier to craft."

"No!" Rahki says, and snatches it from me.

"Careful!"

"He can't use this!" she snaps. "It's forbidden. Absolutely not allowed."

Orban shrugs. "Why not? It's not like the Hotel's in any position to argue."

Nico agrees. "I'm pretty sure the rules got a little more flexible when Cam stuck a sword into the Hotel's heart."

"But it's a *sliver!*" Rahki shouts. "It's in our contracts. If Cam uses that sliver, he breaks his bond of Law with the Hotel."

Nico tosses up his arms in frustration. "The Hotel is dead!"

"You don't know that for sure. I didn't see what you did in there, but the Hotel has survived a lot over the years. We won't know what happened until more time has passed, and that means you *can't* break that contract, Cameron."

"I did," Cass says, shrugging. "I used Bee's sliver, and the Hotel let me back in just fine. Besides, our options are kinda running out."

"Just because you can doesn't mean you should." Rahki crosses her arms. "There are some lines we should never cross."

"Rahki," I say, "I already broke my word to you, and I don't want to do that again. I respect your opinion. I trust you. But . . . we have one shot to make this right."

She glares at me for a long moment. "I am *not* the bad guy here. You all try to make me out to be the bad guy because I like rules, but I'm not. I only want to do what's right."

"I know," I tell her, "and most of the time we need that, but sometimes . . . sometimes you have to break the rules to do what's right."

Rahki exhales, long and slow. "This is a terrible idea." She bunches up her lips in frustration. "Fine. But *only* this time. Never again."

"Great." I clap my hands together, a little shocked by how happy I am to do something that's by all accounts awful. "Now, how does it work?"

33

The Shape of Things to Come

My world explodes in a riot of color and sound.

I expect to feel some kind of compression as my body is folded up into the tip of the sliver, but the reality of it is so much more. Weight and wind press into me from all sides. Everything aches and burns, and the light is so bright. I scream—not from pain necessarily but from the *ahhhhh!*-ness of it all. I'm nowhere. I'm everywhere. I'm zipping across the sky and slipping through cracks underground and bouncing across the surface of water, all at once.

There's something else in the chaos with me. A presence. I remember sensing this once before, that first week in the Hotel—a darkness hiding in the abyss between the doors. It wants something, but I can't tell what.

Then the light brightens, pain flares, and all of a sudden, the swirling vortex of loudness stops. The world is quiet, save for a single, screaming voice.

My voice.

I close my mouth and breathe in the smell of my bedroom,

which still bears a whiff of *eau de* cat—or is that me and these stinky clothes?

When I check my limbs to make sure everything's still in place, I notice the small pinprick of blood on the muscle at the bottom of my thumb. I'm okay.

Now, to stop Stripe.

I race for the living room, but Oma stops me in the hall. "Cammy, I heard shouting. I thought—"

"Out!" I shout. "Get out of the house. Go, now!"

Oma grabs her purse from her bedroom, peppering me with questions, which I dutifully ignore.

Another pained yawp emanates from my room, and Nico comes running out soon after.

"Couldn't let you do this alone," he says, winking as though he didn't just get squished and ripped across the globe to get here. He's followed by a third shout, and Sana stumbles into the hall after him.

When we reach the front of the house, Oma's running around the living room grabbing photo albums.

"We've got to go!" I urge.

Another cry. Cass's voice. "Hurry, Gogo! Oh, come on. . . . She can't fit through the door!" We should have thought of that before slivering Cass and her icon-beast across the Atlantic.

Oma's still gathering her things when I peek through the curtains next to the front door.

My breath catches. Stripe's already here, standing in the street, leaning on his rope-shaped cane; his pin-striped suit is perfectly pressed, and his red-banded boater hat is on his head. I thought we'd have more time.

I lock the dead bolt.

Nico peeks through the window with me, the MC's sword tucked under his arm. "Great."

"If it isn't my two favorite urchins," Stripe calls from the porch, just beyond the door now. "When my old friend said it had a gift for me, I never expected that the gift would involve the two of you. My House made it sound like it has broken free of Nico's control. Is that true, Mr. Flores? Did you let my House go?"

Nico growls. There's something else in his look too. Something he's remembering, maybe, or a question he doesn't like the answer to.

Stripe raps his cane against the door. "Little pig, little pig, let me come in."

"Not on your life," Nico shouts.

"Ah, 'life.' You're all so worried about protecting things like Life and Nature and Law. I can show you a world without those limitations. The bonds were created, and that means they can be destroyed. Once I break these chains, I'll make you both kings. All you have to do is let me in. Help me claim the deed to the Hotel, and we'll unlock its mysteries together."

He still thinks the deed to the Hotel is inside it. At least we have that going for us.

Stripe knocks again. "Come on, Nico. Make a deal with me.

Think of all the good times we had. You want more than this world has to offer you—you always have. There are things that only I can give you."

Nico leans his back against the door, staring blankly at the couch. He's never told me what his life was like before the Hotel. Not the whole truth, anyway. Stripe raised him, taught him. In all the ways that matter, Mr. Stripe is Nico's father. But Nico betrayed him to save us.

Which gets me thinking—the Blight never did try to influence me directly. I kept expecting it to because of what happened to Nico, but nothing ever happened. It tricked me, sure, but it never had any form of control. Just like our contract with Stripe said.

Why was it able to influence Nico? Was it because he was locked in that drupe with it for so long? Or was it something else?

Oma steps up beside me and places a hand on my arm. "Cammy—"

"I know what I'm doing, Oma," I tell her, and for once I mean it. I pull the Key of Lost Things from my pocket. Everyone's here now. I need to finish this. And this time I won't leave any back doors open.

"Sorry, Stripe," I proclaim as loudly as I can. "We're not accepting reservations at this time. The Hotel's closed for repairs."

I insert the key into the door and turn.

Rays of green light burst from the keyhole, pass over the house, and ripple over the walls and furniture like a curtain opening for a play. The glow intensifies, lime-green particles wafting in the air around my friends.

At last the key vanishes from my hand and the floor drops out beneath us before everything goes dark.

I find myself gazing up into a cloudless Texas sky.

Our home is gone. The whole house just vanished, leaving us exactly where we were, but without a floor beneath our feet. The door, the walls, everything from the roof to the foundation of Oma's house is . . . lost, and with it our last point of entry into The Hotel Between.

"Are you okay?" I ask Oma as she stands up in the wet clay earth where the house's foundation once lay. I can see the neighbors' houses just over the edge of the dirt wall that surrounds us. Thankfully it was only Oma's house that disappeared.

"I'm fine," Oma says, attempting to brush the mud off her capris—smearing it, really. She stops mid-smear to stare past me.

At Stripe, who's glaring a fiery hole through my skull.

Rage radiates off the man in the pin-striped suit as he looms over us from his place on the edge of the earthen wall. My heart pounds, right next to the deed in the inner pocket of my vest. He's standing right there, on the raised porch that was left behind when the house vanished. Close enough to touch. Close enough to take the deed away from me.

The last time I saw him this close, he threatened to beat me to death with that cane of his. Mom protected me then, but she's not here now. I don't even know if she's anywhere, anymore.

Stripe raises his hands, and I stand and back away, bracing for some kind of attack—some world-splitting act of rage that will wipe us out.

But instead he claps. Slowly at first, then faster. He laughs, too—a mocking sound that makes my neck itch.

"Well done," he says, popping his cane up into his gloved hand. "The Hotel remains out of my reach, for now." His tone darkens. "But you haven't stopped me, boy. What's lost can always be found."

His eyes dart to something behind me.

I turn to find Nico gritting his teeth, the MC's sword leveled at Mr. Stripe.

"Don't you have somewhere better to be?" Nico asks, jaw set in anger. How could I ever have doubted him?

Stripe's smile widens. "Marvelous. Very impressive." He looks back to me. "It's a race, then. You and your little band of hoteliers versus me and my . . . resources. We'll see who arrives at the Hotel first." He squats and leans over the drop-off, close enough for me to smell his rancid breath. "And this time it'll be winner take all."

He tips his hat and turns to leave.

We should stop him, go after him, *something* to keep him from going back out there into the world, but what can we do? He's a magic, and we're just people.

Stripe pauses when he reaches the sidewalk "Oh, and, Nico, don't presume that I don't know where you stand, boy. Keep pretending, and you might fool yourself, but you'll never fool me. Not again."

We watch as Mr. Stripe disappears around the street corner, whistling a show tune.

I look over at my blood-brother, and he locks eyes with me. There's always something he's not saying; always more to his story. Like how the Blight got so much influence over him, or what he meant when he said that he and I could be powerful.

But he proved himself again by helping us protect the Hotel, didn't he? It's Stripe who's trying to manipulate and deceive us.

"That's . . . not good," Orban says after Stripe is gone.

"We were going to have to find our way back to the Hotel anyway," I say. "To save the people we left behind, like Dad."

"We need to find Agapios, too," Sev adds. "We must secure the deed so that Mr. Stripe never gets his hands on it."

Elizabeth meets my gaze. She's the only one left who knows that Agapios gave the deed to me. I hope she understands how much we need to keep that a secret. The more people who know, the more likely it is that Stripe will figure out we have it and come after us. After me. Elizabeth's not the best at keeping secrets, though, and like Sev always says, "A chatterbox is a treasure for a spy."

"Then it's decided," I say. "We'll search for a way to clear the Blight, find the Hotel, and make sure Stripe never sets foot through its doors."

"Can we eat first?" Nico says. "It's been two months since I've had real food. I'm literally starving."

. . .

The 7-Eleven down the street provides enough "real food" for everyone. I hadn't realized before how hungry I'd gotten. We sit at the picnic tables outside, chowing down on hot dogs and spicy cheese taquitos in silence.

Oma steps aside to make some phone calls and figure out what to do about her missing house. I'm pretty sure that call with the insurance company is going to be a little weird.

Nico and Bee head around behind the gas station to use the door to the Museum and have the Hoppers prepare some rooms for us. Meanwhile Orban ropes Elizabeth, Sana, and Cass into a card game—a good distraction. Cass is back to her chair now that Sev has had a chance to recover a bit too. Can't exactly take a gorilla to the local corner store.

Rahki sits at the other picnic table with me, watching as I write on some napkins. She pulls her cat-ear headphones off when she sees me looking at her.

"What are you doing?" she asks.

I fake a smile at her. "Finishing something."

"'Orban, Most Likely to Point Me in the Right Direction,'" she reads aloud. "'Sana, Most Likely to Have Great Ideas.' 'Sev, Best Dresser.' . . . What is this?"

"It's everyone's Hotel award for doing a good job," I tell her. "Agapios wanted me to come up with awards to give everyone at a staff event once the summer was out—a lesson I think I learned a little too late." I shrug. "Anyway, we may not have the Hotel's resources to make the awards anymore, but I can at least do something. We need a morale boost."

"Good idea." She pauses. "Don't think that just because I let you get away with breaking your word to me this time, you're off the hook for good."

The promise. "I know. I shouldn't have made a promise I couldn't keep."

"You'd better not do it again. Got it?"

"What if I told you that I promise not to break promises?"

Rahki laughs. "Fine." She scans the parking lot, watching the cars come and go. "What happened to the key, Cam?"

The Key of Lost Things vanished from my hand when I used it on the door at Oma's house. "It disappeared," I tell her. "I didn't want there to be any way left for Stripe to get in, so I think the key took that as me wanting it gone too."

"So there really is no way left to reach the Nightvine?"

I shake my head. "Not that I know of. And Mom's key is still inside the Hotel too, along with everything else."

She sighs. "It's going to be a long road home."

A long road indeed. "We'll find our destination. Eventually."

"Cam!" Nico peeks around the corner. "I need to show you something. Now."

He leads me to the door at the back of the 7-Eleven, where Bee and Sev wait with stern faces.

"What's wrong?" I ask. "Why aren't y'all inside?"

Bee turns the doorknob, and the door opens to a storeroom.

That's strange. "Okay? Where's the Museum?"

"That's the problem," Nico says. "The doors aren't linked anymore."

Wait, what? "None of them?"

"None of them," Sev confirms, unrolling his pin organizer to reveal dozens of pins in their sleeves. "I tried them all. Forty pins, bound all over the globe. Not one managed to open a door."

"So what does that mean?" I ask. "Does the binding not work anymore?"

Sev shakes his head. "The binding is still there. I can feel it. It simply . . . does not work as it once did. The magic has changed its disposition toward us."

"You mean it doesn't like us anymore?"

Without the doors, how will we find the Hotel before Stripe? And how will we track down a way to cleanse the Blight? We don't even have a way back to Nico's Museum.

We're homeless.

It took me this long to get used to the idea that doors could lead to anywhere, but now they only lead to where they're supposed to. The rules have changed. Our destination is set, but now the only question is, how do we get there?

"Cheer up, kiddo," Nico says, giving me a pat on the shoulder. "You know your buddy Nico's always got a plan."

That's what I'm afraid of.

ACKNOWLEDGMENTS

The creation of a book requires many cooks and taste testers and teachers, and they are as responsible for the meal as the one who wrote the recipe.

To everyone at S&S BFYR, you are the very best kitchen anyone could hope for. Krista Vitola, the editor virtuoso whose skills with a knife are unmatched—there will never be another like you. Let's keep making exquisite meals for readers together. Catherine Laudone—thanks for managing the kitchen and being such a great sous chef. Chloë Foglia, whose presentation is so sublime—this book is almost too beautiful to eat. Katrina Groover, Chava Wolin, and Bara MacNeill—thank you for ensuring that the dishes we serve are always of the highest quality. Lisa Moraleda, Chrissy Noh, Christina Pecorale, Victor Iannone, Emily Hutton, and all the rest in publicity, marketing, and sales—thanks for telling folks where to find the good stuff. Michelle Leo, Sarah Woodruff, and Amy Beaudoin—you bring in the most cultured diners (teachers and librarians, who are my most favorite readers). Justin Chanda—thank you so much for welcoming me to your restaurant.

Pétur Antonsson, whose illustrations are the sweetest, most delectable complement to any meal. Let's face it, people mainly come for the dessert anyway, and your art is the richest.

Jim McCarthy, agent extraordinaire—thanks for getting my dish on the menu, and for helping out in the test kitchen. Your refined taste is more appreciated than you know.

Gerardo Delgadillo, Lindsay Cummings, Brad McLelland, Samantha Clark, M. G. Velasco, Mckenzie Price, and Jessica Leake, who all encourage me when the dishes don't turn out quite right—thank you for your endless support. To the Electric Eighteens and the Pitch Wars community, you are the best coworkers in the world. Mary Virginia Meeks, thanks for being a champion of reading, and of me.

Jason and Carley Stevenson, David and Jamie, Becca and Lizzie Ake, John Paine, Dave and Natalie, Daryl and Deborah Miller, Jack, Emma, and Dean… you all give me so much life.

Mom and Dad, thank you for teaching me about the world and the people in it. Brandi, here's another book for your shelf. I hope it's worthy. Love you, Sis. Kevin, make sure she displays it with her customary extravagance of twinkling lights. Kendrick, I am so proud to call you my son. Thanks for keeping my head in the clouds. God, you know all I have to say. And Shelly, no matter how you count our years together, they're far from enough. You are my roots, and my branches, and my leaves that blow in the wind. Thank you for choosing me and making me a better man.

And to my dear readers, librarians, and teachers: thank you for choosing to dine with us. Without you, there'd be no one to eat the food, and I have so many recipes I want to try.